STRAITJACKET & TIE

STRAITJACKET & TIE

A NOVEL BY

EUGENE STEIN

ALYSON PUBLICATIONS
LOS ANGELES

Reprinted by special permission with Houghton Mifflin Co.
Cover design by C. Harrity.

Manufactured in the United States of America.
Printed on acid-free paper.

This is a trade paperback from Alyson Publications Inc.,
P.O. Box 4371, Los Angeles, California 90078.

First published by Ticknor & Fields: 1994
First Alyson edition: June 1996

ISBN 1-55583-358-6
(previously published with ISBN 0-395-67031-4)

Library of Congress Cataloging-in-Publication Data
Stein, Eugene.
Straitjacket & tie : a novel / by Eugene Stein.
p. cm.
ISBN 1-55583-358-6 (pbk. : acid-free paper)
1. Young men—New York (N.Y.)—Fiction. 2. Gay men—New York (N.Y.)—Fiction. 3. Family—New York (N.Y.)—Fiction. 4. Mentally ill—Fiction. I. Title.
[PS3569.T3653S77 1996]
813'.54—dc20 96-14617
CIP

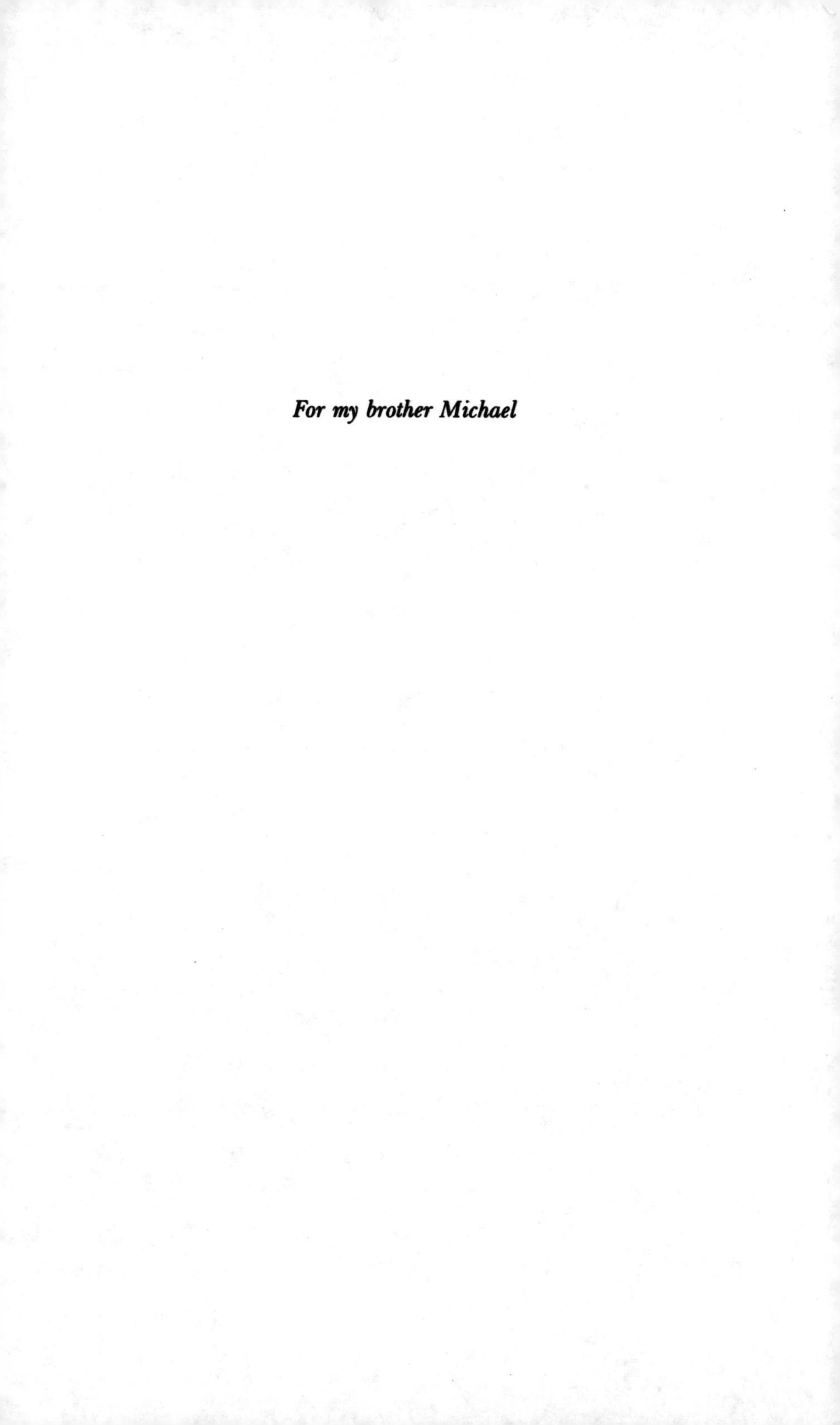

For my brother Michael

"I'm missing the proper feelings. And old Niemeyer told me that once when he was still in his prime, when I was still half a child: it's a question of the proper feelings, and if one had them, then the worst could never happen to one; and if one didn't have them, then one would be in eternal danger, and what we call the Devil would have sway over us."

— THEODOR FONTANE
Effi Briest

THAT'S MY HOME

The Mysterious Stranger

▾▾▾

BERT WAS SIXTEEN when his brother had his first psychotic break. Philip was a freshman at the state university in Stony Brook. At first, there had been a delicious sense of lightness. When Philip walked, he felt as though he were floating through clouds. But then background noises began growing louder and louder, obscuring the more important sounds in the foreground. Philip refused to return to school the following September, pleading for a year's grace to stay at home and decide who he was and what he wanted. His parents let him stay.

Sometimes he felt reborn, renewed. Sometimes he felt touched by God. He was fascinated by out-of-body experiences, astral projection, and telepathy. "If someone wanted to insert thoughts in you, they could do that," Philip told Bert.

"I don't think so, Phil," Bert said gently.

"They can. They can make you think a certain way. That's why homosexuals are so bad. They can put thoughts inside you." Philip despised homosexuals, the very idea of homosexuality sickened him.

Every day Philip listened to the radio, searching the static for a station that remained slightly out of reach. "There are radio stations we don't even know about. The government has them," Philip assured his parents, Joseph and Evie. "Sometimes you can just barely hear them." Maybe there were broadcasts to make people gay — Philip laughed at the idea, he knew it sounded strange. But he believed it.

At random moments, Philip would call out lines from songs,

from television shows, from whatever. Bert would announce the sources — not because he wanted to, but because he felt it would put people at ease. He didn't know why he felt this overwhelming sense of responsibility, why it was his duty to make his brother's behavior palatable. Looking back, he found his efforts a little ludicrous.

WAITRESS TO PHILIP: What can I get you?
PHILIP TO WAITRESS: You and I are of a kind. In a different reality, I could have called you friend.
BERT: *Star Trek,* isn't it, Phil?

WOMAN ON A BUS, TO PHILIP: We're moving so slowly.
PHILIP TO WOMAN: Time is a jet plane, it moves too fast.
BERT: That's Dylan, right? What song is it, Phil?

Philip and Bert Rosenbaum looked very much alike: at their best, more happy than handsome, but affable and wry. They had the same auburn hair, threaded with shocks of red, and greenish brown eyes — cat's eyes, their father called them — that changed in the light. They were both lefties, and both agile, great climbers of trees, able first basemen, decent dancers. They shared the same beautiful smile and the same full lips, only lately Philip smiled less and less.

But he still fiddled with his radio. He had started searching for evidence that extraterrestrial life forms were using the radio waves. "Do you really think you'll be able to hear them?" Bert finally burst out. "On your stupid AM/FM clock radio?"

Philip turned toward Bert and stood there, lost in thought.

"Well?"

Philip still didn't answer.

"Did you hear what I asked you?"

"Do I think I'll be able to hear them on my stupid AM/FM clock radio," Philip rattled off.

Bert waited.

"No," Philip said. "But it's interesting . . ." He pronounced "interesting" slowly and in four distinct syllables, like a German scientist lecturing American students about the intriguing properties of electrons.

Growing up, Philip and Bert loved watching movies that featured special animated effects. Their favorites were *King Kong* and *Mysterious Island.* In *Mysterious Island,* Union prisoners escaped from a Confederate jail in an observation balloon, were blown off course during a storm, and ended up with two female castaways on a Pacific island inhabited by animals of Brobdingnagian proportions. Joseph would join them in the living room whenever they watched the film on TV; no matter how many times he saw the movie, their father would forget the plot and be surprised anew by the sudden emergence of a gigantic crab hiding beneath the sand. Evie, cleaning and dusting, would hover nearby, especially if Joan Greenwood was on screen, until the movie or the music scared her too much. She was frightened most of all by the climactic battle with an octopus, an underwater sequence with silent screams but no dialogue. The soldiers, weighed down by the water and their lead boots, fought sluggishly against the creature; the sequence had the slow, masochistic rhythm of a dream, and in fact inspired some of Bert's most horrific nightmares.

For Chanukah one year, Joseph presented his sons with an eight-millimeter camera, and Philip began making his own films. With infinite patience, he animated a war between Bert's red and black plastic toy soldiers. He used firecrackers as mortar; he used a hot plate to melt the soldiers and simulate nuclear conflagration. Next Philip filmed Bert's wood turtle, in extreme close-up, chewing on a piece of lettuce — the turtle was terrifying as it filled the screen. Evie couldn't watch. She didn't even like looking at the turtle in its bowl after that.

Bert broke the camera a few days later. "You're such a goof," Philip complained, but he didn't really get angry. He didn't have enough money to buy another camera, so he started working weekends at the concession stand at the RKO Fordham movie theater. Bert began saving his allowance, too, but then

Philip decided he wanted a stereo and ended up buying them a cheap, tinny, Sears record player, which they placed, with great reverence, on top of their desk, right under their antiwar and Marx Brothers posters.

Back at home, after his year at college, Philip began jogging around the Jerome Park Reservoir every day. Once Bert was walking home from school with his friend Alison when Philip came running by. Philip was wearing shaggy cutoffs and a T-shirt. His aviator-style glasses were slipping down his nose. "Phil!" Bert called. Philip was running with his eyes closed and didn't hear Bert. "Phil!" Bert called louder. His eyes still closed, Philip pushed his glasses up the bridge of his nose, and ran right by them. Alison laughed. Bert called Philip a third time, but Philip still didn't hear him.

Bert tried to shrug it off. "You know my brother — he's weird."

"Yeah, he is."

Bert wished she hadn't agreed so readily.

Philip embarrassed them all so much: laughing out loud in public for no particular reason (or at least no reason the other Rosenbaums could fathom), gesturing wildly with his hands and then stopping just as suddenly, or rocking back and forth on his chair in a restaurant, food dripping down his chin. His hair grew long and straggly. His parents begged him to see a doctor. Bert begged him. Philip refused. He said he didn't need a doctor. He said he was perfecting his astral projection techniques and soon would be able to escape from his ego. He had already learned to fly over Yankee Stadium, he reported, where a Graig Nettles foul ball had nearly clipped him.

He began writing poetry; he invented words, inverted words, split words, put words inside other words. He signed all the poems "Philip Traum." He listened to Bob Dylan all the time, then suddenly hated Dylan and threw all the Dylan records out — including some of Bert's. Bert was furious that his records had been tossed in the incinerator.

"Philip, those were my records!"

"Those were my records!" Philip imitated him. And then he lectured Bert: "They're not records, they're albums."

Bert knew he was being absurd — given that Philip was crazy, it seemed ridiculous to insist on property rights over his copy of *The Freewheelin' Bob Dylan.* (But he loved the cover so much: Bob and a girl at his side, huddling against the nip of winter.) Still, he tried to reason with his brother; he always tried to reason. "Phil, if you don't want to listen to Dylan, that's your right. But you should give the albums to a hospital or something. Why just throw them out?"

"I have to throw them out because they're bad for people," Philip replied. "They're not just bad for me, they're bad for everyone. I can't let little kids hear this. It's so bad for them."

As boys they were close. Bert always wanted to be in the same class at school, and have all the same friends, and play in the same stickball games in Van Cortlandt Park. He resented that his brother and he were separated so often simply because Philip was two years older. When Bert was four, Philip broke his arm slipping on the floor of their Bronx apartment; Evie had just waxed the long foyer. Seeing the cast on his brother's arm, Bert demanded a cast too, but no matter how much he begged, the doctors refused to give him one. Finally, to placate Bert, his father bought him a toy crutch — Bert found the arrangement highly satisfactory. Bert was twelve when Philip grew pubic hair; that same year, Philip started high school, and the brothers, once inseparable, began spending less and less time together. Bert missed Philip — he felt that something had come between them. Sometimes he blamed high school; sometimes he blamed the pubic hair.

Philip stopped watching TV. He could watch with the sound turned off, or he could listen in another room, but if both the sound and the picture were on, he felt bombarded. At a Yankees game Bert took him to, Philip was lost, distant. After the game, he asked Bert who had won.

He believed that various random events were related to him

personally: a cracked mirror, an open door, a haircut. Philip was certain the mind could be controlled by outside authorities and agencies. Occasionally he felt that he could control other people's minds too. He heard auditory hallucinations: he cocked his head to the side and listened. Or his face broke out in a wild grin while a fantasy, a little playlet, was staged inside his head. He repeated whatever was said to him. He felt his thoughts being withdrawn from his brain; he clasped his hands over his head to prevent the leakage.

For a while Philip stopped wearing his glasses, hoping to improve his vision through practice. He placed on the bookshelf a placard with the word "LOVE" written on the first line and "LOVES" written on the second line, in block letters. He eyed the placard for hours, squinting, straining to improve his eyesight.

One winter day he decided to give up shoes, too, and he walked to Fordham Road and back in the bitter cold wearing only three thin pairs of cotton socks. Years later, Evie would say that of all the crazy things Philip had done when he was sick, it was this episode, this ridiculous, shoeless moment, that had broken her heart. Bert's heart had been broken earlier, when a local channel broadcast *Mysterious Island* one Sunday afternoon, and Philip was too ill to watch.

Pretty Persuasion

▾▾▾

OF ALL OF THEM, Joseph had the most patience with Philip, but even Joseph sometimes snapped. Philip was spending most of his time in bed. He lay there for hours, tossing a small, pink Spalding ball up and down, throwing it, catching it, throwing it, catching it, throwing it, catching it. He just lay there. Bert's father pleaded with him to get up. At times the pleading grew desperate: "Please get up, please get up, can't you please get up?" At times the pleading grew a little angry: "Get up! Come on! Get up!" Once Joseph screamed at Philip for ten minutes. "Damn it, get up! Get up! Get the fuck up! Get up!" Bert had never seen his father so angry. Joseph's forehead was scarlet, and the color seemed to bleed into the roots of his sandy-red hair. Shaking, his voice nearly gone, he still croaked horribly, "Get up! Get up!" Evie tried to pull Joseph away. Joseph was fifty-five; Bert was afraid his father would have a heart attack. Philip just lay there. He could not move. The effort was beyond him. He looked as though he felt sorry for his father, and he looked bewildered too, but he could not get up. "Get up! Get up!" Evie was frantic now too. "Stop it, Joe, just stop it." Bert felt as though he were in the Loews Paradise, watching a movie.

Afterward, sick with himself, Joseph sat on the living room couch and flipped through back issues of *Newsweek* and *Mother Jones*. He worked long hours as a typesetter, for a company that specialized in the labor press, but now the words were a blur to him. He went out for a walk to smoke a cigar (Evie didn't allow him to smoke inside the apartment) and then sat through an impenetrable Brazilian film playing on Fordham Road.

When he returned from the movie, he stuck his head in the boys' bedroom, made a point of greeting Philip effusively — Philip was still lying in bed — and then retreated to the living room. There he turned on the stereo and put on his Listen & Learn foreign language tapes, which promised to teach him to speak Portuguese or Hebrew like a native. He listened to the tapes while he ate peanuts and cashews compulsively. Thin to the point of emaciation at his wedding, Bert's father had put on weight over the years; to his own surprise, he had grown chubby in middle age. With his coiled energy, his appreciation of beautiful women, and his surprising grace on a dance floor, he reminded Bert of a gentler, heavier, less libidinous Jimmy Cagney.

A couple of days later, by way of apology, Joseph bought Philip a really nice turntable.

Philip told his father that he had had incestuous relations with Evie. (Not true.) He told Evie that Bert was a transvestite. (Not true.)

He was smoking pot whenever he could get his hands on some. From his grandfather — an eighty-six-year-old C.P.A. who still had about twenty clients, mostly widows — Philip received an allowance, which he converted immediately into marijuana. Evie made her father stop giving him money, but not before Philip had wrapped small stashes of dope in aluminum foil and hidden the neat squares around the bedroom. Chancing upon one of these, Bert would wonder whether to leave it, throw it out, or smoke it himself. Generally he left it. No matter how distracted Philip became, somehow he always remembered where he'd hidden his pot.

Bert's brother had made a few new friends in the neighborhood — large, laconic, vaguely dangerous young men who came up to the apartment to smoke dope with him when Evie wasn't home. Philip had never had many friends growing up, but he always had a few companions, three or four interesting, introspective boys: a class clown, a coin collector, an outcast, a would-be astronaut. Most of his old friends were now away at college, and the few that called when they came home were soon alienated by his odd behavior, if he could even get out of bed to visit them.

One day Evie came home unexpectedly early from shopping and surprised Philip and Hector, one of his new friends, in the bedroom. They were smoking pot through a huge purple bong. Evie stood there and glowered. Hector, abashed, grabbed his bong and fled. Evie checked the silverware and the pockets of her good dresses, where she hid her best broaches, but nothing was missing. "He was with me the whole time," Philip protested. "He's a good guy."

"Yeah," Evie said, "he's a model citizen. I don't want him here. Do you understand?"

Their mother was a tiny, intense, lean woman. A worrier, but competent and shrewd, Evie was amazingly adept at crossword puzzles, Double-Crostics, and cryptograms. She ran a small typing business out of their apartment on Bedford Park Boulevard. Prodigiously efficient, she could work feverishly for days at a stretch, subsisting mostly on coffee, then collapse into bed. She seemed to thrive on working herself into exhaustion. She exulted in her overwork, even when it made her sick.

She was often sick. Suffering hugely from hay fever, Evie also had frequent colds and flus, so that a box of tissue was never far from hand. Curiously, the allergies had subsided while she was pregnant with her sons, but she'd caught the worst flu of her life while carrying Philip. A frustrated doctor, she was attending pharmacy school part-time and kept a well-thumbed *Physicians' Desk Reference* in her bedroom. Now she looked through the tome and wondered what medicine Philip should be taking. But Philip refused to see a psychiatrist. Joseph and Evie were sick, not he. Bert was sick. Psychiatrists were the sickest of all. That's why they were drawn to the field.

"It's like he's not my son anymore," Evie told Bert sorrowfully. "It's like Philip's gone and someone else has taken his place." She rubbed her fingers, swollen with arthritis. Her knuckles were so large, she couldn't remove her wedding and engagement rings. She looked up at Bert and smiled at him. "But you're the same."

She had always seemed needy, and hungry for Bert's company. Growing up, Bert had been close to his mother; Philip was closer to Joseph. When Bert was young, his father had been not so much distant as absent. Joseph often worked double shifts during the week, and on weekends he took Philip to Yankee games and magic shows, leaving Bert with his mother. Evie hated to be alone.

Bert hated spending any time at home, hated sharing a room with Philip. Mornings and afternoons, he worked at the doughnut counter in the cafeteria of the Bronx High School of Science. In the evenings, he'd go over to Alison's to do homework; she lived a bus ride away, in Riverdale.

They played a drinking game while watching *Star Trek.* The rules were arcane, but Alison knew them all. You had to drink whenever certain strains of theme music played. You had to drink whenever Spock showed emotion. You had to drink whenever other Vulcans appeared. You had to drink whenever Klingons appeared. You had to drink double-time whenever Romulans appeared. You had to drink whenever Yeoman Rand or Nurse Chapel appeared. You had to drink whenever the cast ran back and forth in place, simulating damage to the *Enterprise.* You had to down a bottle whenever the Prime Directive was trampled upon a little too ridiculously. You had to drink a lot. It could get very messy. Playing the game, drunk, Alison had leaned over and kissed him, more than once — but Bert never kissed her back.

Bert had met Alison in his trigonometry class. She was an ace math student, unlike Bert, who had to struggle just to stay afloat. She wanted to be a physicist, and she loved, in order,

Einstein, Niels Bohr, Dostoevsky, *Star Trek,* Arthur C. Clarke, and Phil Ochs. Her dark brown eyes were set close together, giving her a melancholy look, even when she was quite cheerful. She had thick, curly, ash blond hair, a long, pale white neck, and a small, thin, shy smile. She wasn't beautiful, but she was pretty, and Bert wondered why he wasn't more attracted to her. He worried about it sometimes.

He could tell Alison everything — except about Philip. He didn't want people to know how sick Philip was becoming. He wanted to protect his brother; he wanted Philip to get better and then to lead a normal life. If Bert confided to his friends about Philip, then even if his brother got well, he would always be scrutinized, always be suspect.

He could tell Alison everything — except that he was ashamed by Philip. He was ashamed by Philip's antics, his oddness, his greasy hair and scrungy beard and thin mustache. He was ashamed that Philip talked to himself, cursed himself, cursed the world, communicated with space aliens. He was ashamed that his brother was crazy. And most of all, most most of all, he was ashamed that he was ashamed.

He could tell Alison everything — except that he wasn't attracted to her. He knew she liked him; he knew his classmates thought they were boyfriend and girlfriend, and he did nothing to correct them. Even his parents wondered if they were dating, and each time they asked, his stomach tied up in a knot, and he wanted to shout at them to leave him alone. It wasn't any of their business. He didn't know why he wasn't interested in her, he just wasn't.

He couldn't tell Alison anything.

What Bertolt Knew

▼▼▼

PHILIP STILL REFUSED to see a psychiatrist. His thinking grew fuzzy. He had a hard time responding to questions — he groped for answers. Sometimes he knew the answers but forgot to say them out loud. He couldn't concentrate.

He began buying Dylan albums again. He became convinced that Bob Dylan was broadcasting a secret message to him. He pored over the lyrics and wrote messages to Dylan on the album covers. Bert tried to break through to his brother. "Philip, does it make sense that there's a message only for you?"

Philip, lying in bed, didn't answer.

"I mean, of all the people in the world, why should there be a message just for you? It doesn't make sense."

Philip didn't answer.

"Do you hear me?" Bert asked, a little sharply.

"Do you hear me?" Philip repeated, mocking Bert. "Do you hear me?"

The imitation was superb. It was as though Bert were hearing his own voice. But thrown into the mimicry was a certain viciousness, a characterization of Bert as an effete, mincing boy. Now it was Bert who was silent.

"I'm sorry." Philip rolled over to face the wall and curled up into a ball. "I didn't mean it."

"Phil," Bert finally said, "there's no message on the Dylan albums."

Philip folded his pillow around his head. "But I want there to be" came the muffled reply. Philip was almost crying.

I miss you, Bert thought again and always, pining for his brother lying in the next bed. I hate you, Bert thought, for getting sick. I love you, Bert thought, there's no one I'm closer to.

The doughnut counter at Bronx Science where Bert worked was a private concession run by a jittery man named Juan Carlos Ramirez. He joked that he wanted Bert to call him King Juan Carlos — "Like my cousin," he explained. Deeply religious, he went to Mass every Sunday. He was tall, dark complected, a good businessman, and a good friend to Bert, but he would lose his temper if he felt Bert was forgetting the limits of their friendship and showing him disrespect. "I'm the boss," Juan Carlos would say angrily. "I make the decisions, I take the risks. I'm the boss. You got that?" And then, feeling guilty for snapping, he'd slip Bert a five-dollar bill. "Kiddo, get yourself a haircut."

"That won't even pay the tip," Bert complained.

"Redheads." Juan Carlos sighed. He said his life had been ruined by redheads.

"How's that?" Bert asked.

"You know how I'm nervous and how I have a nervous constitution?" Juan Carlos began rhetorically. "Well, when I was still working for the phone company, I had this boss, a young guy, Irish, with red hair and freckles. He looked just like you. Hey, kiddo, who's Irish in your family?"

"The milkman."

"Anyway," Juan Carlos continued, "it just got worse and worse between us. He was making me crazy, and I was scared he was going to fire me. And one night, I tried to go to bed, but I couldn't sleep, thinking about him. I couldn't get him out of my head, I couldn't get his face out of my brain. I got so angry, I thought I was going to explode. Finally I couldn't stand it anymore and I squeezed my body as hard as I could, squeezed it inside of me if you know what I mean, and I cried like a baby. I ran to the window and I was going to throw myself out, but I thought, before I die, I want to hear '*Dies Bildnis ist bezaubernd schön,*' from *The Magic Flute.* I listened to the music, and then, I don't know how it happened, but suddenly I was on my knees and clasping my hands, and I cried, 'Lord, save me from this pain.' I didn't even know I remembered how to pray. But you know something? The pain went away. I found God. Then I found my girlfriend, Marisa, who's much too good for me. I pray and listen to opera every night, and I'm still here."

"Marisa's a redhead, isn't she?"

Juan Carlos smiled sheepishly. "Yeah, kiddo. She is."

Sometimes while he was working at the doughnut counter, Bert would sense he was being watched. Turning to the cash register, he'd catch Juan Carlos staring at him. Juan Carlos, flustered, would look away, or say he was daydreaming, or insist, again, that Bert needed a haircut. He told Bert that he had a beautiful smile. "You're going to break some hearts with that smile."

"Really?" Bert was pleased, and a little embarrassed.

On the anniversary of her brother Buddy's death, Evie lit a *Yahrzeit* candle for him. Buddy had been killed a few weeks before his fortieth birthday when his Volkswagen Beetle hit a truck on the Deegan Expressway. Philip was mesmerized by the flickering light of the candle. He looked at the flame for hours, occasionally swirling his hands in the air like a sorcerer preparing a spell. Bert wondered if he was trying to summon up a genie, a demon, or perhaps Uncle Buddy himself. Then Philip brought his index finger closer and closer to the lighted wick, to see how long he could stand the heat. He burned himself slightly.

Bert smoked a lot of pot with Alison at the end of their senior year at Bronx Science. Bert had been a diligent student all along, but grades didn't matter so much his last term — he'd already mailed off his college applications. At night, he liked to get high. When he smoked pot, Bert felt a secret thrill, a secret link to Philip's madness.

Alison and Bert started hanging out at CBGB and Club 57 on weekends. Bert felt very grown up with his fake I.D., buying cigarettes, listening to a band, not thinking about Philip, trying Quaaludes for the first time. A friend, Peter Fortunato, described him as a Bronx nerd punk rocker. Bert would come home at three in the morning and find Joseph waiting up for him. Did he have a good time? Were he and Alison dating, or were they just friends? Did he really like that music? Wasn't he tired? Go to sleep, it's late. And then they'd both shuffle off to bed.

For the first time in his life, Bert began skipping his homework. He had to write a thirty-page paper on the Treaty of Tordesillas for his Advanced Placement history class, but he procrastinated. Finally, at two-thirty in the morning, the same morning the paper was due, Bert finished writing the report. He still had to type it, but it wouldn't take long. His mother had taught him how to touch-type.

Evie was still up, sitting at the kitchen table with her large checkbook, paying the monthly bills, and drinking coffee. Bert was exhausted. He told her he was going to take a nap and asked her to wake him in an hour, so he could begin typing the paper.

"You drink too much coffee," Bert observed sleepily.

"If I didn't drink coffee," Evie said, "I'd get fat."

Bert went to his bedroom. Philip was snoring. Bert lay down and began timing his breathing to match Philip's snores. The next thing he knew it was daylight. His mother was kissing him on his forehead and telling him it was time to go to school. Philip was still snoring.

Bert felt a strange heaviness on the bed. Wearily, he patted an extra quilt on top of him. "What's this?"

"I gave you a blanket," Evie told him. "I was cold."

"Oh." And then he remembered his paper. "Oh God, why didn't you wake me!" He jumped out of bed.

"I typed it for you," Evie told him. She had typed all thirty pages and bound the report in a plastic cover. "Bert, it's wonderful."

Bert looked at the deep black circles under his mother's eyes and felt guilty. "Ma, I could have done it."

"You looked so tired, honey. I wanted you to sleep."

The senior society at Bronx Science had arranged a screening of *Once Upon a Time in the West* in the school auditorium. Alison had gotten hold of some hash and wanted Bert to share it with her. Bert had never tried hash before. He hated the smell. But he agreed to eat the hash forty-five minutes before the movie began, which meant he would have to ingest the drug during his English class. Just as his class was about to decide whether the governess in *The Turn of the Screw* was hysterical or not, Bert snuck out and found an empty stall in a bathroom. He sat on the toilet, opened the neat tinfoil pancake he'd hidden in his pocket, sprinkled a gram of hashish on top of two Kit Kat bars he had purchased especially for the occasion, and munched and munched and munched. He returned to the class to find that James's ghosts did in fact exist, but that the governess was hysterical anyway.

He loved the opening of the movie, a slow sequence that ended with the arrival of Charles Bronson at a train station. In the second scene, a homesteader and his children were preparing a welcoming feast for their new wife and stepmother. Shots rang out, and the family members were killed one by one, except for the youngest child, a redheaded boy, who was inside the house. The assassins walked out of the underbrush, and the leader turned out to be — Alison gasped, Bert gasped — Henry Fonda. The little boy came running out of the house into a full close-up, and the score began with a tremendous guitar twang.

Bert was suddenly, dramatically, and overwhelmingly stoned. He could feel the chords of music surge through his body, and tears rolled down his cheeks. As the film continued, Bert began noting themes, patterns, and rhythms. But if he told people about his observations, and they found his comments interesting or apt, would it be because he was perceptive or because he had stated the obvious? Perhaps his observations were so obvious that no one had thought to state them before. What if he wasn't seeing more than anyone else, but much less? Not more, but less? Not more, but less?

He felt himself descend each time he repeated the phrase. It was as if he had discovered some horrible mantra or satanic incantation, and now he was falling. His mind was being sucked down into a vortex.

Bert sank.

"What's the matter?" Alison asked him. Bert was dimly aware that she was speaking. "Are you falling asleep?"

Asleep? He was wide awake; he had never been more awake; he was losing his mind. What if this mad tumble never ended, what if it continued for the rest of his life? His parents were already taking care of his brother. . . . He didn't want to go crazy. And he was going crazy right now.

Bert sank.

Ever since Philip had returned from college, Bert had felt as if there were a miniature version of himself inside his head, analyzing his every thought, his every word — monitoring him to make sure he didn't do or say anything crazy; and inside this homunculus, there was yet another Bert Rosenbaum, and another, and another. The series continued infinitely, as though he were caught between two mirrors that faced each other. But now the homunculi had given way; it was the only explanation. There was nothing to protect him. His mind had never been this unsheltered, this indecently exposed. A scrawny, palsied, helpless, worthless agglutination: that shape, that thing am I, Bert thought. And if he was as scrawny, as weak and deformed, as he thought he was (Bert remembered a severely brain-damaged child he had once seen; his stomach knotted itself tighter), he could take only so much. His mind was already exhausted by its effort; he felt battered. There were things outside pushing in, and things inside pushing out.

Bert sank.

"Hey, wake up, you're missing a good part."

Bert felt he needed to hold on to something. Desperate, he reached for Philip — not the sick Philip, but the big brother who had taught him how to bunt, how to carry in addition and borrow in subtraction, how to juggle, how to balance a salt shaker on its edge. . . . He reached for Philip — and Philip saved him.

Gradually the audience came into focus before him, and Alison beside him, and the movie screen in front and above, and even the images on the screen. No one was looking at him; he had been quiet in his distress. Bert was glad. Eventually (it seemed a lifetime later), Alison leaned over to him and whispered, "Here we go." It was the famous, final, grandiloquent flashback, with Charles Bronson and his brother. The scene was magnificent, and Bert was awake enough to appreciate it.

He refused to smoke pot for a week after the movie, but soon enough Alison passed him a joint, and Bert took a hit. His brother smoked too much pot, now Bert was smoking too much pot. It was as though Bert were skating on the edge, constantly testing himself, flirting with craziness, then proving to himself that he wasn't crazy. His brother's illness had shaped him, Bertolt knew.

Philip said he'd astrally projected himself from Yankee Stadium all the way to Shea. He'd seen Lee Mazzilli ground out to third. He said he knew he was having some minor emotional problems, but as soon as the Yankees met the Mets in a subway series, all his problems would disappear; it was no use trying to get him to see a psychiatrist — they should try to get the Mets some decent pitching.

Bert came home from Alison's and heard his mother typing in the back office. He poked his head in to say hello. She smiled at him, revealing her crooked teeth. She had had orthodontia as a child, but her overbite had returned in her twenties. She looked tired to Bert, and old: her hair had gone completely gray, except for a patch at the back of her head, where the hair was still raven black. She was wearing a gray cardigan on top of a pink pullover — she was always cold.

Her clients were mostly lawyers who worked in or near the Bronx County courthouse. The office was actually a maid's room off the kitchen. Evie dusted, swept, and vacuumed the office — indeed, all of the apartment — relentlessly, but she let her papers pile up in a jumble on top of the high wood desk. Evie vowed she would clean her desk up, but it remained the one confined area of mess she permitted herself.

"Hey, Mom."

"Have fun at Alison's?"

"Yeah. I guess."

"You know, your father was asking me if you and Alison are just friends." Straightening the typing paper in the typewriter, Evie tried to sound casual. "I said you were."

"Right," he said curtly.

"Finish all your homework?"

"Yeah." They'd finished all their homework and then they'd finished a Thai stick. He was still a little high.

"You know, I was telling Nina how wonderful your paper was — you know, the one on that treaty?"

Bert cringed. His mother was proud of him, but in an aggressive, almost boastful way.

"Nina wants to read it, Bert. Can I show her a copy? I made a carbon."

Nina lived down the hall; Evie, unlike most New Yorkers, knew all her neighbors. She said she'd been shy as a girl, but Bert found it difficult to believe. In a doctor's waiting room, on a bus, in the laundry room, in any social situation, his mother would strike up a conversation immediately with whoever was around.

"Ma, you know I don't like people reading my papers."

"I know, and I told her that. I told her the only way I got to read it was because I typed it for you. I guess she'll understand . . ." Evie let her voice trail off.

Bert didn't so much mind his mother's attempt to make him feel guilty. What he minded was the incredible transparency of the effort. She thought she was being skillful at manipulating him, and really, she was very obvious. But she *had* typed the paper.

"Okay, she can read it. Just don't show it to anybody else. It's just a stupid paper."

"Thanks."

"Where's Philip?" Bert asked.

"Guess." She meant he was in bed.

"You're working late," he said.

"They need this tomorrow." Evie went back to her typing and Bert watched her for a moment. Her hands were ugly. She bit her nails down to the quick. Her fingers were still swollen and looked like they belonged to a pensioner in an old age home. The typing bothered her arthritis more and more. Because Evie worried that eventually she'd have to give up the business, she had decided two years earlier to go back to school to finish her pharmacy degree. She liked knowing about drugs, she liked knowing their side effects and their dosages. Somehow, while going to school, she managed to keep up the typing business. Bert helped out on weekends.

Bert left the office and went to his bedroom. His brother was there, asleep. He tapped a few times on the small plastic turtle bowl where he kept his snapping turtle. (The old wood turtle had died years earlier.)

Philip rolled over, opened his eyes, and saw Bert. "Hey, little bro."

"Hey, big bro."

Philip murmured something, closed his eyes, and fell back asleep. Bert kicked off his sneakers, picked up Philip's Spalding ball and lay on his bed a long time before getting undressed. He threw the Spalding up and down, throwing it, catching it, throwing it, catching it. And Bert remembered that once, when they were very young, Philip had lost his grip on a helium balloon Joseph had just given him and watched forlornly as it rose into the sky. He told Bert to let his balloon go, too, so it could keep the other balloon company. Bert complied at once.

Later, they played a game called Psychiatrist. Whenever Philip had a headache, Bert told him to lie down, put a cold washcloth on his brother's forehead, and asked him to describe his dreams. Bert took copious notes on a pad of yellow paper. Philip was always the patient. Bert was always the doctor.

Don't Be That Way

▾▾▾

THEY DIDN'T KNOW what to do about Philip. They could force him into a hospital since he was still a minor, but it would be a long, bitter legal battle. They could throw him out of the house, but how could they throw their son, his brother, into the street? They could persuade him to get help — and they tried, they tried every day. But Philip insisted he wasn't sick; they were sick for thinking he was sick. Homosexuals were trying to take over the planet. King Juan Carlos was a homosexual. Nina, their neighbor, owed him thirty thousand dollars, not to mention all the interest due. She was a lesbian, but Wayne, her husband, didn't know. The cleaning lady kept trying to seduce him. (The fearful cleaning lady stopped coming altogether.) Philip liked Nina's dog, a Weimaraner, but the schnauzer down the block had an electrical implant in her molars which made her bark at him.

The night before Bert's high school graduation, Philip began burning all his Bob Dylan albums in the kitchen sink. The curtains over the sink caught on fire, and Philip burned his hand badly. Joseph dashed in, tore the curtains down, threw them in the sink, and turned on the cold water. Evie put ice on Philip's burn. Joseph and Evie told Philip it was time to go to the hospital for treatment. Philip, afraid, agreed, and Joseph drove him down to Mount Sinai Hospital. The psychiatrist there spoke to Philip for an hour. Philip told him he felt like the devil sometimes and sometimes like God. The doctor persuaded Philip to commit himself.

Bert stayed at home with his mother. He put on some Ramones and Neil Young records (*albums,* he corrected himself) and tried to read a magazine, but he couldn't concentrate. He had thought he'd feel better once Philip was in a hospital, but he stood in the middle of his bedroom, looked at Philip's empty bed, and felt empty himself. He decided to go to a graduation party to get his mind off his brother. As he was about to leave, he found his mother sweeping up the ashes in the kitchen, and crying. It was only the second time in his life he had ever seen her cry; the first was when his uncle Buddy had died. "Please don't go," she begged him. She was scared to stay home alone and very worried about Philip. "Please don't go," she said. Bert called Alison and told her he'd forgotten he had to go see his grandparents, so he wouldn't be able to make the party.

"I must have been a terrible mother," Evie was saying. "I must have done something terrible to deserve this." Her fingers trembled nervously.

"It just happened," Bert said. "They think it's genetic."

"Genetic," Evie repeated. She tried to take a sip of coffee, but her hands were shaking too much and she couldn't hold the mug. Bert held the cup to her lips and she took a sip. "I meant to make decaf," she told him, "but it doesn't matter. I'm not going to sleep tonight anyway."

"He'll get better," Bert told her. "You'll see."

She nibbled at some toast. "I shouldn't eat, I'll get fat." She wiped her eyes and smiled at Bert. "You're such a good boy."

The next day they skipped graduation to visit Philip in the hospital. His hand was bandaged. He was doped up on antipsychotic and antidepressant drugs, and it took him longer than ever to respond. He noticed the delay himself and began to laugh. When Philip smiled his beautiful smile, his whole face lit up, like an incandescent bulb. It made Bert feel warm inside.

Juan Carlos called Bert the next day. "Where were you, kiddo? I go to the Felt Forum for graduation, just to see you, and you're not even there."

"I got food poisoning." Another another another lie. "Can

you believe it? It was probably one of your doughnuts," Bert teased. "The lemon custard tasted a little funny."

They snapped at one another all summer long. They argued about money. They argued about Bob Dylan. They argued about the meaning of "a rolling stone gathers no moss." They even argued about the death penalty. Bert and Joseph were against it. Joseph thought it was barbaric. Bert thought innocent people might be executed. Evie was in favor of capital punishment: she believed in an eye for an eye, a tooth for a tooth. Philip said the death penalty should be allowed if there were eyewitnesses to the crime.

For three months, Bert visited Philip every night so they could watch *The Odd Couple* and *Star Trek* reruns together. His parents usually visited Philip in the morning. Bert would take the D train to 161st Street, and then the Number 4 express train to 59th Street, and then the Number 6 local back uptown to 96th and Lexington. Then he'd walk to Madison Avenue, where the hospital was located. A few times, when he left the ward, the guard would mistake him for Philip and refuse to let him go. Fighting down his panic, Bert would have to convince the guard he wasn't Philip.

During the day, Bert worked at the typing business in his mother's office. He split the work with his mother, who was finishing up her classes, studying feverishly for her licensing exams to become a pharmacist, and visiting Philip in between.

Evie graduated at the end of the summer term, only three weeks before Bert would begin college. Graduation was held outdoors, under the August sun. Bert sat with his father; the sun beat against their backs, drenching them with sweat. Someone nearby said it was ninety-seven degrees. Campus do-gooders came by with enormous thermos containers, dispensing little Dixie cups full of water. Every so often the medical squads carted off people who had collapsed in the heat.

Watching some undergraduates get their diplomas, Bert started thinking about college. He was worried that Philip, who was now coming home from the hospital on weekends, would want to drive to Princeton with them when he left for school. Bert didn't want to bring him. Philip's behavior was still too unpredictable, his hair still straggly — he didn't look normal. He'd embarrass Bert in front of his new roommates. But what if he wanted to come? His brother had such a miserable life, Bert didn't want to deny him anything. He felt guilty about going to Princeton and leaving Philip behind. He wouldn't be able to say no.

At last Evie received her diploma, and though the audience had been told to save its applause for the end, Joseph rose to give Evie a standing ovation. They were quite far from the stage, but Bert, half embarrassed by his father's action and half pleased, was sure Evie would know who was applauding. She was fifty-one years old, the oldest by far in her graduating class.

When they got home, Evie stretched out on the sofa in the living room, resting her head on her arms. "So who's making dinner?" she wondered aloud, an old family joke, because no one but Evie ever made dinner. Joseph said they should go out somewhere nice to celebrate, but Evie said she was too tired to go out.

"Okay, we'll go on the weekend," Joseph suggested.

"Not on the weekend," Evie said. "It'll be too crowded." She got up from the sofa. "Maybe on Monday."

Bert understood. She didn't want to go out with Philip. He told his mother he'd make dinner, but Evie wouldn't let him: she said she wouldn't get to make dinner for him much longer. Anyway, she'd just whip up some salmon croquettes, it would only take a couple of minutes.

"Salmon croquettes?" Bert groaned. "Dorm food's sounding better and better."

"I think there's some Spam in the pantry," Evie said dryly.

After dinner, Joseph volunteered to do the dishes. He wore his official New York Yankees barbecue apron while he scoured the pans and sang Yiddish songs of insurrection.

*

Alison was leaving for Radcliffe. On their last night together, they went to the Thalia to see a movie and then had a farewell dinner at the Hunan Balcony. She was jumpy at the meal, laughing and exuberant one moment, teary the next, drinking cup after cup of the thin Chinese tea. They took a cab back to her house in Riverdale (Alison's father had sprung for the cab fare), and then it was time to go. Bert didn't know whether to hug her or kiss her goodbye. He tried to kiss her, but she had expected a hug. Then he tried to hug her, but she, changing tactics, was trying to kiss him. Supremely awkward, they both backed away, looked at each other, and then, moving forward, tried one more time, but got it wrong again. Then they just laughed. "Hold still," Bert said, and he squeezed her, then ran to the bus stop without looking back.

The night before he left for college, Bert had a strange dream. In the dream, Philip had insisted on going with him to Princeton. They were driving down the New Jersey Turnpike, and then the dream got fuzzy: a car accident, police sirens, an ambulance crew, green trees forming a canopy over the highway, and Philip lying dead in the middle of the road. Pounding on Philip's chest, Bert wished with all his heart that he might be dreaming; and then, miraculously, he forced himself awake. But it was an enormous effort to wake, as though he were deep beneath the ocean, struggling to reach the surface. And even when he had finally awoken, he wasn't sure he was really awake; he seemed in an odd, indeterminate, in-between place. The room was blurry. He had a terrific, pounding headache, and his heart was pounding too. But he saw Philip in the other bed, asleep, and then the room settled into focus, and he was back in real time. He remembered that Philip wasn't coming to Princeton; sensing Bert's discomfort, Philip had decided to stay home, although he would help them pack.

They packed all morning: clothing, books, his Yankees pennant, the arrowhead he'd found with Philip by the Bronx River, his Abbott and Costello poster, his deluxe Scrabble set, linens, blankets, towels. Evie had prepared a special small suitcase crammed full with medical supplies and over-the-counter pain-killers and antihistamines. The suitcase embarrassed Bert, but he knew it would hurt his mother's feelings if he didn't take it.

The Rosenbaums had no car; Evie had made Joseph give up his old Rambler after her brother died. Juan Carlos had lent them his Rabbit hatchback. The King was nervous about the trip to Princeton. He helped them pack the car, and then he flitted about, tightening knots, thumping valises, pleading again and again for Joseph to drive carefully.

"You know what, kiddos?" Juan Carlos finally said. "I can drive."

"It's a little out of your way," Joseph reminded him.

"No, no. I like the drive. It's beautiful."

Evie laughed. "The New Jersey Turnpike is beautiful?"

"Juan, there's no room," Bert said.

"Sure there is," Juan Carlos maintained, hurriedly repacking the back seat, smashing the boxes into a smaller and smaller area. "Bert, you can squeeze in the front."

"I'll be very careful," Joseph assured the King.

"Oh, I'm not worried," Juan Carlos told them. "You're a very good driver, I'm sure. . . . When's the last time you drove?"

"Thanks for everything," Joseph said, getting into the car.

Bert hugged Philip goodbye. "Be good," Philip said.

Juan Carlos grasped Bert's hand tightly. "Bert," he said, suddenly overcome with emotion. "Bert, listen to me."

"What's the matter, Juan?"

"I just want to tell you something." He was trembling and there were tears in his eyes. "*Dios que da la llaga, da la medicina.* God who gives the wound gives the medicine. Remember that, please?"

Joseph honked the horn, they waved goodbye, and then they were off. They drove south along the Grand Concourse. Bert thought their neighborhood looked beautiful in the September sun. Art deco buildings presided over the boulevard; the streets were lined with elms and maples. But south of Fordham Road, the concourse grew dingy: the heat had plastered scraps of paper to the sidewalk, shards of glass lined the curbs, rotting sneakers dangled indecorously from telephone wires overhead. The storefronts seemed inhospitable: cheap dress shops, superettes, numbers joints, a couple of hot dog and pizza places. They passed Yankee Stadium. Bert watched it whir by.

"Einstein taught at Princeton," his father reminded him.

"Big deal," Bert muttered.

Evie said, "It is a big deal."

"Einstein," Joseph breathed, ecstatically.

"Watch the road," Evie advised.

"A Princeton man." Joseph turned around to beam at Bert.

"Watch the road," Bert repeated.

"Just don't take the crap courses I did," Joseph told him. "Political science, anthropology, sociology — crap courses. Don't waste your time. Remember, you're not a rich man's son. Take accounting —"

"You want to lead his life for him," Evie said.

"I want him to avoid the same mistakes I made, that's all."

They were still worried about money. Bert had won a small scholarship, Evie had surprised him with two thousand dollars she'd saved for him secretly, and Bert had taken out loans to pay for the rest. He closed his eyes and tried to relax. A Louis Armstrong song buzzed in his head. Philip loved Louis Armstrong (not as much as Dylan, to be sure, but Armstrong ranked a close second). It was hot in the car, even with the windows rolled down. On the inside of his eyelids, Bert tried to see nothing but white, a white wall, a snowstorm. Whooping like an Indian, Philip turned around in the snow and grinned at him. Bert opened his eyes.

"What were you daydreaming about?" Joseph asked. They had just crossed the George Washington Bridge. (Judge to immigrant: Who was the father of our country? Immigrant to judge: I know, I know! It's — George Washington Bridge.)

"Nothing," Bert answered. "What's on the radio?"

"Noise," his mother said. She put down the Iris Murdoch novel she was reading and fiddled with the dial for him.

"Great, eighty minutes of static," Bert complained.

"And now," an announcer on the radio broke in, "WIWW will play Hank Williams's *Forty Greatest Hits.*"

"I can't believe it!" Bert shouted.

"Should I change the station?" Evie asked dryly. On the radio, Williams was singing, "My Bucket's Got a Hole in It."

They drove south along the New Jersey Turnpike. Evie went back to her book, then nodded off. When they were five miles from Princeton, a Buick driving in the opposite direction began swerving from lane to lane, sometimes entering the wrong side of the highway, forcing the drivers in Joseph's lane to scramble out of the way. The car's swerves grew more and more unpredictable. Joseph switched lanes, trying to get farther away. "He must be drunk," Joseph said. In the back, Bert put on his seat belt. "Jesus, what's with this guy," Joseph said. He clutched the steering wheel and swung into the rightmost lane. The Buick ahead, facing them, continued to swing from one side of the road to the other. "He's going to hit us," Joseph said quietly.

A swerve of the car woke Evie. "We'll be all right," Joseph said. He tried to get out of the way, but the Buick slammed into them, cutting into the front of the engine with a horrible crunching sound, slicing the hood along the diagonal—just the way Evie used to cut Bert's sandwiches to make them taste better (Bert remembered thinking). Juan Carlos's car, which was lighter than the Buick, spun around, the hatchback flew open, and all of Bert's belongings flew out. Traffic slid to a halt around them. People helped Bert out of the car. Where had these people come from? Bert was confused, his head hurt. Joseph ran around to the other. Bert was confused, his head hurt. Joseph ran around to the other Bert was confused, his head hurt. Joseph ran around to the other Bert was confused, his head hurt. Joseph ran around to the other side of the car to see if Evie was all right.

"I never will desert Mr. Rosenbaum," Evie said.

"Are you okay?" Joseph asked anxiously.

"You look a little dizzy, Mom." Bert was rubbing his head.

"Like son, like mother," Evie said, laughing.

HIGH
LOW

Physical

▼▼▼

BERT SPOTTED PATRICK BUTLER in front of a newsstand on Church Street. Patrick, handsome, broad-shouldered, and slim-waisted, like a marine cadet in an old Hollywood movie, was leafing through a golf magazine. It was a misty September day, and the owner of the kiosk had put up a plastic awning to protect the magazines. Patrick balanced an umbrella between his legs while he flipped through the pages. He looked up and smiled when Bert approached.

"You golf?" Bert asked.

"Yeah," Patrick said sheepishly, and put the magazine back on the rack. "I guess it's in my blood." He told Bert that he had grown up across the road from a golf course in Dearborn.

"I don't know how to golf," Bert said. "It's not that big a sport in the Bronx. Rape, murder, mutilation — that's more our bag. Although there is a course in Van Cortlandt Park . . ." He rattled on inanely about the park and realized he was nervous. Patrick worked on the floor above Bert, in the Department of Highways, and Bert didn't know him very well.

"Well, if you want to learn, I'll teach you."

"Thanks," Bert said. "I don't think I'd be very good."

"Do you know how to hold a club?"

Bert shook his head no.

"I'll show you."

Patrick demonstrated a grip on his umbrella. His red hands were strong and veined, but chapped. He was only twenty-four — Bert's senior by two years — but his hands looked older, and there were already faint lines around his eyes. He offered the umbrella to Bert, who tried to copy his grip, stance, and swing. "Imagine you're sitting on a bar stool," Patrick said. As Bert squatted in the street, a car honked at a passerby, and he was suddenly aware that he was being observed by hundreds of people. Patrick corrected his grip, lifting Bert's fingers and rearranging them on the handle, then putting one hand on the small of Bert's back and pressing down gently so that Bert would bend his knees. Bert eyed the ground, eyed his grip, and enjoyed the pressure of Patrick's hand on his back. . . . He realized he wasn't listening to Patrick.

"I quit track and field so I could go to band practice. Then I quit band practice because I wanted to keep golfing. I dreamed of being a pro, but I wasn't good enough. So then I just started working at the mall."

Patrick continued to talk about Dearborn. His tales of suburban Michigan sounded sweet, safe, and, Bert thought to himself — watching a young Latino teenager on roller skates pushing a garment rack before him, knocking down people in his path, and fleeing from a cop — rather exotic.

Bert had graduated from college in the middle of the 1982 recession, and nearly three months passed before he could find a job. Eventually his father talked to a friend in one of the municipal unions, and Bert got an interview at the New York City Department of Sewers. Sewers was looking for a staff analyst to beef up its personnel department. At his job interview, Bert had argued persuasively (he felt) that many of the personnel skills he'd learned working on the campus newspaper were transferrable to civil service. Later he found out he'd been hired because they needed a good typist.

Then Alison, who was staying in Boston to attend graduate school, helped him find an apartment. Alison's father was an electrical contractor, and a landlord on the Upper West Side owed him a favor. The landlord had a building on Ninety-seventh Street which was going co-op; one of the apartments was vacant, and he had planned to keep it empty so he could sell it for its market value. But he let Bert live there for very cheap rent, as long as Bert promised to move out at the end of a year. The studio apartment was tiny and dingy, but Bert loved the neighborhood. He could see a thin sliver of the Hudson River out the window. Once or twice, magically, the image of the river bounced off the windowpane and reappeared on the mirror over his bureau. Entranced, he had dimmed the lights and watched the water surge in the silvered glass.

It had rained again the night before, and as Bert walked to the corner candy store to buy a soda, the air was bracing and clean. The only other customer was a boy with Down's syndrome, who was looking through the comics on an old, squeaky metal rack, turning the rack round and round, occasionally picking up a comic book and then putting it back neatly into place. He finally picked an issue of *X-Men* and paid for it with pennies and nickels. Philip had loved the X-men. Bert didn't want to think about Philip.

Bert walked back home. In front of his building, two children were singing as they splashed around in a puddle of rainwater, sending water flying in every direction. The girl was about eight years old, the boy a year younger. A stocky, middle-aged woman in a brown dress, with large brown circles under her eyes, was sitting at her kitchen table on the first floor of the building, watching them through her window and listening as they serenaded her. The children were singing Olivia Newton-John's "Physical."

"Do you like the song?" the girl asked Bert, who had also listened.

"Not so much," Bert said. "But I think you sing it very well."

The girl was jumping up and down in the puddle. "The aliens hate it, too."

"You mean the Romanians?" Bert asked. The superintendent of the building and his family came from Bucharest.

"The *aliens,*" the boy insisted.

"You know, UFOs, spacemen, E.T. We see them all the time," the girl told Bert.

The boy kicked some water. "You don't believe us, do you."

Bert said, "Oh, I don't know."

"We're not supposed to talk about them," the boy said. "But we can't keep our mouths shut."

The woman in the brown dress got up slowly from the table, crossed carefully to the window, and shut it loudly. Then she drew the curtains and walked back into the dark interior of her apartment.

The girl's name was Isabel, the boy's name was Lars. Lars told Bert that the aliens were bald, wore mustaches and sheriffs' badges, and left a trail of green slime wherever they crawled.

"They crawl?"

"Yes," Lars told him.

"No," Isabel said.

"*Yes,*" Lars maintained.

The debate deteriorated into a shoving match before Bert finally interceded.

"We'll show you the aliens, and then you can decide," Isabel told him.

"Fine," Bert said.

"Fine," Lars said.

Patrick had a thin, sunburned face and bright blue eyes, and wore his crisp blond hair long and jagged in the back. They were spending more time together, going out for lunch at the dozens of cheap restaurants around city hall, although they still hadn't golfed.

Patrick loved rock music. Detroit was a hard-rocking town, he told Bert. When Lou Reed played a concert downtown at the Ritz, they decided to go. The floor was sticky, the music incredibly loud. More and more people poured into the room, and the room got hotter and hotter, until Bert could feel beads of sweat dripping, drop by drop, down his back. The walls and the floors of the Ritz vibrated, and small throngs of dancers formed within the larger mob. The crowd churned with the music, like roiling water. Bert and Patrick found themselves in a group of East Villagers: skinny men and women, pierced, tattooed, and clad in black. Sometimes Patrick danced with a woman in a black miniskirt, sometimes he danced by himself, sometimes he seemed to be dancing with Bert. They danced for hours.

At work the next day, Bert was exhausted. His body was sore, and he had a headache. "Did we have fun?" Diana asked him, watching him swallow some aspirin. Diana had just started working at Bridges and Tunnels, on the same floor as Bert but on the other side of the bullpen. She came from Calumet City, Illinois, outside Chicago, and had a flat midwestern accent that got under Bert's skin.

"Yeah, I had fun."

"I bet."

Diana was very pretty, about twenty-seven, with a perfectly oval face, and short blond hair buzzed bluntly in the back. She had attended Catholic grade school and high school and then studied history at Northwestern for two years. Her husband, who was Jewish, had just been transferred to New York from Chicago, and they had moved into an apartment in White Plains. She asked Bert for books to read, and she read them on the train during her commute. She liked to read the ending of a book first. She said that way it was like a puzzle, to see how the writer could navigate all the way through a book to get to the final point. She said she hardly saw her husband. She said she saw Bert more. She said her husband never read. She said she liked Jewish men. She had a wonderful sense of humor, she liked to laugh, and she liked to tease. She had a wonderful, throaty laugh, a husky laugh, deep in her body.

"I never have fun," she complained to Bert. "I should spend time with you. I bet you could show me a good time."

"I could try," Bert said, and realized, a beat late, that they were flirting.

Bert had avoided the trip for two weeks, but Lars and Isabel finally dragged him to the back yard behind the apartment building. (Bert called it a back yard only because they took offense when he termed it an air shaft.) The children cleared a path through the bags of garbage that had piled up in the basement and then pushed open the heavy iron door that led outside.

"The aliens like this place," Lars told him. Bert looked around: concrete, a few blades of grass forcing their way up from the cracks, a dirty puddle of water.

"They enjoy their privacy," Isabel explained. "People can't stare at them here."

"Oh, would people stare?" Bert asked politely.

"Well, they're alien-looking," Isabel said.

"They look like chairs," Lars informed him.

"Lawn chairs," Isabel amended.

They paused for a moment. "Green lawn chairs," they said in unison.

"But most people can't see them at all," Isabel told Bert.

"No?"

"Just some people," Lars agreed.

"Their heads look like rectangles," Isabel said.

Lars stared pointedly at his sister. "Triangles."

"Whatever," Bert said.

Isabel and Lars stood four feet apart from each other and began to chatter away in an unearthly, low, guttural tongue. Goomalay, they called it. "They're almost here," Isabel panted, reverting to English.

"Almost," Lars called out. "Almost . . ."

They broke off at the same time. "It's no good," Isabel said. She turned toward Bert. "You're holding back."

"Me?"

Lars was miffed. "They were almost here, and you blocked them."

"I didn't," Bert insisted.

"We'll try again tomorrow," said Isabel.

Diana's favorite period of history was the Russian Revolution. She loved the passion and the bloodshed. Two nights a week she was taking a beginning Russian class at N.Y.U., not for credit but for fun. She had taught Bert the Cyrillic alphabet so that he could quiz her on her vocabulary words; in return, she tested Bert on Soviet history. She challenged him to name the triumvirate who succeeded Lenin.

"Stalin," Bert began.

"Obviously."

"Zinoviev."

"Good."

"And . . ." He struggled to remember.

"Oh, Bert. I'm so disappointed."

"Kamenev!"

She kissed him on his forehead. "Good boy." Bert thought she should finish college. She was too smart to be satisfied as a clerk. But Diana said she wasn't ambitious. She liked having a job she didn't have to think about too much. She got her work done and put her energies elsewhere. Diana and her husband, Rob, were scouting out houses in Westchester and Connecticut on weekends. They wanted to buy their own place.

Sometimes Diana said she didn't know why they were even looking for a house because she expected they would get divorced. She said her sex life was dwindling. Rob was losing interest in her. He said he was just tired, and he did have a stressful job, marketing software programs, but Diana worried that he didn't find her attractive anymore. She said she missed the sex.

She decided she was going to get back into shape. "Then I'll be cute again, and all the boys will go wild." After work, on the days Diana didn't go to N.Y.U., she took an aerobics class. She usually changed in the ladies' room in the office and modeled her tights for Bert — red, orange, green, purple. She showed Bert the different steps she followed in her class: running in place while drawing the knees high up, stretching left, then right, dancing from side to side, squat-thrusting. He grew hard, once, watching her.

Patrick and Bert went out again, to hear a band playing at Pier Three. Afterward, Patrick was wired. He said music got him hopped up. He was always so wildly enthusiastic: about golf, rock and roll, skiing, Indian food, chocolate, sambas. Once, when Rob had gone out of town on business, Bert had gone dancing with Diana, Patrick, and Patrick's coworker Kathleen at Sounds of Brazil. Patrick had danced like a dervish, like someone possessed. His passion frightened Bert. Patrick seemed out of control. "I don't think I can sleep tonight," Patrick said. "You don't have any pot, do you?"

Bert said he had some Valium, left over from college, when he'd gotten stressed during exams. Patrick came over to the apartment, and Bert gave him a couple of pills. Patrick took one and washed it down with a beer. "Thank you so much."

He walked around Bert's small apartment. The tiny bathroom was off to the right of the entryway. Next came a hall closet and then the narrow kitchen area — double sink, oven, refrigerator, and cabinets, all along one wall. A tall Formica island, used as a counter and table, separated the kitchen from the living area. A pair of high metal chairs faced each other across the island. The living area barely had room for Bert's double bed, a chest of drawers, a bookcase, a compact stereo, a portable television set, and the three small cactus plants he constantly overwatered. Wherever there was wall space, and in the corners of the mirror over the chest, Bert had placed photos — of his parents, Philip, his uncle Buddy, friends from school.

"I know it's not the greatest apartment in the world, but the rent's cheap." Bert was often embarrassed by how small and dark the room was.

"And it's in Manhattan. Sounds pretty good to me." Patrick sat on the down comforter. Bert had treated himself to the double bed as soon as he moved in. It made him feel like a grown-up.

Bert put on some Van Morrison, *Astral Weeks*. "This'll relax you."

"Great." Patrick lay on the bed with his eyes closed.

Bert lay down beside him, so that his left leg brushed up against Patrick's right. His nerves were jangling. They didn't speak for a while, then Bert rolled closer. Patrick didn't move away. "Patrick?"

"Hmm?"

Bert moved closer still. Patrick put his hand on Bert's thigh. Bert could hear his heart thudding slushily. He felt as though he were swimming underwater. Patrick used Bert's thigh for leverage and sat up. "I guess I should be going. I don't want to crash on you."

Bert sat up too. "You can stay over if you're tired." Patrick and his cousin shared an apartment in Queens, a long subway ride away.

"Nah, I'll be okay."

Bert walked him to the elevator, then hugged him good night. Patrick clapped him on the back a few times. "Night, buddy."

"Good night."

"You're such a good friend," Patrick said. "Thanks."

The elevator came and Patrick left. Bert walked slowly back to his apartment. He got undressed and lay in bed awake for a long time. He thought about his girlfriend in college, Stacey, a sunny, placid premed student. Initially she had pursued him. He hadn't been interested, and she had withdrawn, but once she'd withdrawn, he found he was attracted to her. They had dated for two years. The longer he'd known her, the better he could anticipate her actions; and the more he anticipated, the more annoyed he became, until all his time with her was spent calculating what she would do next. He would seethe when she did what he predicted or blow up at her and accuse her of chicanery if she failed to conform to his expectations. Then he would buy her presents because he felt guilty. With their roommates and her long hours in the lab and his long hours on the newspaper, they had had sex only rarely. She had never really excited him. Their lovemaking was pleasant yet somehow remote. Bert had come to believe that sex was always remote. As they made love, part of him was always watching, always in control.

When he thought about how he had behaved toward Stacey — about the hundreds of petty, ambiguous, easily deniable injuries — he was ashamed of himself. They had broken up at the beginning of senior year. Their relationship settled first into an uneasy truce and then into a friendly comraderie. But when the friendship deepened, it threatened to turn into romance again, and then they had both backed away, until by graduation they were barely speaking.

He couldn't sleep. He remembered going to Stacey's eating club, and how happy she'd been — how happy he'd made her, and how little it had taken. He remembered Patrick rearranging his fingers on the umbrella and pressing the small of his back. He remembered Diana modeling her tights — he forced himself to remember. He remembered Patrick clapping his back just a half hour earlier . . .

He tried not to think about Patrick, but Patrick kept pushing through. Patrick grinned at him on Church Street like Philip had grinned at him once in the snow; Patrick's thigh grazed Bert's thigh the way Bert's and Philip's thighs had touched when they Indian-wrestled; Patrick mixed music and drugs into Philip's favorite cocktail.

Bert was sweating and threw off his blankets. He couldn't control his thoughts, as Philip hadn't been able to control his. This new, unwelcome urge for Patrick was crazy, diseased, pernicious. Bert was confused, his head hurt: Patrick reminded him of Philip, and Philip reminded him of himself. What if all this time, Philip and gay desire had lurked inside him, dormant, like a slow virus?

He was shaking. He took a Tylenol for his headache and a Valium so he could sleep. Well, fuck all of you, Bert thought as he swallowed the pills. Fuck all of you for making me feel different. You don't know who I am, so don't tell me what to do.

He lay down and rearranged the covers. Philip, different. Patrick, different. Crazy, different. Gay, different. He wasn't gay. He'd had a girlfriend in college. Philip, different. Patrick, different. Crazy, different. Gay, different. The words formed a pattern, and although the words were threatening, the pattern calmed him. To give in to the pattern, to the repetition, was easy, was comforting. Gradually he sank into sleep, and from sleep into a dream, and then he heard screaming. At first he incorporated the screaming into his dream, but the screaming seemed to gather force, until at last it woke him. "I'm not keeping you up," a woman was screaming at the top of her lungs. "You're keeping *me* up! No one knows what Jane goes through! If you want me to sleep, stop burning my genitals! Stop burning my genitals and I'll sleep!"

Bert heard the sound of glass shattering. He sat up in bed and looked at his clock. It was four in the morning.

"I broke your mirror? I broke *your* mirror? It was Jane's mirror! Stop torturing Jane! You and your FBI plots! Oh God, let me sleep! Stop burning and mutilating my genitals! Burn and mutilate your own genitals!"

Bert opened the window and tried to figure out where the noise was coming from. He couldn't believe how piercing the voice was. It seemed to echo from the building next door, across the air shaft. The woman was crying, noisily. "God, God, please let me sleep. Kill me if you want, but don't mutilate me little by little . . ."

Bert got back into bed but couldn't get back to sleep. The woman had started moaning, like an animal. Bert put his head under the covers, trying to block out the noise. Every time he was about to fall asleep, she started screaming again. At around six A.M. she stopped, and Bert slept fitfully for an hour or two.

In the morning, he stumbled into the shower, got dressed, grabbed some juice, then went downstairs to buy a bagel and the Sunday paper before heading to Riverside Park. He felt shaky and slightly nauseated. He found a quiet part of the park, and lay down, half under the shade of a maple, half in the warm October sunlight. Bert relaxed. The grass was very green, and for a few minutes at least, he allowed himself to be off his guard. Bert felt his eyelids close, opened them resolutely, felt them close, pried them open, felt them close.

He felt a humming around him, and the air seemed to grow heavier, and when Bert opened his eyes a small cigar-shaped craft was landing at his feet. The lid of the ship opened and three space aliens emerged.

The aliens were green, short — about three feet tall — and squat. Their oily skin gave off a wet, fishy smell. They had four legs, and at rest, their bodies angled backward, like lawn chairs. Their faces were large and round, but their mouths were thin and tight. Their big, doleful, light green eyes seemed to see inside him. On each hand they had three fingers and an opposable thumb. Their arms were very flat, like armrests.

Two of the aliens were — Bert assumed — nude. On these two, what would have been the seat of the lawn chair was darker green than the rest of their bodies, and had the obscene, engorged protuberance of a hamadryas baboon's hindquarters. The third alien, hairier than the others, was wearing a mauve Norma Kamali outfit that Bert had seen in the window of Bloomingdale's. Green mucus oozed out of their mournful eyes and tiny nostrils.

"Greetings," said the tallest. "My name's Herbert. Also known as Harold." His tongue was long, green, and narrow and poked nervously out of his mouth even after he had finished speaking.

"Oh God," Bert said. His hands were sweating. He wanted to run, but he felt frozen, as in a nightmare. His limbs wouldn't respond.

"We've been trying to get in touch with you for quite a while," a second one told him in a clipped, cool, yet feminine voice. "But you were always blocking. We had to make some changes before we could reach you." She touched him and left a thin trail of fishy, viscous green slime on his skin. "You don't mind, do you?"

"It doesn't matter if he minds," said the third (the one wearing Norma Kamali) in a basso profundo voice. "It's too late now." The creature crept up to Bert so that its tongue was nearly against his ear and sang in a husky, bitchy, insinuating whisper: "It's too late, baby, now it's too late . . ."

"I suppose it is," the first said quickly. "But here we are."

Bert was starting to shiver. He wondered if he had the flu. He wondered if he had a high fever. He wondered if he was hallucinating.

"You're gonna like us," the third assured him, still up against his ear, dripping green saliva onto Bert's neck.

"Oh God," Bert said again. "Please don't hurt me."

The third continued to taunt him. "You're gonna like us sooo much."

"Stop it, Ribsy," the second one commanded. And then she introduced herself: "Call me Evelyn." She was plump and had softer, rounder features than the others.

"Evelyn's my mother's name," Bert noted vacantly.

"Isabel and Lars told you about us, yes?" Herbert asked him.

"Yes, but, but —"

Evelyn interrupted his stammering. "You know, I don't think he's ready for us," she told the others in her measured, clinical tone.

"Almost," Herbert said. "He's almost ready." He approached Bert slowly, carefully, like an orderly in a hospital quieting a disturbed patient. "Bert, I'm afraid we're going to have to rewire your circuitry."

"Ooh," said Ribsy, suddenly squeamish. "I don't want to watch."

Bert backed away from them. He wanted to fly from the park, into the city, where he could merge into the crowds. "Get away from me," he half ordered, half begged. "Get away from me."

A miniature schnauzer, off its leash, came running up and started barking at the aliens. In a flash the aliens and their spaceship disappeared. Bert was left alone with the dog and a small pool of green slime.

Sugar Honey Iced Tea

▼▼▼

THEN SMOKE STARTED BILLOWING out of the car and a state trooper took a fire extinguisher and started spritzing it everywhere. The car didn't catch fire, though. Which is good because it wasn't even our car. We borrowed it." Somehow they'd started talking about car accidents, and Bert was telling Diana and his coworkers Barbara and Harry about his first trip to Princeton, four years before.

"It wasn't your car?" Harry laughed. "I'd like to have seen the guy's face when you brought it back."

"Me too." Bert felt guilty: he hadn't called King Juan Carlos in a long time. "Luckily, the other guy had insurance. He was drunk. I think he lost his license for about thirty days, that's all."

"And no one was hurt?" Barbara asked.

"We thought my mother might have had a concussion, and I was dizzy, too, but it turned out we were fine. It's a good thing my brother didn't come with us. I think if he'd sat next to me in back, he would have been killed."

Philip was living in California, sharing an apartment with a friend from his freshman year at college. He worked at a bookstore in Santa Monica. When he stayed on his medication, he functioned well, but sometimes he'd stop taking his pills and then his behavior would become erratic again. He didn't know how to drive so he had to take buses everywhere, but otherwise he liked Los Angeles. He said he was a little lonely, and he was teaching himself to play the guitar, so he could join a rock band.

"No one hurt — well, that's a miracle. The Lord was watching over you. That's right, and don't you laugh at me," Barbara said, turning to Harry, "or I'll slap your fanny."

"I didn't say anything," Harry protested.

"But you thought it. The Lord was keeping his eye on you, Bert. You know that, child."

"Testify, Bert," Harry prompted.

Bert ignored him. "People figured out from my luggage we were going to Princeton, and five or six cars stopped to ask if we needed any help. My mother went on ahead with one of them and brought some of my stuff to my room. By the time I got there, she was already best friends with my roommate and had told him all about me. I was so pleased."

Diana did an imitation of Bert's mother: "This is Bert's typewriter. He's an excellent typist."

"That's not bad," Bert admitted.

"You're too hard on that woman," Barbara said.

"No, he's too hard on me." Diana walked back to the other side of the bullpen.

"I don't trust that girl," Barbara muttered.

Barbara and Harry both worked for the Department of Sewers. Harry Lamartine Fourdrinier was a budget officer, about thirty years old, part Creole, part Native American, but mostly black. He had been a dancer in the Merce Cunningham dance company ("All Osage Indians are superb dancers," he assured Bert); he had played drums in a jazz group; he had studied Arabic at Columbia University; now he was getting his M.B.A. part-time. He was slim, fit, and tall, about six feet two. His face was lighter than the rest of his body and slightly pocked by acne scars. He still took dance classes and carried himself like a dancer.

Barbara Pitt was also black, a thin, freckled woman in her late forties who worked as a secretary to Bert's boss, Steven. She had two grown daughters, one a painter and graphic designer, the other a bookkeeper, but she looked much younger than her age. Her hair was cropped close to her scalp and she wore small hoop earrings.

Bert sat between the two. Long white fluorescent tubes

hummed overhead. The desks in Sewers were all battered wood or battered metal; Bert's was metal. On one side of the bullpen, three small offices gave the occupants some privacy. Bert's boss worked in the cubicle in the corner. On the opposite side of the bullpen, the Department of Bridges and Tunnels had three identical cubicles. Tall steel file cabinets lined the side walls; papers and plants were piled on top. The walls had been painted a violently cheerful canary color after an analyst in the comptroller's office read an article suggesting that yellows boosted productivity. The ceiling was still beige.

The phone rang. The call was from a research firm that Bert had hired to field a survey for him. The company needed someone to approve the budget. Bert had asked his boss who needed to sign, but Steven didn't know and seemed incapable of finding out. Bert had gone then to Steven's boss, the assistant commissioner, but he had just sent Bert back to Steven. The deadline for the survey results was looming, and Bert knew he'd be blamed if the survey wasn't completed in time.

"Just sign it yourself," Barbara advised. "That's what I always do."

"What if they sue me?"

"What could they get?"

"My portable TV." He grabbed the contract, signed it, sealed it in an envelope, and put it in his out basket. It seemed to Bert that Barbara knew better than anyone — better than Steven, the assistant commissioner, or even the mayor — how civil service offices worked.

He hadn't told anyone about seeing the aliens, not even Isabel and Lars. Over the course of a week he had managed to convince himself that it had all been a dream.

He had met Lars and Isabel's parents, Jorgen and Luisa Heiberg, several times in the elevator. Luisa was a dark-skinned Latino woman. The children were much lighter, and Isabel had blond hair, like her father, a Norwegian. Luisa worked as a ticket agent for American Airlines. Jorgen was a taxicab dispatcher. He had been an air traffic controller — Luisa liked to describe their romantic first encounter, in a La Guardia Airport employees' lounge — but had lost his job during the strike.

Luisa invited Bert for lunch one Sunday. Isabel, excited, showed Bert the slime molds she collected. Lars, a budding lepidopterist, took Bert on a guided tour of his pressed butterflies. And Jorgen, the proudest of all, bragged to Bert about all his recent purchases: a Leica camera, fantastically expensive stereo speakers, and a computer. When Luisa teased Jorgen about his childlike enthusiasm, Jorgen sank into a chair in a corner of the living room and sulked. Because Jorgen seemed to spend so much money, and because his mood swung so erratically, Bert wondered if his Norwegian neighbor took and dealt drugs.

Diana told Bert she had been heavy as a girl, "a blimp." She said she had worn an awful, scratchy gray woolen uniform and looked like a horse. She hated Catholic school and she hated nuns. She was thin now, even thinner after all the aerobics, sleek, like a cat. She sat in her chair like a cat, too, with her feet curled underneath her.

They liked to trade dirty jokes. "What's white and ten inches long?" she asked him.

"What?"

"Nothing."

Bert wandered upstairs to the Department of Highways. He was always doing that, shuttling back and forth between Diana and Patrick. Sometimes it was hard getting any work done. "Hey, Pat, what's white and ten inches long?"

"My dick."

"In your dreams," Bert said.

"Well, what's the answer?"

"Nothing's white and ten inches long."

"You're a goof," Patrick told him.

They had dinner together that night, at an Indian restaurant on Chambers Street. The waitress brought them their food and smiled at Patrick. She was pretty, maybe nineteen. Bert watched his friend smile back at her. Patrick was wearing a sweater, but the restaurant was hot and the food was spicy. When he took off his sweater, his shirt slid up with it, and Bert caught a glimpse of Patrick's stomach, and a thin trail of hair crawling up his abdomen. Bert wanted a flat stomach like that.

"How's your dad doing?" he asked. Patrick's father had been laid off at Chrysler.

"I feel bad for him. He's trying so hard to find work. I offered him money." Patrick winced. "It was awful."

"He turned you down?"

"Yeah, but my mom said yes. They need the money. She's worried they're going to lose the house."

"You know, there's a Yiddish saying," Bert remembered. "When a father gives money to his son, both laugh. When a son gives money to his father, both cry."

"In Dearborn, I didn't have a single Jewish friend."

"Want to see my horns?"

"Don't even say something like that."

Bert and Harry had seen a movie near Lincoln Center and then had walked a mile and a half uptown to Bert's apartment. Now they were getting high and listening to *Blood on the Tracks*. Bert didn't smoke much, but Harry liked to get stoned on weekends and always seemed to have a supply of pot.

"Pat's really a great guy," Bert told Harry. "You should get to know him."

"I just want to impale myself on him. God, I miss dick. Two months of celibacy and I'm going crazy." Harry put his hands over his mouth. "Listen to me, I'm so bad."

"You think he's gay?"

"I can't tell," Harry said. "With him, I can't tell." They smoked in silence for a while. "This is a great album."

"This is great pot."

Bert bought a quarter ounce from Harry. He wanted to have

some around the house — like a host who stocks good-quality gin and vermouth.

After a long, listless day at work, Diana, Patrick, and Bert walked over to J&R's record store on Park Row. They stopped first to buy cans of iced tea from an elderly black man with an ice chest in front of City Hall Park. Patrick and Diana argued about music, then about who had taken more drugs in their reckless college days, and finally about whether it was good for children to grow up in the suburbs. The last debate grew testy because Diana wanted to bring up a family in Westchester and Patrick insisted New Rochelle or Mamaroneck would destroy a child's soul. "I'm still getting over Dearborn," he told them. "It's like a disease." Bert, the only one who hadn't grown up in a suburb, remained neutral.

The three separated when they got to J&R's; Diana went to the classical section, Patrick to the rock and roll, Bert to the jazz. He ended up buying a Louis Armstrong–Earl Hines album, then went downstairs to wait for the others. Diana came down first. She hadn't bought anything, and she said goodbye and left before Patrick returned.

Patrick, who was broke but had bought a half dozen albums anyway, ended up going straight home, too. Bert walked him to the subway stop near the store. Patrick patted Bert's back goodbye and then let his hand trail down Bert's spine to his ass, where it rested for a moment. Then Patrick hurried down the subway steps.

Bert, startled, his heart hammering, started walking across City Hall Park, toward his own subway stop. The space aliens were waiting for him in the park.

"Greetings," Herbert said again.

"Stop doing this to me." Bert backed away from them. They seemed cleaner than before — there was no more mucus on their faces — but they still terrified him.

"What's the matter this time?" Ribsy asked him. Ribsy was wearing the same Norma Kamali outfit.

"I don't want you to rewire my circuitry." Bert realized how ridiculous it sounded.

"We won't have to. It seems as though you've rewired it on your own. Sometimes that happens after an initial contact," Evelyn told him, matter-of-factly.

"Now, Bert, listen to me very carefully," Ribsy said, grabbing his wrist and holding on so tightly it hurt. Bert stared at Ribsy's green arm and the wristwatch Ribsy was wearing. The numerals on the watch were written in a strange, alien script consisting of wedgelike forms. "Have you told anyone about us?"

"No. No one. I promise."

"All right then." Ribsy let go of Bert's wrist.

In the seat of their chairs, the aliens had what looked like a built-in storage area, on a hinge. It reminded Bert of a piano bench with room for music inside. Herbert opened the lid. "We're marsupials," he explained. He removed a release form for Bert to sign. The contract stated that Bert would never reveal the existence of the aliens or discuss them with anyone but Lars and Isabel. If he didn't sign, Herbert said apologetically, they would never contact him again, but they'd have to remove portions of his memory.

"Wh—— what do you mean 'remove'?"

"I mean, we go inside your cranium and eliminate all the relevant peptides. It's painful, I'm afraid."

"Sorry," Ribsy said.

Bert read the document quickly and then signed.

"You're a lefty," Ribsy observed. "It figures."

After he had signed, the aliens seemed more at ease. Herbert opened his dark green seat again, took out his pipe, lit it, and began to smoke contentedly. Ribsy, who had long green hair, began manicuring his or her nails and painting them with green nail polish. Evelyn took out knitting needles and busied herself with a wool blanket. The clacking sound of the needles reminded Bert of his mother's typing. Indeed, Evelyn worked with his mother's same intense concentration.

"We're from the planet Debbie," Herbert informed him,

"though one of Evelyn's mothers was actually born on Enoch, our brother-sister world."

"You have more than one mother?" Bert asked.

"It gets confusing when we speak in English," Evelyn said. "We have a male mother, a female mother, and a *malchick* mother."

"Malchick," Bert repeated.

"It's the word for my gender," said Ribsy.

Herbert explained the usage: " 'Give the ball to Ribsy. Malchick wants the ball.' "

"Malchick wants *to* ball is more like it." Ribsy laughed uproariously at malchick's own joke. It was a strange laugh, "tee hee hee tee hee hee" repeated over and over again in what sounded to Bert like a joyless, flat monotone. Ribsy's mane of green hair shook back and forth.

"Actually, we're all *malchiks.*" Herbert varied his pronunciation somewhat and then spelled out the word. "But Ribsy is malchick-malchik, or malchick for short."

"It's not so difficult, really," Evelyn said. "You'll get used to it."

"You'll keep quiet about us, won't you, duck?" Ribsy asked. "No one's supposed to know we're here."

"Yes, sorry for the formality of the contract, but we have to maintain some safeguards," Herbert told him. "According to the Federation's Prime Directive, we mustn't influence the history of another planet."

"The Prime Directive?" Bert muttered. "The Federation?"

"We got the idea from *Star Trek,*" Evelyn said.

"Oh dear." Ribsy was looking at malchick's cuneiform watch. "We're late. We'd better go, but we'll be in touch."

The aliens walked away, Ribsy sashaying in front. Bert was perturbed by Ribsy's confusing sexuality, like a taxonomist troubled by a platypus: the creature didn't fit into any established category. Malchick's flamboyance made Bert uneasy, as if malchick were mocking him or mocking sex itself. Then Bert decided he was a bigot, fearing Ribsy only because malchick was different.

"I like your dress," he called lamely after Ribsy.

Ribsy turned around. "This old thing?" Malchick modeled the Norma Kamali outfit coquettishly, and then the three aliens vanished.

The next night, Patrick and Bert went out to hear another band. Patrick was buzzing afterward. Bert asked him if he wanted to go back to his apartment — he had some pot.

"Well, thank you, Mr. Rosenbaum. This is an unexpected treat."

When they got to his studio, Bert brought out the bag of pot, and Patrick rolled a joint dexterously. "I was never very good at that," Bert confessed. "Harry had to do it for me last time."

"Harry was here?"

"Yeah."

They lit the joint and started smoking. Bert put on the radio, then brought Patrick a beer and some pretzels.

"We're friends, right?" Patrick asked.

"You know we are."

"But I'm not your best friend."

"I don't know if I have a best friend."

Bert sat next to Patrick on the bed. "Bert," Patrick said, "do you think I could please have one of those pills? I'm still wired."

"I'll give you one later."

"Thanks," Patrick said. He leaned back on the bed, closed his eyes for a minute, then opened them. He put his hand on Bert's thigh and scratched Bert's jeans. Bert scratched Patrick's jeans. Patrick squeezed Bert's penis through the jeans. Bert put his hand on Patrick's chest, then rubbed Patrick's neck softly with his other hand. He kissed Patrick's neck.

"Do you like this?" Bert whispered, so his voice wouldn't shake.

"You look so scared," Patrick said.

Bert pulled down the window shade, and they started kissing. Patrick's lips tasted salty from the pretzel, and his tongue tasted sour from the beer. They kissed, and Bert felt his lips melt into

Patrick's lips, until his own lips tasted salty, too. Patrick kicked off his pants, then Bert kicked off his pants. Patrick took off his boxer shorts. Bert still had his Jockey underpants on. Patrick gave a tug on them, and Bert slipped out of these, too.

"You've got red pubic hair," Patrick said.

"I've noticed."

Patrick asked for a Valium. He said it relaxed him. "I wonder what you'd do for a Quaalude," Bert said, handing the pill to him.

"You've got Quaaludes?"

"I was kidding." He peeled off Patrick's socks while Patrick swallowed the pill.

"Bert, you're not going to tell anyone at work, are you?"

"Of course not."

"You won't tell Harry?"

"No."

They lay on their sides, their bodies intertwined, like two pairs of scissors. Bert rubbed his cheek against Patrick's stubble. "Did you shave this morning?"

"No."

Bert worked his hands down each vertebra of Patrick's back. "That feels good," Patrick said. He kissed Bert. "Are you still scared?"

"Yeah," Bert said.

But he got less scared as the night progressed. They kissed and came, kissed and came, then cuddled on Bert's down comforter. Bert felt so light, so lithe and limber, as though he'd been doing yoga. A feather from the comforter somehow ended up in his mouth.

Patrick got up at dawn so he'd have time to go back to Queens and change his clothes before going to work. Bert stayed in bed. On his sheets he could still smell the faint sweet odor of Dial soap and almondy Vidal Sassoon shampoo — Patrick's soap, Patrick's shampoo. Bert took a shower, then made breakfast for himself, and he thought, This is the same cereal as yesterday, the same milk, the same package of cheap paper napkins, the same cheap stainless steel spoon. Yet everything was different, everything had been Doppler-shifted to a higher, more perfervid frequency. He was spent but intoxicated.

"Honey," Barbara told Bert at work, "you look like something the cat dragged in. Here you go." She brought him a cup of coffee.

"Thanks," Bert said. "You didn't have to do that."

"I know. If I had to, I wouldn't." She set the coffee cup down but accidentally sloshed some of the liquid over the side. She quickly dabbed it up with some tissue. "Sugar honey iced tea."

"I never heard that before," Bert said.

"Nowadays kids say 'Snap.' Have you heard that? They say 'Oh, snap.' But they mean 'Oh, shit.' That kills me."

"We used to say 'Oh, sweat,' " Harry recalled.

"Sure, we used to say 'Oh, sweat,' " Bert said. "But I never heard 'Sugar honey iced tea.' "

"In my family we weren't allowed to curse," Barbara recounted. "My daddy wouldn't have it. And we weren't allowed to call someone a liar or use the word 'lie.' People told stories. People were storytellers. My daddy was so old-fashioned."

"Feel free to talk as though to a neighbor," Evelyn suggested. "We're very conversant with Earthly cultural references: Jesus, Rembrandt, Lenny Bruce . . ."

"Uh huh," Bert said. It was all so bizarre. After work, he had taken the subway to Coliseum Books, and then walked into Central Park, where he had run into the aliens again.

"Evelyn's doing her Ph.D. on Lenny Bruce," Herbert said proudly.

"Well, not solely on Lenny Bruce," Evelyn corrected him. "I'm calling it 'Modes of American Jewish Humor,' with a concentration on Lenny Bruce and Robin Williams."

"But Robin Williams isn't Jewish," Bert pointed out.

"Oh, shit," Evelyn said. "Now you tell me?"

Bert was still feeling wobbly around the extraterrestrials, and he was tired from staying up all night with Patrick, so he sat down on the grass, and the three aliens settled in a circle of chairs around him.

"We're here on a special mission," said Herbert. "I'm an anthropsychologist documenting patterns of Earth behavior in preparation for eventual full-scale contact between our two worlds. Evelyn's researching her dissertation. And Ribsy came —"

"I came because I wanted to sample your delightful illicit substances and fuck your divine Gary Cooper," Ribsy announced.

"Gary Cooper's dead," Bert said.

"I was misinformed," Ribsy complained bitterly.

Be Aware, Avoid Stumbles

▾▾▾

DIANA SAID she'd forgotten to wear a bra. Her nipples showed through her sheer silk blouse. "Don't get me excited," she warned Bert, "or they'll get erect."

He was getting an erection himself. "How could you forget to wear a bra? That's like forgetting to wear underwear."

"Sometimes I forget my panties, too."

"Go study your Russian." Bert wanted her to go back to her side of the bullpen so his erection would go away.

His boss, Steven, came over with a memo he wanted Bert to edit. Steven was a pudgy man in his forties, with a round face, long, graying sideburns, and a salt-and-pepper mustache. He was always very apologetic when he interrupted Bert, even if Bert was just shooting the breeze. Diana said he looked like a goose, rocking back and forth, waiting for Bert to finish speaking.

The memo was another of Steven's masterpieces. It was entitled "Be Aware, Avoid Stumbles" and warned people not to fall. "Most people have fairly good balance, and the majority of us probably won't fall in the near future," Steven wrote. "Yet, employees continue to fall and hurt themselves." Bert told Steven it didn't need much editing. Steven, pleased, went back to his office.

After work, Bert took the express train to Ninety-sixth Street, then walked north toward his apartment. He passed a broad, lethargic woman in a brown pants suit who carried a shopping bag in each hand while she trudged slowly up Broadway. She had jowly cheeks and dark brown rings around her eyes. Her dark hair was tied in a bun. Bert was sure she was the woman who lived on the first floor of his building.

He turned around to face her. "Do you need some help with those?" He gestured toward the shopping bags.

"No," the woman said. "No, NO, *NO!*" She shouted at him, as though trying to scare off a mugger.

"Sorry, sorry," Bert apologized quickly. He hurried home so they wouldn't meet at the lobby door.

The Van Cortlandt Park golf course was going to close soon for the winter, so Patrick and Bert arranged to go that weekend. The course was mostly empty. They spent their first half hour at the park talking about golf etiquette, and then they rented some clubs and headed to the driving range. Bert proved a disastrous student, but Patrick remained an extremely patient teacher. Patrick kept telling him to ease his grip on the club. Bert gripped it more and more lightly, until on one swing, it flew out of his hands and nearly bludgeoned the seventy-year-old man next to him.

"Sorry," Bert said meekly.

"You goof."

On a few swings, Bert hit the turf and sent dirt flying into Patrick's eyes. "Hey, don't worry, that happens to everybody," Patrick reassured him. On another swing, the club plowed deep into the turf and embedded itself there. Bert had to struggle to free it. "Well, that's a first," Patrick admitted.

Bert managed one beautiful drive, two hundred twenty-five yards dead center, with a bit of a draw. The ball seemed to hang in the air — Bert could hardly breathe — and all at once he understood why the game could be so addictive. But he was never able to duplicate the shot.

They returned the clubs, then walked over to his parents' apartment on Bedford Park Boulevard. Bert had come to an agreement with himself not to tell his mother and father about his interest in men. He wasn't sure what to make of it himself, and his parents had enough to worry about with Philip. Then, too, he was scared of their reaction and scared that telling them would give his gay desires a kind of permanence. "I hope it's not too weird for you, meeting my parents," Bert told Patrick.

"What do you mean?"

"Well, it's not your standard second date."

Patrick jiggled coins in his pocket nervously as they took the elevator up from the lobby. Bert assumed he was apprehensive about meeting Bert's parents, but Patrick was a wonderful guest, politely admiring the Rosenbaums' apartment, making small talk, even showing his appreciation of the family photo album — although he did laugh too hard at Bert's naked baby pictures. Like Joseph, Patrick had attended the University of Michigan, and the two were soon talking about Michigan's football team and the prospects of the Tigers, while Evie pried Bert with questions about his job. She thought Sewers was a dead end and wanted him to get out as soon as possible. Bert knew she was right, but the discussion irritated him anyway. Then Evie wanted to know if the boys were hungry — they were starving — and ended up making them fat, juicy hamburgers.

"This is the best burger I've ever had, Mrs. Rosenbaum," Patrick told her.

"It's because it's kosher. It's very good quality meat." Evie sipped coffee and watched them eat. She wasn't eating herself. She said she'd been gaining too much weight lately. Bert reminded her she was still thin.

Patrick insisted on doing the dishes for Bert's mother. Evie dried them and somehow got Patrick to talk about his old girlfriends. Joseph, in the living room, was describing to Bert a magazine article he had just read about a bitter strike by copper miners. Bert pretended to listen to his father but mostly strained to hear the conversation in the kitchen because Patrick was telling his mother more than he'd ever told Bert. When Bert asked him about previous relationships, Patrick refused to discuss the subject. Now he told Evie that he had dated a woman named Sharon seriously, and also a woman named Lily. He'd even been engaged once. Joseph had evidently heard part of the conversation, too, for when Patrick and Evie emerged from the kitchen, he told Bert's friend, "You have to help us find a nice girl for Bert."

Bert was horribly embarrassed. Evie chastised her husband. "Joe, I'm sure Bert can find his own girlfriend. He doesn't need our help." She straightened the antimacassars on the chairs and swatted Bert's feet off the couch. "How's Alison doing?" she mused. "She was such a lovely girl."

"She's fine."

When they left, his mother kissed him goodbye, turning her head to the side and pecking his cheek, terrified as always that she might accidentally brush his lips with her own. "You didn't shave," she complained good-naturedly.

"Come over more often, will you?" his father asked him. "We miss you."

Afterward Patrick told Bert how comfortable he'd felt with Joseph and Evie. "My mother would have just served highballs."

They took the subway home and sat in the first car, the car Evie never wanted him to ride in, Bert told Patrick, in case of an accident.

"You think you're more like your mother than your father, don't you?" Patrick said.

"Yeah. I do."

"I think you're more like your dad."

"Why do you say that?" Bert was surprised but pleased.

"The way he's quiet sometimes, and really outgoing other times. . . . Maybe it's genetic. What was your grandfather like?"

"My dad's dad? I never met him. He was a barber, a linotype operator for a Yiddish newspaper, and an anarchist. My grandmother was a Communist." He smiled at Patrick. "I hear they fought all the time."

Bert wanted Patrick to come back to his apartment but didn't know if he should ask; so when the train pulled into Ninety-sixth Street and Patrick got up from his seat even before Bert did, Bert was delighted. As they walked up Broadway, Bert grew weak in his legs and in his groin. And he had a strange feeling that they were being watched: that people could tell they were going to have sex, that people could tell they were lovers, just by looking at them.

He opened his apartment door, and then Patrick closed it behind them and started backing Bert toward the bed. He pushed Bert down almost roughly and began to kiss him. But Patrick stopped almost at once, raised his head nervously, like a coyote startled by a noise, and then sat up on the bed. Bert understood. He brought out a joint and a bottle of beer and searched the radio for a station playing mellow rock and roll. Patrick smoked the joint quickly, drank the beer greedily, and then their kissing resumed.

The next few times Bert suggested getting together, Patrick acted oddly, said he was busy with friends, said he wasn't busy but he was tired, said he wasn't tired but had to help his cousin clean their apartment. Bert tried to occupy himself with crossword puzzles, television reruns, and magazines, but though they'd had sex only twice, he already felt lonely without Patrick.

He ran into Ribsy at the Red Apple supermarket. Malchick made him buy four milk chocolate bars with hazelnuts and some mocha almond fudge Häagen-Dazs ice cream. He went with Ribsy to the back yard of the building, where he joined the aliens for a snack.

"So, was it a big honor that you three got to come to Earth?" Bert asked.

"Well, not that many people really wanted to come," Evelyn told him. "You hear so much about the crime in New York."

"But since we're married and were willing to visit," Herbert said, "we got to be the first, well, I suppose you'd call us tourists, from the planet Debbie."

"How come no one knows you're here?"

"We snuck in during the air traffic controllers' strike."

Ribsy took a pair of scissors out of malchick's seat and handed them to Evelyn. Then malchick removed an emery board and started filing away at an armrest. Evelyn began cutting the green plastic strands of Ribsy's hair.

"Tell me, love, do you swing both ways?" Ribsy suddenly asked.

Bert turned bright red. "I beg your pardon?"

"Listen, we can always tell, can't we?" Ribsy said confidentially. "Shakespeare, John Dos Passos, James Dean. We can always tell."

"I suppose so. Is that why you guys were interested in talking to me?"

"Not really," Herbert said. "We were interested in Lars and Isabel, who were so receptive. They led us to you. After we met you, we decided you'd make an appropriate case study."

"You mean, you wanted to study a representative sexually confused postadolescent?"

"No, someone who watched a lot of TV," Evelyn replied brightly.

"You really seem to like television."

"We pick up all your broadcasts," Herbert said.

Evelyn eyed Ribsy's strands to make sure the bangs were even. She snipped first on the left, then on the right, then on the left. It reminded Bert of a Marx Brothers routine. Finally she gave up. "Here." She handed the scissors to Herbert. "You do it. You're better at cutting hair."

Herbert took the scissors and began styling Ribsy's tresses expertly. Bert suddenly remembered watching his father cut Philip's hair when they were boys. "It takes a little while for the broadcasts to reach us, of course," Herbert said. "But you'd be surprised how attached other planets have become to fragments of your culture."

"On Valensylvia, there's a radio station that broadcasts excerpts from the Uniform Commercial Code, thirty-six hours a day," Evelyn reported. "And another station that only plays Donovan songs."

"We love your music," Ribsy told him, brushing locks of hair off malchick's shoulders.

"Perhaps you'd enjoy listening to some Yiddish songs?" Herbert offered. "I could sing 'Di Grine Kuzine.' "

"My father always liked that one."

"Yes, well, Harold loves to sing it." Ribsy rolled malchick's eyes.

Herbert put down the scissors, cleared his throat, and then began singing. Bert watched with fascination as the green strands of Herbert's hair vibrated gently. Herbert changed color as he sang, from light green to beige back to green again. He sang the song in a weird, wobbling, reedy voice, somewhat high in the register, like an oboe slightly out of tune.

"Aren't you afraid someone's going to hear you?" Bert asked when the song had ended. "Or see you?"

"They can't hear us unless we want them to," Evelyn said.

"And we're invisible," Herbert told him. "Except to infants and the extremely aged."

"And dogs," Evelyn said. "Dogs can spot us."

"And substance abusers," Ribsy added.

"Twins, quite often," Evelyn said. "Scandinavians. Some brothers and sisters who are almost pathologically close. Jewish lefties with a family history of mental illness."

"Dogs are the real problem," Ribsy told Bert. "Most are friendly, but a few don't like us. Especially schnauzers. Schnauzers hate us. I mean, what did we ever do to schnauzers?" Ribsy took a mirror out of malchick's seat and admired malchick's haircut. "Stunning."

Harry was dating a seventeen-year-old black kid he'd met somewhere. The boy, whose name was Chuck, said he was straight and made money sleeping with women. He wouldn't let Harry visit him, he wouldn't give Harry his address. If he wanted to see Harry, he waited outside Harry's apartment, sometimes for hours on end.

"I guess I'm a father figure to him," Harry said. Harry told Bert that after they'd had sex the first time, Chuck wanted money. Harry told him he'd give him some money, but it was just that, a gift, this time only, and if Chuck wanted any other arrangement, he could forget about it. But Chuck kept coming back — he said he wanted to spend time together. They always ended up in bed, Harry said, and they went at it for hours. It was incredible, Harry said.

Bert was swamped by lust, not for Harry, not for the seventeen-year-old Chuck, but for the creaking of bedsprings, the smells of sweat and sex, damp pillows, exhausted sleep, a sense of danger, crazy energy spiraling through him. He felt like an addict, waiting for Patrick to call him, waiting for Patrick to touch him, waiting for Patrick.

"I don't even like you that much," he told an imaginary Patrick. Bert was lying with his face in his pillow, speaking into it. "I don't even like you. But I do like you." He changed his mind quickly, stumbling over the word "like" in his haste so that it came out "lick." He laughed into the pillow at the ridiculously Freudian mistake, and then he grew quieter, almost sullen. "I do like you. I like you, Patrick, so shit on you." Now he was churlish. "Shit on you if you don't like me. Fuck you, Patrick. I like you, so fuck you."

And wasn't it amazing, Bert thought at night, finally nodding off, the way you could rest your head in your arms, and look down the length of your arm, and see your pulse beating in your wrist? It was your heart that was beating, but you could see it in your wrist.

"You fascist!" the woman started screaming. "You prima donna! Stop burning my genitals, you pile of shit, you big nothing. No wonder you keep me drugged! No wonder you sell drugs! If I wasn't drugged, would I take action against you, you murderer, you lunatic. Oh God." She was crying now. "Why don't you let me sleep? Don't abandon Jane. Oh God, God," she moaned, "why won't you help me? Help Jane. Help her.

Help her." She screamed all night long. Bert still couldn't tell where the noise was coming from. He never ceased to be astonished at how loud it was. She had the lungs of an opera singer. He was so tired. He stumbled over to the phone and called the cops and, later, half asleep, he heard them battering on somebody's door.

Little Rooster Crowin'

▾▾▾

YOU PEOPLE have no more sense of beauty or feeling than Donald Duck!" the woman screamed. "Why won't you let me alone, just for one minute! Just for one minute, let me breathe! Stop burning my genitals, you piece of shit criminals. You should be in jail! Stop burning Jane's genitals!"

Bert ran into the Heibergs in the elevator the next morning. "Do you hear that woman screaming?" he asked them. She had settled into a regular pattern of screaming every night from three or four in the morning until dawn. About half the time, Bert was able to fall back asleep. He would have moved if his rent wasn't cheap.

"Hear her? Yah, her voice is busting my fahcking skull, damn sure, betcha," Jorgen said. "All I want to do is put my hand around her throat and yerk and yerk her devil head until I snap her neck like a piece of fahcking lutefisk." He put his hands around Isabel's neck and shook her for a moment, then laughed and let go.

Luisa ignored Jorgen's demonstration on Isabel, so Bert decided to ignore it, too. "What building is she in? It sounds like she's next door."

"She's in *this* building," Luisa said. "On the first floor. Jane Alley."

"The woman with the bags under her eyes?"

"Yah. She is a devil woman." Jorgen paced back and forth in the elevator like a caged tiger. "I could smack that fahcking bitch so hard her face falls on the floor. I could take a hot pipe and yam it up her cunt. Then she could burn, yah, damn sure, then she could yell all she wants." Isabel and Lars held on tight to Luisa during their father's tirade.

Bert saw Jane Alley at the mailbox a few days later. Jane was sitting on a low bench, wearing a brown skirt and a white blouse, smoking a cigarette, waiting for the mailman. He said hello to her.

"Yes," she said, not looking at him. "I know who you are."

"Ms. Alley, I have to tell you, the screaming's really a problem."

"I can see how it would be." Her voice was calm, but her stained fingers trembled as she smoked the cigarette. She looked tired.

"Can you stop?"

"I don't think so."

"I hate calling the police."

"Be my guest, call them. You're not telling me anything I don't know."

Diana had done a lot of cocaine back in Chicago ("mostly to get thin") and dated a drug dealer for a while. Once, in a restaurant, a deranged supplier ran in with an Uzi and pointed it at both of them. "That's when I decided it might be a good idea to get out of the relationship." She gave up drugs, began working for an advertising agency in Chicago, and started dating Jewish men — "because they don't get you killed, and they're animals in bed."

Steven, Bert's boss, walked in at the tail end of the conversation. He stood there, holding a floppy disk, embarrassed to interrupt them, and embarrassed to have overheard their discussion.

"Hey, Steven. What's up?"

"I've found some really wild trends in Brooklyn. A huge turnover rate in April. And Bert," he added enthusiastically, "it's statistically significant!"

"I'll take a look," Bert promised him. "Right away."

One of Bert's main projects for personnel was to determine why turnover was so much higher in April than any other month. He thought it probably had something to do with the weather. Winter was over, and the sewer workers didn't want to be underground anymore. Also, construction jobs were opening up and other civil service tests were being offered. But Steven wanted him to perform complex statistical studies to determine the reason. Statistics made Bert's head swim. Harry usually had to help him out. Bert wrote some of Harry's project reports to repay the favor.

"And Bert," Diana mocked, once Steven had left, "it's statistically significant!"

She had started using cocaine again, she confessed to Bert — not on a regular basis, only when someone offered, or sometimes when she had sex with her husband, or when she wanted to lose weight. When she talked about having sex with her husband, Bert felt a confusing quiver of longing in his stomach and chest.

"Do you have any cartwheels?" Ribsy asked him.

"Cartwheels?" Bert didn't know what Ribsy was talking about.

"Copilots," Ribsy said.

Malchick could see that Bert was confused.

"Crystals. Footballs. Meeny-miny-moes."

Bert was still at a loss.

"Amphetamines. Jeez." Ribsy shook malchick's head. "What a maroon."

"I like spooky pictures," Barbara told them. "They scare the hell out of me. When *Dark Shadows* was on TV, I used to bring a TV to work. When I saw *The Exorcist,* I slept with the lights on for a month and kept my Bible open to the Twenty-third Psalm."

"Listen to her, she likes to be tormented," Harry said.

Diana had wandered over to hear Barbara's story. Bert was

editing, or supposedly editing, another one of Steven's memos.

"I remember, *Jaws* scared me so much, I wet my bed at night," Barbara continued. "When I was a little girl, I used to wet my bed every night. And my father used to give me a beating every time. I used to beg my sister, Please don't tell Daddy. No, she'd say, I'm tired of you pissing on me. We shared a bed. So I'd get up at five in the morning and wash the sheets, and put on new ones, so my father wouldn't know. But after my mother passed, I was afraid to get up in the dark. I used to see her in my dreams. Before I'd go to bed, I'd pray, Please God, don't let me pee. And when I was wide awake after seeing my mother in my dreams, I'd cry to my mother, 'cause I saw her right there in the room, Please let me alone, Momma, 'cause I'm scared. My mother passed when I was seven and a half. My sister used to have bad dreams, too, used to see ghosts. Once she woke me up, she was rustling the sheets so much. What's the matter, I asked her. The devil's riding my back, she told me, and her back was moving up and down, like it was galloping. Get the hell off me, devil, she shouted, and pretty soon she quieted down."

"That's quite a story," Bert managed.

"No story, it's the honest-to-goodness truth," Barbara insisted. "Later, my sister told me the devil cooked in her pots and slept in her bed. She showed me one time how the sheets were all mussied up. I thought it was her husband that did it, but she said no, her husband was visiting his brother."

"It must have been so hard for you, growing up without a mom," Diana said. She put her arm around Barbara.

"Hey, I grew up without a dad," Harry said. "Put your arm around me."

"In your dreams."

"My daddy had his hands full with us," Barbara reflected, patting Diana's hand. She was softening lately toward Diana. "We were something else."

Bert looked at Barbara's black hand on Diana's white hand, and at Diana's white shoulders and white breasts, visible beneath her gray cotton dress as she leaned forward. He watched her breasts swell as she breathed, and he wondered what her pink nipples looked like under her bra.

The aliens told him that they were worried about being under constant surveillance. "How can you be under surveillance if no one can see you?" Bert objected.

"You think there's no conspiracy?" Ribsy said. "They hire people. Identical twins. Drug addicts who'll do anything to get their next fix. Dolphins. And dogs."

"Who does? Who hires people?"

Evelyn whispered confidentially, "Air Traffic Control."

"I can't believe they're using dolphins," Bert said. "Dolphins are so nice."

"You must be joking," Herbert said. "Don't you know that dolphins are the world's worst scabs, that they steal jobs from Peruvian peasants, dump toxic waste for the Bechtel Corporation, smuggle cocaine for the Medellín cartel, and make illegal campaign contributions to Aryan Nation?"

"A dolphin would stab its own mother in the dorsal fin for an extra piece of squid," Ribsy maintained.

And there was another problem. Ribsy had somehow stumbled upon a cocaine deal that was going down, deftly (and invisibly) nabbed the cocaine, and left a miniature drug war in malchick's wake. But Ribsy was petrified that an addict had seen malchick do it and would drop a dime on them.

"Just give back the cocaine," Bert advised.

Ribsy put an armrest over each nostril in turn and sniffed. "Ever hear the Everly Brothers sing 'Long Time Gone'?"

"I see," Bert said.

"We're a little worried about Rivka," Evelyn told him.

"Rivka?"

"That's what people close to me call me," Ribsy explained.

"Should I call you Rivka?"

"No."

*

They made love, then lay in bed together and listened to Bob Dylan. "He's still my favorite," Patrick told Bert.

Meet me in the morning, 56th and Wabasha
Meet me in the morning, 56th and Wabasha
Honey, we could be in Kansas
By time the snow begins to thaw.

They say the darkest hour is right before the dawn
They say the darkest hour is right before the dawn
But you wouldn't know it by me
Every day's been darkness since you been gone.

Little rooster crowin', there must be something on his mind

This was Bert's favorite part:

Little rooster crowin', there must be something on his mind
Well, I feel just like that rooster
Honey, ya treat me so unkind.

For Bert, sex was like truth serum; afterward he felt so open, so incapable of lying. "I like this even better than sex," he told Patrick. "You know, just lying here, talking."

"You're like a girl," Patrick said.

Bert felt as though Patrick had just punched him in the stomach, as though Patrick saw him as a ridiculous Zuni man-woman. Well, he knew how to gain back some ground.

"I got a letter from my brother," Bert told him.

"Yeah?" Patrick sat up, suddenly attentive.

Bert had begun telling his friends about Philip. The aliens had informed him that ten percent of the population on the planet Debbie was schizophrenic, and Bert had realized that there was no reason to hide Philip's illness. The great shock to him was not how calmly everyone took the news; the shock was how interested everyone was, Patrick and Diana especially. They weren't scared away from Bert after learning about his brother. In fact, hearing about Philip seemed to turn them on.

Bert thought their interest was almost pornographic — but he used it.

"He says he's going to be a great guitar player. He says he's going to be another Bob Dylan."

"Really?" Patrick's eyes lit up with excitement.

"Yeah, really." Bert turned away from Patrick and ran his finger along a crack in the wall. He felt disgusted with himself, yet he needed to talk. "Sometimes," Bert said, still not looking at Patrick, "sometimes when I was in high school, and Philip was so sick, I used to think we'd be better off if he died. Isn't that horrible?" Patrick kissed his back. "I don't feel that way anymore. I don't want to. I love Philip." His body tensed because Patrick was kissing a sensitive spot on his shoulder, and he was growing hard again. "I think he's brave, the way he never complains. I don't want him to die. I just want him to get better." He turned over and faced Patrick.

"I want to apologize," Patrick said. "I didn't mean it, when I said you were like a girl. I'm just an idiot. I didn't mean it at all."

"I know."

"Forgive me? Please?"

"Of course."

They made love again, and later Patrick asked him if he knew where he could buy some speed. "Why do you want speed?" Bert wondered. Patrick never took speed with Bert.

"I just get tired sometimes." He squeezed Bert. "You tucker me out."

Harry and Bert were eating lunch in a TriBeCa diner, surrounded by teamsters from the warehouses on the West Side, would-be hipsters who had moved to the area for the lofts, vent men and bag ladies, and a few suits from the financial district, slumming.

"Do you date guys much?" Harry asked him.

"Not much." So often Bert wanted to tell him about Patrick, but Patrick had sworn him to secrecy.

"You should. There are all kinds of people out there to meet. Let me ask you something else." Harry scooped up the last of his tomato soup. "Did you ever go through a sleazy period?"

"I never did."

"You will. Someday, someone's going to break your heart, and then you'll get all sleazy on us."

"Great. Something to look forward to." He didn't want to be sleazy; the prospect frightened him. He'd feel out of control, out of his carefully planned orbit. And anyway people were starting to get sick — starting to die. Patrick said he had slept with only one man before him, in high school. Bert thought he was safe with Patrick. He didn't know if he'd be safe with anyone else.

"Just how much intelligent life is out there?" Bert asked the aliens, whose spaceship had hovered overhead in the back yard of his building, and then glided to a halt beside him.

"That's a very interesting question," Herbert said. "I've made a study of your planet's own attempts to grapple with the issue. "You've heard of the Green Bank equation?"

Bert shook his head no. "Green Bank?"

"I *love* that color." Ribsy applied some green lipstick to malchick's green lips.

"The Green Bank equation seeks to determine how many advanced communicating civilizations, *n*, can be detected in the galaxy," Herbert said. "The estimates for *n* — the pessimistic, the cautious, the optimistic — have varied from four to a trillion."

"Four?"

"Well, actually, we know for sure that *n* is at least thirty-six, because on the planet Debbie we've received communications from thirty-five other planets," Evelyn said.

"We were fairly sure there was life on Earth centuries ago, even before we received transmissions," Herbert told him, "because our spectroscopy analysis revealed there was so much H_2O. There was such an abundance, in fact, that we thought only aquatic life forms lived here. And when we contacted the aquatic life forms, they never mentioned there were intelligent terrestrial life forms as well."

Ribsy put away malchick's lipstick. "They just kept complaining about 'extremely vicious parasitical land-based organisms.' "

"They meant human beings?"

"Precisely," Herbert said.

"A little later, of course, we were visited by Gypsies," Evelyn added. "From Romania."

"How could Gypsies visit?" Bert was incredulous.

"It's not really clear, is it, Harold?" Evelyn said.

"It must be similar to the way we travel through space, though," Herbert-also-known-as-Harold proposed.

"And how is that?" Bert asked.

"When a sun dies and becomes a black hole or a neutron star, space gets very dense," Herbert said. "Time slows down enormously. We use the gravitational force of a neutron star to accelerate us. It's like skating on superfast ice. No friction. As you skim closer and closer, you speed up."

"I guess if you're not careful, you can get squashed by all that gravity."

"You ain't kidding." Ribsy reached into the seat of malchick's chair, took out a razor blade, and began to cut up what appeared to be cocaine.

"The Gypsies must have trapped oxygen in a vehicle, and when a comet swung by, they grabbed a ride to the nearest dense object. They rode each planet or asteroid to the next one. Finally they swung from star to star and ended up on Debbie. It's like what you call hitchhiking," Evelyn explained.

"It sounds more like Tarzan," Bert said.

"The Stellar's sea cow, now extinct on your planet, began emigrating to Debbie on Christmas night, 1758, when Halley's comet returned," Herbert lectured. "They grew tired of being slaughtered all the time, especially since no one responded to any of their lawsuits against capital punishment or their impassioned speeches in favor of vegetarianism. Manatees and sea cows are really the perfect space travelers, by the way."

"No luggage," Ribsy told him.

"And who are the worst space travelers?"

"I'd imagine pre-Batista Cuban businessmen," Herbert said.

"Why did they carry such big trunks?" Evelyn asked him.

Bert went out for a drink with Diana after work. Her husband would be meeting them there later. He was taking her to see a Charles Ludlam play in Sheridan Square. Diana got very girlish when she drank, and very flirtatious. "Now, who are you dating, Bert?" She snuggled next to him. "There must be all kinds of women after you."

"No. Nobody. I'm like a monk."

"Or do you like boys?"

"I like you."

"You're going to go to my head. Like this drink." She was most of the way through her second vodka and tonic. "I'm glad we did this." She held his hand. "You have nice fingers. Warm."

"Thanks." Bert's palms started sweating.

"Like a sculptor." Diana loved sculptors. She said she'd dated a sculptor once, he was like an animal.

"You know, when my dad was in college, he used to model his hands and his feet for a sculpting class," Bert told her. "To make money. We all have nice hands and nice feet."

"Your feet are nice?"

"They're okay."

"How nice?"

"Nice." Bert was embarrassed.

"And what else? What else do you have?"

"A nice smile."

"Oh, you've got a killer smile, Bert. Don't smile at me too much. I don't think I could take it."

She tilted her glass to get to an ice cube at the bottom of her drink and then started chewing the ice. She looked so beautiful, her face slightly flushed from the drink. Bert grinned at her.

"Help! Help!" she started shouting, her mouth full of ice.

Bert tried to get her to shush. "People are going to think I'm hurting you."

In fact, a waiter came by. Diana ordered another drink. Bert wanted cranberry juice. He had the feeling he was going to need his wits about him.

Diana's husband, Rob, showed up, wearing a three-piece suit and checking his watch. "Sorry I'm late." He was a powerful-looking man, just on the thin side of husky, with a neatly groomed beard and mustache. He worked in midtown.

"Honey, this is Bert." Bert shook Rob's hand. He knew Rob would have a rock-hard handshake, so he tried to shake as firmly as possible. "Sweetie, we've already established that Bert has nice hands and nice feet."

"Oh, really."

"Diana's had a little to drink."

"She does that sometimes."

Bert said goodbye and fled.

Patrick didn't want to stay over — he said he had to be in Queens early in the morning — so Bert kissed him goodbye at the elevator. Patrick didn't kiss him back. His lips hardly parted.

"No one's going to see us. No one's up. It's four in the morning."

Patrick kissed him, and then the screaming started. "You have no character, no personality, no anything! You're just destroying Jane, not creating a new one in her place! Have I sung you your lullaby yet? You and your FBI cabals! You and your CIA conveniences! Stop running an illegal mental facility here! Stop selling drugs! Stop burning my genitals!"

"What," said Patrick, "is that?"

"My neighbor," Bert said.

Somehow Patrick had never heard her before. "I can't believe how loud she is."

Bert went down to the first floor with Patrick and knocked on Jane Alley's door.

"Yes?" she said from inside.

"It's Bert Rosenbaum. From 5B."

She opened the door a crack. Her stout, fleshy body peeked out of her white nightgown. Her long brown hair was down, and her jowly, defiant face was white and careworn. With her white nightgown and white skin, she looked as pale as a ghost, except for the large brown bags under her eyes and a faint black mustache over her upper lip.

"Jane, I know you're in pain, and I'm sorry. But you're keeping everyone in the building up. I can't take this anymore."

"You can't take it." Jane was amused. She opened the door and told Bert to come in.

Bert and Patrick entered the apartment warily. The long hallway was unspeakably filthy: huge dust balls along the baseboards, rotting bags of garbage by the door, dead cockroaches and mouse droppings on the floor. Inside the living room, paper plates covered the chairs and the sofa. And on the paper plates, human excrement. The stench was overpowering. Bert and Patrick headed back to the hallway.

"Jane, I wish there were an easy way to say this." He tried to speak as gently as possible. "I think maybe you should see someone. You know, get some help?"

"I don't need help. You're the one who needs help. You're the one who's crazy. Imagining things. Fantasizing. Pouring poison into the air vents." She wrapped her arms around her chest, suddenly cold.

"I don't want to get into an argument, Jane." He was tired — he was always tired. "I just want you to stop screaming."

"Oh, I'll stop screaming."

"You will?"

"Of course. As soon as you stop running an illegal mental facility out of your apartment."

"What?"

"I know what you're doing in there. Drugging me through

the air vents, in violation of my constitutional rights. Controlling me, so you can produce symptoms of mental illness. Burning my genitals."

"Jane, I promise you, no one's doing that."

"Go ahead, laugh at me. I'm beyond all that. Laugh. Have a nice day." She was laughing herself.

Imperial Bedroom

▾▾▾

PATRICK CAME TO BERT for sex when he was lonely, often. When he was horny, usually. And when he was a little drunk or stoned, always. Bert bought more pot from Harry so he'd have it for Patrick, and he stocked his refrigerator with beer. He didn't know exactly where they were heading, but he was confident he'd end up where he was supposed to, like a sea turtle, borne by ocean currents, somehow finding its way home to spawn.

If Patrick came over on a Friday night, they'd watch cartoons together the next morning on Bert's portable TV. If Patrick came over on a Saturday night, they'd watch Sunday morning news programs. Patrick was a news junkie, and, like Bert's father, during a crisis or during a natural disaster he was glued to the television set, watching report after report, flipping channels to find the latest update. "What can I say? I love carnage."

Diana could always tell when Bert had seen Patrick, as though she could sniff the faint odor of sex on him the next day. "Ooh, we've been busy," she told him. "Who's the lucky girl?"

"I told you, I'm a hermit."

"Yeah, well, you got company in your cave."

Sometimes he almost eluded her. He'd have sex with Patrick, and the next morning Diana would say nothing about it. But by afternoon she'd always circle around him, moving in, closer and closer. "Busy like a bee," she'd say.

"I don't know how you do it. I showered and everything."

"Is she cuter than me?" Diana demanded. "Who is it? You can tell me. I won't tell anyone.

"It's Kathleen," she'd say. Barely five feet tall, Kathleen was the unassuming woman with very straight, straw-colored hair who worked with Patrick upstairs in Highways, and who had gone dancing with them at S.O.B.

"It's your friend Alison," Diana would say. She knew all of Bert's friends, even the ones from college and high school: she had made him draw a tree diagram to show how they all connected and where he'd met each one of them.

"Alison's in Boston."

"It's Ed," she'd say.

"Who?" He didn't even know any Eds.

Now that it was getting colder, they'd get hot chocolate together every morning. Bert was trying not to drink so much coffee. Diana always ordered a big dollop of whipped cream in her hot chocolate. She ate the whipped cream first, before it melted. She said if she didn't exercise, she'd be as big as a house. She loved to eat. She loved to bake, too, and was always bringing in batches of muffins for Bert. She ate only a quarter of a muffin herself, but Bert feasted on them. They were delicious: spongy blueberry or cranberry or pumpkin muffins. She told Bert he was lucky he was thin. Bert said she was thin too. Diana insisted that she was huge. She just wanted to lose five more pounds, then she'd be happy.

"This is as exciting as my life gets, Bert. Doing aerobics, baking muffins for you, and reading kinky best-sellers." She had just finished reading W. J. Jacobs's *A Field Guide to Madness*. She said the sex scenes got her hot. "Pathetic, huh."

Bert asked her about her husband. He was boring, Diana said.

"I thought he was an animal."

"He was. Now he's just old." He was six years older than she. "I bet you're an animal, Bert."

Bert scratched under his armpits like a chimpanzee.

Patrick came downstairs and nodded hello to Bert, then sat on the edge of Diana's desk, drinking coffee out of a Styrofoam cup. Diana seemed miffed. She didn't really like Patrick, she'd told Bert — she thought he was too full of himself. Bert said she just wasn't giving him a chance. She admitted he was good at his job: she'd worked closely with him, so she knew. Bridges and Tunnels and Highways had collaborated on a grant application to the federal government, and she said Patrick had written a terrific proposal. Of course, she added archly, he was late turning the application in, and on the day it was due, poor Kathleen had to race to the post office to make sure it was postmarked by five P.M.

"My cousin finally bought a car," Patrick told Diana.

"Yeah. So?"

"A BMW 320. Candy apple red."

Diana couldn't hide her enthusiasm. "That is such a hot car! I want a ride in it."

Harry wandered in. "What's all the commotion?"

Patrick stood up. He always seemed uncomfortable around Harry. "Kenny's getting a BMW."

Harry laughed and said that if he had a BMW, maybe he'd still have Chuck. Chuck, his seventeen-year-old, had flown the coop. Harry had no way of getting in touch with him. Desperate to find him, he had started taking walks through the Hub, 149th Street in the Bronx, where he thought Chuck lived. He hadn't realized how attached he'd become. "I miss him. I miss teaching him things. I miss his dick," Harry told Bert. He put his hands over his mouth. "I'm so bad, just listen to me." Harry said he couldn't eat, thinking about Chuck. He said he was going out of his mind. "He's just a kid, he needs me." He hadn't slept in five days. It sounded crazy to Bert.

But with Diana and Patrick, Harry put on a brave front. "On second thought, fuck him. He doesn't deserve a BMW."

"There you go," Bert said.

"Did you shave today?" Diana suddenly asked Patrick.

"No."

"Slob."

Steven came over, interrupting their coffee klatch. He bobbed until he was sure they were done speaking, then asked Bert if the personnel surveys could be sent upstairs to Assistant

Commissioner Truby. Bert reminded Steven that they wouldn't even be returned from the field until Wednesday. "That's too bad," Steven said. "I told him they'd be ready today." Steven had a habit of creating artificial deadlines that made them all look foolish.

Later in the day, Bert finally got Steven to read a memo that had been sitting on his desk for a week. "You know what would go great at the back of this memo?" Steven said with gusto.

"What?" Bert was already dreading the answer.

"Those questionnaires."

"Steven, I'm afraid they're not ready yet," Bert told him. "I called and tried to rush them through, but they'll be here Monday at the earliest."

What bothered him most about Steven was his procrastination. Even though he loved his job, Steven could never bring himself to finish or approve something until the last minute. Bert liked to prepare everything ahead of time, so that he could relax and forget about it. But he couldn't forget about it with Steven because Steven wouldn't approve whatever Bert had done until the deadline was breathing down his neck — and then, at the eleventh hour, Steven would make dozens of changes so that Bert had to kill himself to hand the project in on time. Half his day was spent managing his boss, imploring Steven to read something before it was actually due. The other half was spent visiting Patrick and Diana compulsively. He felt like a moth fluttering back and forth between two flames.

Later in the day, they went upstairs to meet with the assistant commissioner. At the last minute, Steven turned to him and said, "Maybe we should bring those questionnaires with us."

During the Tylenol-tampering scare, Diana had a headache and asked if anyone had any aspirin. Patrick, who also had a headache, had some Tylenol, but Diana wouldn't take any. "Come on, these are pills, not capsules," Patrick pointed out.

"I don't care, I'm not taking them."

"Just pretend it's a diet pill," Harry teased her.

"You're a nasty boy."

Patrick swallowed one in front of her. "See? I'm still here."

"White people are crazy," Barbara said.

"That's what I always say," Harry agreed.

"You gotta watch yourself," Barbara said. "This is a crazy planet — people killing each other all the time with pills, knives, and guns."

"I'll take one," Bert offered.

"Don't you dare," Barbara commanded.

Bert swallowed a pill to show he wasn't afraid. "They're not capsules. They're perfectly safe." Diana still wouldn't take one. Patrick and Bert grinned at each other.

"There have been lots of cultures as violent as the Earth's, quite a few even more violent," Evelyn told Bert. "But most of them annihilated themselves. The others evolved, adapted. Few planets have reached Earth's level of advancement and remained so violent."

"I must say, your planet's really an anomaly in this respect, something unaccountable." Herbert, adopting his professorial tone, was puffing away at his pipe.

"I think it's because no other planet is so sexually fucked up," Ribsy suggested.

"Is that true?" Bert asked the other two.

"Probably," Evelyn said.

Herbert took his pipe out of his mouth, banged it against his armrest, put it back in his mouth. "It is true, but to be fair, other planets are just as repressive, but about different issues. On Earth, sexuality has become enormously fetishized. The most elaborate taboos center on the family and sexuality. That's very unusual. On most planets, most taboos and neuroses center around food and eating."

"Really?"

"On some parts of the planet Debbie, as little ago as a century, being overweight was considered a crime against the state," Evelyn said. Her face was blushing a dark green hue. "And some crazy people would like to make it a crime again. You have your fascists, we have ours. Where I come from, in the north sector, I would be subject to the most persistent ridicule for my weight. Even in this day and age. And even though I know it's crazy, I can't help feeling fat and ugly sometimes. I see myself the way they do, and it kills me. I'm trying to lose weight, though, I really am. But anyway" — Evelyn was suddenly defiant — "why do people care how much people weigh? Whose business is it anyway?"

"I don't know," Bert said. "I think you look fine." All three aliens looked peculiar to him, but Evelyn didn't look any more peculiar for being a few pounds heavier than the others.

"You're beautiful, you know that, don't you?" Herbert told her.

Ribsy took one of Evelyn's armrests and kissed it. "Evelyn was a weight liberation activist on the planet Debbie," malchick told Bert proudly.

"But I turn out to be as oppressed as any *babba.*" Evelyn laughed.

"What's a *babba*?"

"An old benighted peasant malchik, who worries and worries about every half gram she eats," Evelyn said.

"I don't think you're like that at all."

"He's a charmer, this one," Evelyn told Ribsy.

In bed, Patrick would spell words with his fingers on Bert's skin, and Bert would try to decipher them; or Bert would drum melodies on Patrick's chest, back, sides, butt — "Over the Rainbow," *"La donna è mobile,"* theme songs from television shows like *Bewitched* and *I Dream of Jeannie* — and Patrick would have to guess what music Bert was playing. Often, Bert would tap the same songs over and over again; he always found pleasure in repetition. They'd quiz each other on license plate mottoes, too: SPORTSMAN'S PARADISE, THE OCEAN STATE, LAND OF ENCHANTMENT, FIRST IN FLIGHT. Bert loved holding Patrick, because it was nice to nestle in bed next to somebody, like two spoons, and listen to the other person breathing, and go to sleep.

One evening an official from the Department of Mental Health visited Bert at his apartment. With his gray beard and avuncular face, the man looked like the kindly owner of a children's day camp. He apologized for bothering Bert and spoke so softly that Bert had to lean forward to make out what he was saying. When Bert finally understood where the official worked, he was delighted to see him. "You've come about Jane Alley," he surmised.

"Yes, I have."

"Thank God. I mean, I feel sorry for her. But she can't keep screaming like this."

"I understand that you see patients here at night." The man still spoke in a measured tone and checked his reflection in the mirror over Bert's bureau.

"Excuse me?"

The official explained that Jane Alley had charged Bert with running an illegal mental facility out of his apartment. He was investigating the claim. "We don't want anyone to receive substandard care." He coughed quietly and then apologized for coughing.

"I can't believe this," Bert said. "Look around. It's a studio apartment! Where would anyone fit?"

Apologizing for invading Bert's privacy, the bearded man checked the closet, under the sink in the kitchen, behind the shower curtain. "I hope you understand that we're committed to meeting the health needs of all New Yorkers. It's a sacred trust."

"But do you understand that she's ill? That she screams every night and keeps the whole building awake? Do you understand that? Do you have any idea what that's like?" Bert noted the frenzy in his voice and suddenly worried that the man would think he was crazy and lock him up. "Ask anyone," he said. "Really."

The man knocked on the door next to him. No one was home. The man knocked on the door across from him. The woman who lived there said she'd heard about the screaming from Bert but hadn't heard it herself. Bert was getting very antsy. "I guess you can only hear it on this side of the building."

The man went upstairs and knocked on the studio apartment above Bert's. Bert held his breath on the landing below. He was worried: Mr. Watanabe, the quiet Japanese engineer who lived there, had been too polite to complain about the students who lived next door to him for a year and played the Grateful Dead's "Casey Jones" at full volume more or less continuously. Bert worried that Watanabe would be too polite to complain about Jane Alley, as well.

Watanabe answered the door, nervously said yes, she had screamed, on occasion — on how many occasions, he couldn't state — but he supposed all of us lose our tempers now and then.

"Please. Try one more door," Bert begged, calling up to the man.

The official knocked on Jimmy Giannakopoulos's apartment. After the Dead aficianados had graduated from Columbia University's journalism school and left New York, the burly Jimmy G. had moved with his wife and baby daughter into the two-bedroom apartment next door to Mr. Watanabe. He was a bus driver and a stage director, and he said Jane Alley was fucking insane, and the next time she screamed, which would probably be later that night, since she screamed every night, his wife was going to have to tie him down so he wouldn't take his gun and shoot Jane right between her beady brown eyes. "I'm an artist, I need my sleep!" he shouted as the Health Department official fled.

"Love Between Man and Woman . . . Consumes Energy and Wastes Time. On the Other Hand, Love of the Party and of the Chairman, Mao Tse-tung, Takes No Time at All and Is in Itself a Powerful Tonic."

—*People's Daily* (Peking)

▼▼▼

PATRICK SAID they shouldn't see each other so much, he thought Bert was getting the wrong idea. He wanted to be friends, he said Bert was a great friend, he said Bert was his best friend.

"So, when will we see each other? I mean, get together?"

"You know," Patrick said. "Sometimes. Okay? Please?"

"But sometimes, right?"

Diana noticed that she hadn't sniffed him in a long time. Bert shrugged. Well, good riddance, Diana said. She didn't like having a rival.

"A rival?"

"Well, Bert, you know you're my one and only."

He stayed late one night to edit another of Steven's memos. The report was entitled "Drive Yourself to Safety." Steven's logic was ingenious, especially if you were driving uphill: "Keep your foot off the gas pedal at all times and put it over your brake pedal to reduce the time it takes to hit the brakes. When you know you have to stop or slow down," Steven wrote, "don't put it off."

Diana was staying late, too, killing time until she met her husband uptown at Symphony Space. They were going to see *Ruddigore*. She was dreading it.

"No, *Ruddigore*'s great," Bert assured her. "It's my favorite Gilbert and Sullivan."

"Really?"

"Really." His mother loved Gilbert and Sullivan and listened to the D'Oyly Carte recordings with Martyn Green whenever his father wasn't practicing with his Listen & Learn tapes. Bert told Diana about the witch's curse, and how beautiful the overture was, and how much he loved the song about the man who was diffident, modest, and shy; about the character Mad Margaret, and the wonderful patter trio she took part in; about the neat, logical twist at the end which ensured happiness for everyone. She insisted that he tell her the ending, so she could enjoy the operetta more.

Then she challenged him to a game of dots. They took turns connecting two dots at a time, trying to complete the most number of squares. Bert won, but he had the feeling that Diana had let him win.

"Now you get your reward."

She kissed him. He didn't know what kind of kiss it was going to be, so he parted his lips slightly and waited. She slipped her tongue into his mouth. Oh, Bert thought, that kind.

"The devil made me do it, Bert."

They kissed again. "This is a bad idea," Bert said. "You're married."

"Tell me something I don't know." They kissed a third time. "You're right. I'd better go." She grabbed her shoes and ran to the elevator without even putting them on. Bert watched her run. She was beautiful. He knew she was a tease, but somehow knowing didn't help. He jerked off in the men's room.

"Oh God," Herbert told him later. "Those awful years in your early twenties when all you can think about is sex and you go a little crazy. We wouldn't go back there for all the money in the world."

"Speak for yourself." Ribsy smoothed the pleats of malchick's woolen, green-and-blue tartan kilt.

The aliens told him that bisexuality was much more common

on the planet Debbie than on Earth. They were always talking about sexual configuration. Not sexual preference, not sexual orientation: sexual configuration.

"It's the most all-inclusive term," Herbert said. "Because we're configured by our genes, by our families, by our environment, and by the political structures around us."

"Our whole society is more attuned to configuration than yours," Evelyn told him. "Geometric configurations, sexual configurations, configurations of power. In an Earth film, say, *It's a Mad, Mad, Mad, Mad World,* you get a laugh when that loud abrasive woman slips on a banana peel."

Bert supplied the name: "Ethel Merman."

"Exactly. But in a typical comedy on Debbie, a triangle is likely to be bent into the shape of a trapezoid."

"And that's funny?" Bert asked.

"Hilarious. Remember that Aleph-10 movie?" Ribsy asked malchick's spouses. "When Rudolph comes home, and his *brocknee*'s ovoid?"

Evelyn and Herbert shrieked with mirthless-sounding laughter. Tee hee hee. Tee hee hee.

"Can you relate to our comedies at all, then?" Bert asked Evelyn.

"Some easier than others. *I Love Lucy* could be a sitcom on a planet Debbie network. It's all about configuration. Lucy rebels against staying at home. Lucy wants to break into show business. Those are power configurations. Lucy rebels against the constraints of space. That's a geometric configuration. And then all the wonderful pairings: the Ricardos, the Mertzes, the two women, the two men — and the most interesting of all, the diagonal relationships between Lucy and Fred, and Ethel and Ricky. *Leave It to Beaver* is about configuration, too. Again, it's mostly couplings: father and son, mother and son, brother and brother, husband and wife."

"What comedies can't you relate to?" Bert wondered.

"*Gilligan's Island,*" Evelyn said. "To us, it's so sad. All those people marooned on a circular island. A circle's the saddest shape, you know. On the planet Debbie, *Gilligan's Island* is considered a tragedy."

"We love the song, though," Ribsy advised him.

The next day, Diana brought him a big batch of muffins. She put it on his desk without speaking. After he asked, she said she'd liked the operetta. She ignored him the rest of the morning. Bert didn't press her. Finally, around lunchtime, she approached him. "Oh boy, this is hard."

"Want to play dots?"

"Can we just forget about last night?"

"I guess. It's weird, though."

"I was in a strange mood. Rob and I have been having problems. You know that. But after the show, we had a really good talk, and I think we cleared the air."

"That's good," Bert said.

"You know I'm very fond of you, Bert." She stood there, awkwardly, abashed. "I'm sorry."

Bert went upstairs to visit Patrick in his cubicle. He was forcing himself to visit no more than once a day. He usually waited until the late afternoon in the increasingly vain hope that Patrick might come downstairs to visit him, but today he felt depressed and wanted to see him sooner.

"Hey," Patrick said. "How you doing?"

"Hi, Bert." Kathleen waved at him from the other side of Highways.

"You want to go to lunch, Pat?"

"I'm going with Harry."

"Harry?"

"Yeah. Want to come?"

"Nah." Bert didn't feel like going out to lunch with Harry. He felt like going home and crawling into bed. He supposed he was tired, although he didn't think Jane had screamed the night before. She screamed so much, he was losing track. Jorgen and Luisa had finally called a tenants' meeting and hired a lawyer to try to evict her on a nuisance charge. The lawyer warned them that it wouldn't be easy. Bert had phoned a few social service agencies to see if there was anything anyone could do, but they always told him that if she wasn't violent, there was no way to force her to get help. The landlord had tried to contact her family, but apparently she had none, except for a brother who'd disappeared many years earlier. Jorgen and Luisa were starting to despair. Jorgen said he was taking tranquilizers to sleep and speed to wake himself up the next day. Luisa said in the middle of the day she'd just start crying, for no reason at all. She said she was just so tired. And she said Jorgen and she were fighting all the time. Jane was breaking up their marriage. Jane was the other woman.

Bert went back downstairs and checked with Barbara to see if Steven was looking for him. He wanted to make sure to avoid him. He just didn't feel up to facing Steven's enthusiasm.

"Honey, you look as serious as a heart attack. What's bothering you?"

"Nothing."

"You're not going to faint on me, are you?"

Bert smiled. "I don't think so."

"I fainted once. It was amateur night at the Apollo Theater. They had amateur nights back then," Barbara recalled. "I went on, and I was going to do a song. And while I was singing, I looked at the audience, and I suddenly realized, every single one of them people was looking at me. Every single one. I got so scared, I fainted dead away. A doctor came up from the audience. Said it was nothing but stage fright."

"It takes practice to be able to perform in front of people."

"It takes guts, too," Barbara said.

Lonely without Patrick, he went home to visit his parents one Sunday morning. He let himself in with his key. He hadn't shaved since Thursday, and, as he walked down the long foyer of the apartment, he saw himself appear, skinny and half-bearded, in the mirror at the end of the hall. With his tattered jeans and his stubble, he looked like a derelict. His reflection got larger and larger, and then he realized he wasn't seeing his reflection — he was seeing Philip. His brother had returned from California.

Philip walked down the hallway toward him and then clapped Bert on the back. "Hey, little bro."

Bert hugged him back. "Hey, big bro. Wh—— when did you get in?"

"Last night. Late. We were going to call you later."

"You're growing a beard."

"You are too," Philip said. His hands were shaking. Bert could tell immediately from the jitteriness that Philip had stopped taking his medication.

Their mother and father were visiting their grandparents. Philip had been too tired to go. The two brothers talked for an hour before Joseph and Evie returned. On a whim, Philip had left his job at the bookstore and come to New York. He said he was visiting for only a week, but he had brought three big suitcases with him and also his two guitars, so Bert knew he wanted to stay.

Evie kissed Bert on the cheek when she entered the apartment and smiled nervously at Philip. "It's nice having the whole family together. So who's making lunch?"

"We should go out to eat. We can go to Dominick's," Joseph suggested.

"No, we'll eat here. Phil's only going to be staying for a week. I want to cook for him. I think a short trip is always nice. You get to see everybody, and you don't start missing your own apartment." Evie retreated to the kitchen.

But after a week had passed, Philip remained in the Bronx, back in their old bedroom. Joseph had converted the room into a study and piled all the newsmagazines, Jewish periodicals, and left-wing journals that he never had time to read on the bookshelves and beds. But he packed these away happily to make room for Philip. Philip practiced his guitar, loudly, for hours a day — horrible, cacophonous, screeching on the electric, and, more rarely, soft, spare Dylan on the acoustic — until

Joseph or Evie begged him to stop. Then Philip, sullen, would put away the instruments and brood on his bed, cheered eventually by rhapsodic fantasies that made him smile.

The space aliens said that the methods of caring for the mentally ill on Earth were barbaric. They likened it to the treatment of deaf people a century ago. "In those days, the deaf were regarded as morons and imbeciles," Herbert said. "But once sign language was developed for the deaf, their intelligence couldn't be denied."

"On Earth, you lack the language to communicate with the insane. But eventually you'll learn it," Evelyn told him. "Like the Australian aborigines, you'll enter dreamtime. And then you'll discover what pain, what dignity, what wisdom, and what sorrow lies within the mentally ill."

"Can I learn?" Bert asked, imagining one of his father's foreign language cassettes. "Now?"

"If you want," Ribsy said. "But there are no schools yet. So I'm afraid you'll have to become mentally ill yourself."

"N-no," Bert said. "I don't want to do that."

Barbara and Bert were alone in the office. Bert watched as she cleaned her desk, swabbed the phone with Lysol and a tissue, sharpened her pencils. She was always so orderly.

"Barbara, remember you told me you and your sister saw ghosts?"

"Oh yes. Many times."

"Well, this is a strange question, but have you ever seen extraterrestrials?" He sifted through the papers cluttering his desk while he waited for her response.

"I've never seen them," Barbara said, dusting a photograph of one of her daughters. "But I know they're out there."

"I think a lot of people who say they see them don't really see them. Maybe they think they do, but deep down, they know they're not real. And then other people," Bert said, "other people really see them."

"Course they do," Barbara insisted. "They're real. Real as this desk" — she patted the desk — "or this chair" — she patted the chair between them — "or this head." She knocked lightly on Bert's forehead.

"Yeah, I guess you're right."

"Oh, I'm right," Barbara said. "Right as rain. Wait a minute, I'll show you." She opened her desk drawer and removed from a neat, yellow Pendaflex folder an article she had clipped from the *National Enquirer,* "Your Coworker Could Be a Space Alien, Say Experts . . . Here's How You Can Tell."

The article listed ten ways to detect space aliens hidden in the work force. They often wore odd or mismatched clothes; had strange dietary habits; displayed a bizarre sense of humor; took off frequently from work, kept a diary; misused everyday items; constantly questioned coworkers about their customs; were secretive about their personal life-style; talked to themselves; experienced mood changes in the presence of high-tech equipment.

"Wait a minute," Bert cried. "I've done all of these things!"

"Well, you know, I've had my suspicions about you, Bert," Barbara said, and then they laughed together.

Bert arranged to meet Evie for lunch. His mother wanted to talk. She worked in Washington Heights, at Columbia-Presbyterian Medical Center. He took the subway all the way uptown from work, got lost in the labyrinth of the hospital, and finally found the pharmacy. His mother, wearing one of her cardigans, was speaking pidgin Spanish to a Salvadoran customer. When she had finished filling the order, Evie, as proud as a peacock, introduced Bert to all her coworkers, including a twenty-five-year-old pharmacist named Tom Helmer, to whom she seemed very attached. Tom had a neat, dark black beard and a bookish, handsome face — almost a beautiful face, actually. But his nose had been broken in a childhood accident, leaving him with a bump on the bridge, and his teeth were slightly discolored. He had dimples when he smiled and sad, sober eyes. Tom was trying to unionize the pharmacists at Presbyterian, thereby impressing Joseph to no end, Evie reported. He seemed nice enough to Bert, but solemn and somewhat dull. Bert could tell that Tom was gay, but he didn't think his mother knew — or perhaps she knew but didn't want to know, the way Bert sometimes thought his parents knew but didn't know about Patrick and him.

"Is it horrible that I want Philip to leave?" Evie asked him at lunch. "I'm fifty-six years old, I've been working a long time. I just want some peace and quiet. It's not fair." Her hands trembled as she drank some coffee. "It's just not fair. I love him, and I want him to get better. Every day I give people pills and cure them, and I think, why can't I cure my own son? But I come home at night and I'm scared. I don't want him here. Am I wrong, Bert? Am I such a terrible mother?"

"No," Bert had to tell her. "You're not." He understood why she didn't want to live with Philip. He wouldn't want to live with Philip either.

Patrick knocked on his apartment door a week later and asked if he could please come in. Bert had been in bed, wearing only underwear. He opened the door quickly and then jumped back under the covers. Patrick sat next to him and said his father had called him. He thought he'd been hired for a job, but at the last minute, they had picked someone else. His father, a little drunk, had started crying into the receiver. Patrick looked shaken. "Bert, could you please just hold me?" Bert held him for a long time.

Jane started screaming, "First they possess me, now they try to dispossess me! Just wash me with a little bit of tenderness, just open your soul, what am I, a freak for your amusement? Just because I'm barren? I'm burning up. Oh God," Jane screamed, "I'm burning up."

"I've never asked, but do you have children?"

"Three," Evelyn told him.

"They're grown up now," Herbert said. He coughed into

one of his armrests. "I miss them so much. Sometimes I just want to see them, I just want to look at them. But . . ." He lit his pipe again. "Life goes on. Because of relativity, they'll be much older when we get back."

Evelyn shivered, as though suddenly cold, even though she was wearing two layers of sweaters. She had told Bert that she found the Earth chilly. "It's no big deal. Children and parents separate every day."

"Would you like to see their holograms?" Ribsy asked.

"Sure," Bert said eagerly.

Ribsy opened up the seat of malchick's body and removed three cubes. By pressing a button on each cube, Ribsy activated the holograms, which floated in the air. The first was of a young male malchik, wearing a sweater, raking leaves outside a two-story house, then waving at the camera.

"That's Ernesto," Ribsy said. "When he was a teenager. Isn't he a hot one? I love this picture."

The second hologram was of a malchick-malchik, playing the drums in a garage. Malchick's hair was flung wildly from side to side as malchick played. It was a silent hologram, so Bert couldn't hear the music. But the rhythm was distinctly alien and unearthly, judging by the timing of the drumsticks. The beats kept surprising Bert. They seemed to come at the wrong moments.

"That's Robin," Herbert said.

"Robin is Harold's favorite," Ribsy told Bert.

"I don't have favorites," Herbert-also-known-as-Harold maintained.

"Not much you don't," Ribsy said.

The third hologram was of their daughter malchik, Shulamith. Shulamith's skin was light green, and her hair was almost yellow. She was reading a book in a back yard, next to a swing set. Then Robin came over to her. Shulamith put the book down and began tangoing with Robin on the green grass.

The holograms faded. Ribsy put the cubes back in malchick's seat, smiling sadly.

"It must have been hard for you. Leaving your children."

"It was," Ribsy said, "extraordinarily difficult."

"I'm so sorry."

"Why should it matter to you?" Evelyn was indignant. "They're not your children. Anyway, they have families of their own now. They don't miss us one bit."

"Evelyn, you know that's not true," Ribsy said.

Later Bert came across her in the back yard. She was activating her own holograms and weeping. But she made no sound as she sobbed. She hadn't noticed Bert, and Bert backed out of the yard before she saw him.

Ground Control

▾▾▾

BERT HEARD A KNOCK at his door. He thought it was Patrick, and he opened the door wide, trying to wipe the grin off his face. Standing there was a husky, hostile man in a green uniform.

"Bertolt B. Rosenbaum?" the man asked.

Bert nodded.

"I'm from Air Traffic Control." He offered his I.D. card: Sergeant Peter Brown, Special Investigations, Federal Aviation Administration. "Can I ask you a few questions?"

"I guess." Bert was uncomfortable and shifted nervously from one leg to the other.

"My department investigates violations of the FAA code among air traffic personnel."

"What kind of violations?"

"Any number of things. Drug smuggling. Financial improprieties. Unauthorized entries into U.S. air space. Are you familiar with the Heiberg family?"

"Somewhat," Bert said cautiously.

He evaded all of Brown's questions. Brown talked mostly about Jorgen but seemed interested in the entire family, even the children. He had heard that the children saw space aliens and that Bert spent time with them. He had even heard about Jane's screaming. He wanted to know if the children confided in Bert, if the children talked about their parents or about the extraterrestrials. He asked if Lars and Isabel took drugs. He asked if Lars and Isabel spent money.

*

Bert conferred with the aliens.

"How did they spot you?" Bert asked.

"It could have been any of a dozen ways," Evelyn said. "IV drug users, dolphins —"

"Identical twins," Herbert interjected.

"The thing is, they seem to suspect Jorgen, mostly," Ribsy reminded them.

"But Jorgen isn't involved. And why did they ask me questions?" countered Bert. "They must know something."

"Listen, no one's going to be arrested. No one's committed a crime here," Evelyn reassured them.

"Oh really." Herbert glanced at Ribsy, who was smoking some dope. "I'm not worried about us," Herbert said. "We can always blast off."

"But my dissertation!"

"This is a worst-case scenario, duck," Ribsy comforted Evelyn.

"I'm worried about the Heibergs and you," Herbert told Bert. "I don't want to get Jorgen in any trouble."

Bert invited Diana, Patrick, Harry, and Barbara up to his apartment to watch the last episode of *M*A*S*H* and to play cards. He borrowed the enormous TV set that Jorgen had just bought so that they wouldn't have to watch on his small portable. Kathleen asked if she could come. She said she didn't want to play (she was awful at cards), she wouldn't *kibitz* ("that's the right word, isn't it, Bert?"), she just thought it would be fun to hang out with them (if he didn't mind). Bert said of course she could come.

It was crowded in his studio, and they were all talking at once, and it got very hot because Kathleen was in the kitchen making brownies, and Bert was losing more than he was winning, but he enjoyed himself. On TV, Hawkeye was having a nervous breakdown. By the end of the episode, he had recovered completely: a miracle.

"My husband's gonna kill me if I lose any money," Barbara

said. She shuffled the deck expertly. "High Low. High and low hands split the pot."

"The last time I won anything, I was playing Chutes and Ladders with my little sister," Harry said morosely. "And even then, I cheated."

Diana studied her cards: a four, a nine, a ten, a jack, a king. She knew you weren't supposed to draw to an inside straight, but hell, she was going to do it anyway. She threw in the four. Harry didn't like his cards, so he used his ace to get four new ones. Patrick had a pair of sixes. He threw one of them in. He'd go for the low hand. If he ended up with a higher pair, well, he thought, he'd still be better off than where he'd started. Barbara had dealt herself a pair of fives. She threw in the other three cards and prayed for another five or another pair.

Bert looked at his cards. Two of hearts, ten of hearts, jack of hearts, jack of clubs, queen of spades. Now, this was interesting. He could keep the two jacks, pick up three cards, and try for three of a kind. Or he could throw in the queen of spades and the jack of clubs and try for a flush. The odds were against it, but statistics didn't take his emotions into account. He wanted that flush badly. He loved flushes. Still, it was too risky. He kept the pair of jacks and drew three cards.

Barbara and Diana ended up splitting the pot. Barbara had three fives, Diana had the low hand. Then Kathleen served them the brownies with Ben & Jerry's mint Oreo ice cream. It was delicious. As they ate the brownies, Jane Alley started screaming.

"What the hell's that?" Patrick feigned ignorance.

Bert felt a throb of pure rage toward Patrick but dampened it. "That's Jane."

"My God, she's loud," Diana said. "I never believed you when you said it was so loud."

"No one ever believes me." He explained that Jane screamed out her back window into the air shaft, where her voice echoed back and forth as it funneled up the passageway. Even with all his windows closed, he could hear every word she shouted.

Jane was bellowing: "You bastards, you Hitlers, haven't I shed enough blood for you? Murderers! Assassins! Drug addicts!"

"My God, how do you sleep?" worried Diana.

"I don't."

"That poor woman," Barbara said.

"Poor Bert," Kathleen said.

"We're going to court in a few weeks," Bert told them.

Philip's behavior worsened as the weeks went on. He studied the metallic and enamel surfaces of lamps and kitchen fixtures, the lambent blue flame of the stove burners, the luminous white refrigerator Evie scrubbed clean every night, the refulgence of morning sun on the linoleum. The flickering and shimmering of light and shadow fascinated him, seemed to awake in him feelings of incredible intensity which he tried to set to music. But they weren't the right feelings, Philip confessed, not the normal, proper feelings that a normal, well-developed, heterosexual twenty-five-year-old would feel. This worried him. Still, he said, when he jammed on his electric guitar and closed his eyes, he was transported to another world, another planet — a better planet, he thought, even though lesbians there controlled the means of production.

And he explained, quite rationally, that he had changed his mind about the death penalty because he now realized it had no deterrent effect whatsoever and that it made no sense for the state to commit the very crime it was supposed to be punishing. Also, he said, he had been in error when he had condemned homosexuality. With his greater age and wisdom, he understood that homosexuals could not control their feelings and desires and deserved the same civil liberties as anyone else. Support for the death penalty and homophobia showed just how pervasive fascism really was. "If you were gay," he told his brother, "I would love you just as much. I mean that, Bert." And Bert almost wept.

"I'm glad you changed your mind about gays," Bert said. "I'm proud of you."

"I'm not homosexual, if that's what you think." Philip became increasingly agitated. "I am not a homosexual, although Mother will never rest until I become one. Never, never, never, never, never!" he shouted at Bert.

"Have you ever, I don't know, changed anything since you've been here?" Bert asked them. "You know, changed the course of history?"

The espresso Evelyn was drinking shot down her green chin.

Herbert cleared his throat. "We've told you about the Prime Directive."

"Yeah. So now tell me the truth."

The aliens looked at one another. "All right," Herbert decided. "I'll tell you if you swear to keep it a secret. We've made two changes. The first was in Italy, in 1938, just outside Palermo. Mussolini was in power. Two anarchists were about to kill a man who was going to kill himself anyway. The anarchists, good men at heart, would have been driven to the brink of madness by guilt, and would have eventually killed themselves as well. It just seemed so pointless. So we stopped it."

"What the hell were you doing in Italy in 1938?"

"We made a wrong turn at the nearest black hole," Ribsy explained. Ribsy was rubbing malchick's lips with some cocaine. Malchick liked to numb them.

"And the second time?"

"Well, I don't want to go into particulars," Herbert said, tapping his pipe nervously. "It happened several years ago, near the nexus of your planet."

"The nexus? Where's that?"

"Midway between Englewood Cliffs and Camden, New Jersey," Evelyn informed him.

"That's near Princeton, right?"

"Yes," Ribsy said. "That's right."

"Well, what'd you do?"

"It doesn't matter. It was an accident." Herbert smiled sadly to himself. "People love us, or hurt us, or love us and hurt us. Sometimes you want to make things better, and you just make them worse."

Joseph asked Bert if he would share an apartment with Philip. "We can help out with the rent," his father told him. "You can get a bigger place. And maybe you'd like the company."

"I don't think so, Dad."

"He loves you so much. You're the one he always connects to."

"Dad, I'm not going to do it."

Joseph, saddened, tapped his magazine with an unlit cigar. "I understand. It's just that Philip and your mother don't get along so well. Never mind." He looked up at Bert and smiled. "Hey, don't worry about it. Everything's going to work out."

Bert sat beside him on the sofa. "It doesn't seem fair, what our family goes through."

"Hey, a lot of people have it worse off than us. A lot worse." Joseph was adamant.

Philip insisted that he was taking his pills, but they all knew he wasn't. Finally Evie said she wouldn't make him dinner if he didn't take his pill, and she watched him swallow it every night. The medication stabilized him, and the obsessions and lurid fantasies soon faded. Philip started shaving and dressing better. He even looked at the help wanted ads. Bert believed it was imperative that Philip work and that as rational behavior was rewarded, Philip would become more rational. After all, he had held down a job in Los Angeles for two years. The bookstore was willing to take Philip back if he returned, Philip told them. Evie wanted him to move back to L.A.

"I think you'd be happier in California," Evie said.

"But I want to stay here."

"But I know you love Los Angeles. You're independent there," Evie reasoned with him. "If you stayed here, we'd always be looking over your shoulder."

"But I want to stay."

"And of course, it's hard for your father, giving up his study. You've been doing so well in California. I think you'd be happier there."

Philip said nothing. Joseph said nothing. Bert said nothing.

"Don't you think you'd be happier there?" Evie prompted. "I think you'd be happier there."

"Yes," Philip said at last. "I'd be happier there."

Joseph rented a car, and Bert accompanied his father and brother to the airport. "I'll call you three, four times a week," Joseph told Philip, and Bert knew he would.

Evie stayed home to work. She still typed on weekends to make extra money, most of which she would send to Philip in California. But as she typed, the words on the page began to swim in front of her. She closed her eyes and rubbed them. She was tired, she hadn't slept well in weeks. Outside, on the Grand Concourse, a car screeched to a halt, but not in time, for she heard the plaintive shriek of a collision, and she cried out with fear. The memory of the Rosenbaums' own collision was so real and so clear and so plangent that it seemed to Evie as if she were actually experiencing the accident again.

The car swerved sharply and woke her with a start. "We'll be all right," Joseph said. The Buick slammed into them, cutting the hood along a diagonal. The car spun in the opposite direction, the hatchback flew open, Bert's things flew out. She was confused, her head hurt. Joseph ran around to see if she was hurt. "I never will desert Mr. Rosenbaum," Evie said. She wasn't even aware that she was speaking.

"Are you okay?" Joseph asked anxiously.

"You look a little dizzy, Mom," Bert said, rubbing his head.

It seemed to Evie that Bert was rotating around and around, that he was twirling in front of her. Surely he must be dizzy, too. "Like son, like mother," Evie said.

Then space began settling and she was back in time. She heard a police siren behind her. Green patches of trees and blue patches of sky surrounded them. A Goodyear blimp floated lazily over the highway. Another car, with a Princeton bumper sticker on the back, had just pulled up. Bert's clothes and bags lay scattered everywhere. She saw a small valise, a pillowcase, Philip lying in a heap on the road. . . . Terrified, she turned back quickly and saw that it was only a T-shirt of Philip's that he'd lent Bert, and one of Philip's baseball caps, and a pair of blue jeans, crumpled on the ground. Bert's Scrabble set had been flung helter-skelter all around them, and she noted, insanely, that the tiles had spelled the word WOOF at her feet. Then Evie looked from Bert to Joseph and then from Joseph back to her son again. Bert's mother laughed, seeing that her boys were safe.

Evie began typing again, but her fingers were jittery, and she made many mistakes. She remained nervous until Joseph returned from the airport. Philip was safely on the plane, Bert was safe in his apartment, Joseph was safe at home, with her.

Isabel and Lars said they were being followed. They pointed out a large blond woman in front of their building. The next day, as Bert took the subway to work, the same woman waited on the subway platform near him. Bert let the local go by and waited for the express. The woman waited too. He got on the Number 2 train, and the woman got on the same car with him. There were no seats, so he crossed to the next car. The woman followed behind him. He stopped suddenly. The blond woman passed by, squeezed into an empty seat, and pretended to read. Bert looked at the pamphlet she was studying. It was a schedule of incoming flights at La Guardia Airport put out by the Air Traffic Control division.

"Now, if she has an identical twin. And if she's an IV drug user —" Evelyn began.

"If she's a lefty!" the three aliens called out in unison.

"We never told you about southpaws, did we?" Herbert asked. "It's a cofactor."

"There can't be many left-handed identical twin junkies," Bert said.

"They only need one," Ribsy reminded him.

"How did they find her?"

"They've got some personnel department, all right," Evelyn acknowledged.

"What if she's gay or bisexual?" Herbert said. "That would be the last straw."

"Bis have an easier time seeing you?" asked Bert.

"You have to understand, sexual configuration isn't something that can be taken in isolation. It defines the brain's electrical wiring, it establishes your pathways. And some pathways are more conducive to spotting us than others. God, I hope she's not bi," Herbert ended.

"I hope she is," Ribsy said. "It'll mean she's more — open."

"What are you thinking of doing, Ribsy?" Evelyn asked warily.

"Mata Hari, at your service." Ribsy curtsied.

Harry was walking on air: Chuck had returned. One day he came home from work, and there was Chuck, waiting for him. They held each other all night long. Chuck was a kid, just a messed-up kid, but Harry was starting to fall in love. He was scared about Chuck running off again. He knew it was crazy, he knew it didn't make any sense, but he was falling in love.

"I don't know what it is, but there's something sexy about you. Maybe it's that you're always thinking about sex."

"How do you know?"

"I can smell it. You're a skinny, sex-obsessed, Jewish kid," Diana said. "Just my type." She laughed her wonderful, growling laugh. There was a glint in her eye, like a cat welcoming a pigeon to the neighborhood.

He fiddled so much, Patrick. He constructed all kinds of origami creatures — swans, penguins, turtles, grasshoppers, rabbits, butterflies, kangaroos. Bert loved best of all the masks of brides and grooms, witch doctors, astronauts, nuns, and angels which Patrick would make for him out of paper. Patrick made origami the way other people doodled: absentmindedly, while talking on the phone or watching cartoons. He'd worked in a florist shop during high school and learned from a colleague.

He was also handy at repairs, and coworkers would bring in broken radios, toaster ovens, turntables, and typewriters for him to fix. Armed with a screwdriver and wrench, absorbed in his task, he would pass into another world entirely. And then when he was finished, he'd look up at Bert, a smile of beatific satisfaction on his face. He glowed.

Patrick told Bert they needed to talk. They met at Empire Szechuan at three o'clock in the afternoon on a Saturday. "Bert, I don't know how all this got started," Patrick began in a low voice, though no one was around.

Bert was reading *The Ambassadors.* He hated the book, but he was already halfway through it, and he was determined to finish it, in case years later he decided he really ought to read it. He didn't want to put himself through the first two hundred pages ever again. "What do you mean you don't know how it got started," Bert said cooly. "You were there."

"Bert, it's just that I don't want to be the kind of man who sleeps with men."

"But you are that kind," Bert said, quietly resuming his reading. He was amazed at how you could read a page over and over again without the contents ever sinking in. When he read Henry James, that seemed to happen a lot.

"I've had girlfriends," Patrick said.

"This is embarrassing."

"I like girls. I don't know — I liked you, Bert. I was lonely, and I liked you, and that's why it happened. I wasn't choosing a lifestyle. That's what you seem to want from me."

Mostly he'd just wanted to cuddle, Bert thought ruefully. If it was going to end anyway, he wished they'd spooned more. He started reading again.

"It's really helpful, you reading your book."

"What if it's a lie, Pat, what if no one's so completely heterosexual, so completely straight. What if it's a fraud?"

"I don't know why you're acting this way. You make me feel guilty, and I don't even know what I've done wrong. You want something from me I never promised to give you. When it happened the first time, I thought, okay, that was fun, now it's over. I let it happen again, and I thought okay, now it's really over. But you never let it be over."

"Yeah, Patrick, that's exactly the way it happened." Bert was getting angry, and the angrier he got, the quieter he got. "Well, good. Fine. I'm glad we've had this little chat." He started reading the same page again.

"God, you really are weird! Look at you, reading! Don't you have any feelings?"

No, he never had the proper feelings, Bert supposed. Maybe he was different, maybe he was crazy, he didn't know. "I guess you're making more friends," he said archly, because he would rather Patrick think him waspish than weak. "Dating a nice drug dealer or something?"

Patrick ignored the sting. "You'd be great for someone, Bert. You've got incredible traits that would be appreciated by someone. I know you'll find someone."

Traits. Someone. Jesus, it was unfair. Why should Patrick get to make the decisions? Answer: because Patrick was in control. Bert had lost. That's all, he'd lost. He didn't even feel like fighting anymore. He put down his book and looked at Patrick. "Okay. Okay, you win."

"Okay?" Patrick asked him closely, surprised by Bert's sudden capitulation.

"It's over," Bert said, smiling a little — because Patrick wanted him to.

She was wearing a short, tight black dress. "This is my Twiggy outfit," Diana told him. "Except Twiggy was thin, and I'm a fat slob."

"Yeah, you're enormous."

"How do I look in it?" She modeled it for him, turning around. Her breasts were barely contained by the dress.

"Why don't you unbutton one more button."

"I'm not wearing a bra. If I unbuttoned any more, my boobs would fall right out. I don't know, maybe you'd like that look. Would you, Bert?"

"You're such a cock tease," Bert said.

"Well, yes."

They met later in the copy room, by chance. No one was around. The two Xerox machines were running, and the small, windowless room was stuffy. "It's so hot in here," Diana said. "I should just take this dress off."

"Why don't you."

Bert locked the door, then walked up closer to Diana and put his hand on one of the buttons of her blouse. "Buh, buh, buh, Bert," she said. She was making fun of him. Sometimes when he was nervous he had a stammer. He unbuttoned the button. "You're still in there," he complained.

"What are you going to do about it?"

He unbuttoned the next button, freeing her breasts. She wasn't lying, she wasn't wearing a bra. He made little circles around her right nipple. "You're very beautiful," he told her.

"I just play a good game," she said.

He touched her right nipple with the tip of his finger. "This is weird. "We're in the Xerox room."

"Well, Bert," she said, "there's no time like the present."

He took her nipples into his mouth, one at a time, and sucked on them.

She started laughing. "Original."

He put his hand between her legs and worked his fingers into her panties. She wriggled out of her panties so he could play with her pussy.

"Sit on the Xerox machine," he said.

"What?"

"Come on, do it."

She sat on the copier and pressed herself into the glass. Bert pushed the copy button and the machine started humming. "Art in the age of mechanical reproduction," Bert declared.

"You can blackmail me with that."

"I'd like to. It'd be nice to have the upper hand for once." He put his hand back in her pussy and they started kissing. She grabbed his dick through his pants.

Someone at the door rattled it back and forth, trying to get in. Diana jumped down, hoisted up her panties, buttoned her dress frantically, smoothed her hair, grabbed the incriminating photocopy, crumpled it in her hand, started crying, and opened the door.

Bert's boss, Steven, was there. "I'm sorry." Diana was crying. "I've just been going through some personal stuff, and Bert was talking to me."

Steven turned bright red. "I didn't know. I'll come back. I didn't know . . ."

The next day, Diana and her husband left on a ski trip with Patrick and Harry. Kathleen had planned to go, too, but later canceled. Bert couldn't go because the court date had finally arrived for the nuisance suit against Jane Alley.

Bert and the other witnesses testified that they'd repeatedly called the police because the noise was so loud. Jane looked straight at them as they spoke. Her hair was pulled into a bun and she wore a neatly pressed — and for once, blue — dress. Some of the tenants were thrown by Jane's public defender, a young Asian woman: she was a good attorney (better than the one the building had hired) and was generally able to find some inconsistency in their testimony. She eventually negotiated a three-month delay on any eviction proceedings and promised that Jane would seek counseling.

"Counseling, it's a fahcking waste of sunshine and spit," Jorgen complained later, drinking tea out of a small white porcelain cup. They'd all walked over to Chinatown after court adjourned. "One really ought to cut her devil head off, yah sure, you betcha."

"A lobotomy," Luisa suggested.

"They don't do that anymore," Bert said quietly.

"I have no sleep in six fahcking months. The other night,

she has screamed so loud, I have gone to the fridge and have put my head inside, yust for some quiet. The police should lock her in yail." He was starting to yell. "I'd like to fahcking kill her, I would. I'd like to fahcking —" Then Jorgen was suddenly laughing. "Listen to me. Yust you wait, I'm the next who goes crazy, damn sure."

By the time Bert got home, it had started snowing. Good ski weather. Bert phoned Philip. He'd called his brother just a few days before, at the end of February, to wish him a happy birthday, but he felt like talking to him again.

"Hey, Phil, remember that time it snowed and we —"

"I remember."

Philip said he'd started working nights at Tower Records on Sunset Boulevard. He was still working days at the bookstore. He wanted to save up money so he could date more. He said he'd just asked a girl out.

"That's great, Phil."

"She said no. She said I was weird."

Bert said she didn't have good taste in men if she didn't want to go out with Philip. He said Philip shouldn't let it get to him, that he had wonderful traits lots of women would go for.

"I have to get in a rock band, Bert. Then all these girls will want to date me. That'll be so great!" Philip laughed exultantly. Bert laughed too, mostly because he was picturing Philip laugh. When Philip smiled, his whole face lit up — he beamed.

He went upstairs to see Isabel and Lars one evening, but as he got out of their elevator he ran into the blond woman who had been following him. The aliens' spaceship was parked on the landing. Evidently the woman had just emerged from the craft, and she was still a bit dizzy, for she rocked on the balls of her feet. She smiled faintly at Bert, embarrassed, then ran down the stairs.

"Nothing like a little *Moondance,*" Ribsy told Bert, emerging from the spaceship, puffing away contentedly at a cigarette. At first Bert thought the Van Morrison music was coming from the Heibergs' apartment, but then he realized it was pouring out of the spaceship.

"What's going to happen now?" Bert asked.

"I suspect Ground Control won't be bothering us for a while, at least," Ribsy said.

"Are you that good?" Bert asked malchick.

"When I'm good, I'm very good. And when I'm bad"— Ribsy blew a perfect smoke ring into the air — "I'm even better."

The Rising of the Women Means the Rising of the Race

▾▾▾

BERT WAS VISITING Lars and Isabel's bedroom. Against one wall, in a trophy cabinet, Isabel displayed her beloved slime molds. On the facing wall, and also on the ceiling, Lars had hung his butterfly collection. Lying on Lars's bed and staring up at the glass case overhead, Bert watched the insects in their silent, frozen flight. The butterflies were beautiful. The slime molds — well, Isabel thought they were beautiful, anyway. They were certainly colorful enough. Isabel explained that the final stage in the life cycle of the slime mold, when it formed fruiting bodies, was the most vibrant. Yellow, orange, red, white, violet, pink, gray, the bodies rose up out of the slime molds and produced spores that were spread by wind, rain, and insects to begin the life cycle all over again when they germinated.

"Any word from Air Traffic Control?" Lars asked.

"No. That seems to have quieted down."

"There's still a problem," Isabel told him. "Ribsy grabbed some more Bernice."

"Bernice?"

"You know, stardust," Lars said.

"Huh?"

"Cocaine." Lars shook his head at Bert's provincialism. "Jeez."

"And we've seen a junkie hanging around the building, like he's looking for somebody." Isabel was worried.

*

Bert met the aliens in Riverside Park. A golden retriever, off its leash, spotted the aliens sunbathing in the winter light. The dog lunged at Herbert, happy to see him, wagging her tail furiously. Herbert jumped back, terrified.

"She's not going to hurt you," Bert said.

"I know. It's instinctive, I guess." Herbert walked up to the retriever and patted her tentatively.

"What did you want to see us about?" Evelyn asked Bert.

"Isabel and Lars tell me Ribsy's stolen some more coke."

"I did no such thing," Ribsy said.

"Really?"

"Well, all right, I did," Ribsy admitted. "But so what?"

Evelyn was furious. "We're in a precarious position. We've already been spotted once. What were you thinking?"

"A bunch of junkies aren't going to do anything," Ribsy said.

"I shouldn't get mad at you. You've obviously got a problem," Evelyn said.

"What kind of problem?" Ribsy giggled nervously, tee hee hee tee hee hee.

"A drug problem."

Ribsy giggled again. "You're crazy."

"You take drugs every day, Rivka," Herbert said quietly.

"I get a rise out of them. What can I say? I'm just a very sensual person."

"Ribsy only said no once," Evelyn told Bert. "And that was because malchick didn't hear the question."

"One of my mothers was the same way," Ribsy remembered. The alien took out a syringe that malchick had converted into a flute and began playing a horribly dissonant melody. Herbert and Evelyn stood at attention. "The Debbie Planetary Anthem," Ribsy explained.

When Diana got back from the ski trip she told Bert that she and Rob had patched things up, the weekend away had been good for them. Bert wasn't surprised. He buried himself in his work, editing the latest of Steven's memos, "The Higher You Go, the Harder You Fall." Falls from a height were the most serious accidents facing the department, Bert learned. "Stairs are good exercise," Steven wrote, "but only if you don't get injured."

In spite of Jane's "counseling," she was still screaming. One day Bert returned home to find a subpoena. Jane was suing him. She sent him a letter the next day (and forwarded copies to the *New York Times,* the district attorney, the judge of the nuisance case, the governor, the mayor, and the American Medical Association), charging him with his specific crimes: misappropriating her discoveries and ideas; drugging her without her consent; observing her, inside and outside her apartment, twenty-four hours a day, in violation of her rights of privacy under the Constitution; repeatedly and illegally forcing his way into her apartment, with thefts of and damage to her property; so seriously affecting her physical health by drugging her that she was prevented from working and was forced to go on welfare; perjuring himself in court.

Their apartment building on West Ninety-seventh Street, she indicated, was registered as a residential multiple dwelling. Despite this, a number of apartments were used for transients who remained in the building for only a short while — in the Rosenbaum and Heiberg apartments, she'd noticed, sometimes for only a night, for what was probably mental health training. It was all terribly ironic, Jane wrote, since she had recently made amazing discoveries about how to deal with immature, infantile people with less cost to herself.

She noted in an addendum that if the judge didn't support her, he would be party to what could be described only as Nazi-like crimes, crimes in complete violation of the Constitution, crimes in which she had been abused and exploited as an experimental animal. "You would thus be placed among those who have violated and ignored law, justice, ethics, humaneness; among criminals who have destroyed a human life, in an organized, illegal enterprise for their own sick, selfish, obsessed ends," she lectured him. "Such an enterprise is doomed. It is ungodly, inhuman, insane. It violates every ethical value entrusted to civilized persons. Civlization itself is diminished by their activity."

Bert learned from the landlord that Jane had been a teacher, and he noted that not a single word was misspelled in the neatly typed, single-spaced letter. The lawyer whom the building had hired told Bert not to worry, the case would be dismissed as soon as it went to trial — but yes, Bert would probably have to go to court a few more times to get everything straightened out. He didn't want to represent Bert — he worried that Jane might sue him, too. That night Jane screamed, "I can't breathe, oh God, stop the CIA torture of political prisoners on West Ninety-seventh Street! Stop burning my genitals!"

Luisa told Bert that she and Jorgen were considering a separation and were arguing about who got to move out. They both wanted to — neither one wanted to stay near Jane. They worried about the children, but they didn't think they could make a go of the marriage. Recently, things had gotten even worse: "I've been working nights this month, but I came home early last week, and there he was on the sofa, fu——" — she broke off, then continued a moment later — "screwing around with this big blond bitch who works at the airport. And I thought she was my friend."

"I'm sorry, Luisa." Bert didn't know what to say.

"I asked him why, and he said it was because he was so devil tired, yah, sure, betcha." Luisa laughed, but wiped tears out of her eyes. "And I was so tired, I almost understood."

Evelyn and Ribsy were attending an aerobics class, incognito. Bert and Herbert were reading in the basement. "This is so implausible," Herbert complained, putting down his copy of Arthur C. Clarke's *Rendezvous with Rama.* He picked up the Sunday paper and started leafing through the book review section, periodically jotting down titles of books and authors on a little pad of paper. Herbert liked to keep a list of books he intended to read.

"My father does the same thing," Bert said. "But he never has time to read the books."

The elevator doors opened, and Evelyn and Ribsy emerged, still panting from their workout. Ribsy eyed Bert critically. "You're dressed so June 1977," malchick told him. Bert was wearing faded jeans, a T-shirt, a blue workshirt over the T-shirt, red Converse high-tops. "Mid-June," Ribsy pinpointed the matter further.

"Thanks."

"Your planet's so strange," Evelyn said. "We saw two kids fighting on Amsterdam Avenue. One kid called the other a cocksucker."

"So?"

"On our planet, 'cocksucker' is a term of approval," Ribsy informed him. "Even endearment."

"Why should sucking cock be an insult?" Evelyn demanded. "Why should giving pleasure be disparaged?" She shook her head, then picked up the Sunday crossword puzzle and a pencil. " 'Blennoid fish of the family *Zoarcidae,*' " she announced.

"It's on the tip of my tongue," Ribsy lied.

Diana, Barbara, and Kathleen were going out to lunch, and somehow they'd lassoed Bert into joining them. Bert didn't want to go: "All you're going to do is complain about men." They promised they wouldn't. The three women ordered salads. Bert ordered a burger and fries.

"I like men," Kathleen began over lunch. "Theoretically."

"The problem is, they like to take over," Barbara said. "They throw their clothes around, they don't make the bed, and they always leave the damn towels on the floor."

Bert munched a fry disconsolately. "I knew this was going to happen."

"They don't want to tell you what's going on, and when you ask them, they say they have to read the newspaper, they have to go to sleep, they have to watch football," Diana recited.

"I hate football," Kathleen said. The other women agreed.

"I like baseball more," Bert offered.

"I hate baseball," Kathleen said.

"I like baseball," Barbara told them. "My daddy and I saw James 'Cool Papa' Bell hit an inside-the-park home run in 1946. I was eleven years old. Never forgot it."

"I want a man to treat me like an equal — and still hold the door open for me," Kathleen proposed.

"You want too much," Bert said.

"You hold the door open for me." Kathleen smiled at him, pulling back her flaxen hair.

Diana asked for a french fry, and took a few. Kathleen asked for a french fry, and took a few. Barbara asked for a whole mess of french fries. They finished his fries, and Bert asked if they wanted to split another order. The three women insisted they didn't want any more. Bert ordered another batch anyway. The women helped themselves. The waitress asked if they wanted dessert. Only Bert ordered: a slice of chocolate pecan pie. The women divided it neatly into four pieces. Kathleen ate the pie in small bites, savoring it. "Mmm, this is good."

"Men are emotional babies," Diana said. "They're draining."

"Because they're selfish," Barbara went on. "And they plan your life for you."

"Even if you're not that involved," Kathleen reflected. "They think they know what's good for you, and they hardly even know you."

"They're needy," Diana said, digging into the pie ferociously. "And narcissistic."

"Well, what do you like about them?" Bert finally asked.

"They're needy," Diana said. "And narcissistic."

"When you like them, it's not because they're men," Barbara told him. "It's because you get along."

"They know how to do things," Kathleen added. "They can carry heavy things for you and move furniture. They can fix things, they're mechanical."

"They're logical. Women think too much with their hearts,

men use their minds. And they've got a lot of energy," Barbara acknowledged.

"I like their bodies," Diana said.

"Yes, ma'am."

"I like when they surprise you," Kathleen said. "When they're not manly at all. When they grow flowers or write poems or act like little boys."

"I like their clothes," Barbara mused. "Something about a man's clothes I just like."

"I like when they're chivalrous, when they treat you like you're a little weaker — because sometimes you are," Kathleen admitted shyly.

"I like when they do the dishes," Diana said. "But that's rare."

"The best thing about a man is when you have to deal with another man, and you don't want to, they can do it for you," Kathleen asserted.

Barbara had finished her slice of pecan pie and was now flattening the crumbs with her fork, then licking them off the utensil. "They like making babies," Barbara said. "But they don't want to help you take care of them."

Patrick came down to visit him after lunch. He was embarrassed to ask, but he wanted to know if he could borrow ten bucks, just until his paycheck came in. Bert said of course, he didn't have to be embarrassed, everyone got low on cash once in a while. Bert gave him a twenty.

"You're such a good friend," Patrick said.

Later, Assistant Commissioner Truby came downstairs to talk to Steven and started screaming so loudly that none of them could work. Barbara got up and closed Steven's door gently. Truby pulled open the door, ran out of the cubicle into their area, and began shouting at Barbara, who was already back at her desk, "You bitch, don't *ever* do that." Truby was a large, imposing man with large ears, a large chin, and a fleshy nose. Ruddy-faced even at his most relaxed, his cheeks and forehead were now a mottled purple color, and his ears were inflamed.

Barbara got up from her desk and walked swiftly to the assistant commissioner. Bert thought she was going to take a swing at him. He rose, instinctively, hoping to stand between them and calm them down. “Mister, don’t you ever talk like that to me with your fresh mouth,” Barbara said softly. She spoke quickly too, trying to hold her anger in check. “With your filthy disgusting mouth, don’t you say those words to me. I wasn’t raised by hoodlums. My daddy taught us manners. I don’t like hearing words like that.” She turned and sat back down at her desk.

Bert was still standing between them, feeling foolish, since there was nothing for him to do. He sat back down. And to think: Truby supervised *personnel.* Un-fucking-believable.

Truby stood there a minute, glowering, then turned on his heels and walked back into Steven’s office, slamming the door shut. Barbara told Bert that she wasn’t worried about her job. She had so much dirt on people in the department that they wouldn’t dare try to fire her.

Later, Steven bobbed up and down, apologizing to Barbara for Truby’s behavior. “It’s not your fault,” Barbara said.

“We listened to the most wonderful radio program last night,” Ribsy told Bert. “All six sides of Neil Young’s *Decade.*”

“What station?” Bert would have listened himself.

“WIWW,” Evelyn said.

“I’ve never heard of it.”

“You’re kidding.” Herbert looked surprised. “We’ve even heard of it on Debbie. You mean, you really don’t know about it?”

“It’s like they always say: tourists end up seeing more of a city then the people who live there.” Ribsy clucked malchick’s green tongue. “Evelyn, tell Bert about WIWW.”

Evelyn began:

THE LEGEND OF WIWW

A nomad radio station, WIWW can usually be found within the boundaries of the continental United States, but occasionally signals have been picked up as far away as Hawaii, Singapore, Bali, Glasgow, Riga, Rome, Paris.

The station was originally operated by a Jewish anarcho-syndicalist who lived on a side street off the Grand Concourse, in the Bronx. On a clear day, his signal lapped at the shores of Yonkers and the northern tip of Manhattan. Apparently, he had a good view of Yankee Stadium from his tenement apartment, because he often broadcast Yankee games, giving his own play-by-play description.

As the anarchist movement was ruthlessly suppressed in the U.S., the station, a small portable unit, changed hands again and again: now turning up in a Queens coroner's office, now being run by a Hasidic jazz enthusiast, now brought to sudden, ecstatic life by a sleepy young girl's furtive, midnight broadcasts of Jerry Lee Lewis or the Rolling Stones.

The equipment is old, the circuitry hopelessly jumbled. But still, now and then, a spark of life can be drawn from it, attracting a momentary gasp of recognition or attention: the shock of juju music breaking into the Badlands of South Dakota, a back-to-back rendition of "Heartbreak Hotel" and "Hotel California" pouring into Poughkeepsie —

"But I heard that station!" Bert interrupted. "In camp!"

"Was it a socialist Jewish sleep-away camp?" Ribsy asked.

"You bet."

"Then you heard it, all right."

— or the sudden crackling strains of "Bei Mir Bist Du Schon" on a channel that was previously static, jolting awake a bone-weary Teamster nodding off at the wheel of his truck.

The broadcasts are erratic, unpredictable, flung here and there by the antiquated machinery. A truly anarchic radio station, WIWW zigzags across the nation and across broadcast bands, a perennial (and perennially hushed-up) bane to the FCC. The station's very existence is a slap in the face of bureaucratic state-capitalism.

Depending not on contracts, but on trust, each owner knows when his or her appointed stewardship has ended. The station is passed quietly from one to another, emotionally, like a secret Masonic handshake. A hodgepodge of repairs, of ad hoc fuses and temporary hinges, of mismatching microphones and ill-fitting headsets, WIWW appears like manna from the static of heaven. Much like anarcho-syndicalism itself, the station can never be stamped out or silenced.

"What a nice story," Bert said.

"It's no story, it's the God's honest truth," Evelyn insisted.

"*Vive l'anarchie.*" Ribsy toasted them with some cocaine.

"What are the only two man-made structures that can be seen from outer space?" Ribsy challenged him.

"The Great Wall of China," Bert said. "And, and, let me think." He struggled to think what the answer could be.

"Give up?"

"Yeah."

"The Burger King on Fordham Road and the Grand Concourse." Ribsy started laughing mirthlessly, tee hee hee tee hee hee.

"How much coke have you been doing?" Bert wondered.

"Ooh, a lot."

Patrick said he wanted to talk, so they went to the Xerox room for some privacy. He confessed that he couldn't pay back the twenty yet. Bert assured him it wasn't a problem. "I know you're good for it."

"But, Bert" — this was hard for him — "I need to borrow another twenty."

"Don't worry about it. Just pay me back next week."

Bert gave him another twenty-dollar bill. Patrick hugged him tight and, just before letting go, squeezed his ass. Bert was surprised, but it put him in a good mood. He whistled as he walked home from the subway. When he got home, he found a letter from his friend Alison in Boston.

Dear Bert,

The professors who supervise the physics lab here seem to have taken seminars in sarcasm and sexism (alliteration). I thought things would be better in grad school, but they're not.

Other classes are better. I'm the only woman in my math class. Somehow that makes me paranoid. But then, so do a lot of other things. The lecturer (Complex Analysis) has an interesting sense of humor. After a particularly neat development, he'll raise his eyebrows and say, "Thrills," or "Fun and Games," or both, or additional which I can't recall right now, depending on the degree of neatness.

Last night I had to do a Lagrangian with incredibly tedious algebra, first in the library, and then, in fitful sleep, in bed. Also, for several nights running I stayed up till five in the morning, writing two project reports, one of which was good, I think, and one of which was on the wrong topic.

In a film I once saw on Freud, one of his professors said to him, "Anyone who needs more than five hours of sleep a night should study art." I think of this often, usually when I'm about to pass out from exhaustion.

On a sculpture walk recently, I told the tour guide that Henry Moore's *Oval with Points* suggested to me a giant tooth, perhaps a molar. After this, I also told her I could envision a spark leaping the gap between the two points. I often bring physics into art, where it belongs, some of the time, anyway. Cézanne's *Mont-Sainte-Victoire* seems to me an almost flawless example of vector addition.

Heisenberg's book is a lot of fun. It isn't too much in the way of heavy reading. It's all, "I had lunch with Wolfgang and we talked about atomic physics some" (Pauli), or "Albert and I took a walk on the mountain outside of the institute and chatted about quantum theory."

Tuesday I begin my parachuting lessons.

Remember the guy upstairs? I guess I still have a thing for him. I thought it was over. It was, until it started all over again. It's not worth it. I think I am mostly over it, but every now and then. . . . Last week I kept him up really late asking questions and making stupid observations and theorizing when he wanted other things or sleep. I thought it was funny. Perversity prevails. Later I talked to my neighbor Paula about the whole thing and realized how foolish I was being. I decided to break all emotional and other ties with him, and I have, which is a big accomplishment because I've been trying for a long time but couldn't do it. It's made me a lot more confident and has helped my ego because I'm no longer dependent or subject to his whims, etc. And now I can concentrate when I work. And I'm happier. In fact — I'm happy. Yesterday I was speaking on the phone to him about some math-related matter, and I said something that I didn't realize was a double entendre until he took it the wrong way, and I didn't realize he took it the wrong way until I got off the phone. I think I insulted him unconsciously.

Personally, I think things are okay.

I thought I had lice. I worry that I'll get herpes. I used to think I had tapeworm. I always think I'm pregnant.

I had a dream about the starship *Enterprise* a couple of nights ago.

This letter quantum is drawing to a close. Talk about your seas of forlornness. Please write me back in the near future, as I'm sure you have much interesting to relate. I'll write if you write, and even if you don't, but you wouldn't not, would you? Right. Tell me how things are doing, I'm interested. Honestly.

Love,
Alison

Patrick came to see him very late the next night, knocking softly on his door. "It's me, please." He'd been at an after-hours club, Save the Robots, and he'd suddenly felt terribly lonely. He said he'd missed Bert, more than he thought he would. He guessed maybe their friendship was more serious than he realized. He was feeling tense, he just wanted to relax with some pot, maybe a pill. Bert said he had only a couple of pills left.

"But you have some?"

"Yeah."

Patrick pretended to be an ape, barking and scampering around the room, eating bananas, moving around and around Bert in tighter circles, jumping on the bed at last — Bert was laughing — thumping his chest triumphantly, and then diving on top of him.

Waiting for the Plumber, or Someone Like Him

▾▾▾

LOOK. I'll cut down, I promise. But you know how it helps me." He wanted Bert to buy some speed for him from Jorgen. Patrick kissed him on his eyes. ("Cat's eyes," Patrick said.) He could be very affectionate sometimes, although he still seemed scared of the sex. ("So you'll get some?" Patrick said.) Patrick still owed Bert a lot of money, maybe three or four hundred dollars in all, but he wasn't disappearing, so for a while, anyway ("You goof," Patrick said, lying down naked behind him on the quilt, and kissing his shoulder), Bert was content to drift.

Diana said that he was slumming in the Department of Sewers and that he should leave. "You went to Princeton, Bert. Get a grip." The economy was improving. He didn't have any excuse to stay. "You're too good for this place. I'll miss you, a lot, but you deserve better."

One of the drains in his old double sink was completely blocked by a strange fungus that the superintendent refused to clean under any circumstances, and it had started to spread to the other sink. When the toilet showed signs of going, too, Bert finally convinced the landlord to pay for a plumber. Because he couldn't specify what time he'd be there, Bert had to stay home a whole day to wait for him.

A nearly square-shaped man named John finally showed up at four in the afternoon. Cigar ashes flecked his torn pants. His assistant, Tony, a young Latino man, was dressed nattily in a freshly pressed Lamartine Plumbing workshirt and Calvin Klein jeans.

"Busy day," John said, puffing on a cigar. Bert opened a window to let the smoke out. "Busy, busy day."

Bert showed him the fungus first. Tony grimaced, whipped out a surgeon's mask from his pocket, and put it over his mouth and nose. "You don't need a plumber," John muttered. "You need a lawn mower."

Bert ran some water in the other sink and let John and Tony hear the strange hiccuping noises. John turned the water on and off, on and off, listening to the gurgling like a cardiologist studying the arrhythmia of a heart. "I'll take care of this here," John told Bert and Tony, opening his bag and taking out some chemicals to treat the fungus. "Tony, check out the toilet situation."

Bert led Tony to the bathroom. "You're lucky, man," Tony told him. "This guy's a genius."

"Really?"

"Best plumber in New York." Tony flushed the toilet a few times. "What do you know, same problem as in the kitchen."

"How can it be the same problem?"

"It all connects," Tony insisted. He pointed to the pipes. "It all connects."

"I work for the Sewer Department," Bert told him.

"Then you know, man," Tony said. "Am I right?" He began snaking the pipes. "How did that fungus start, anyway?"

"When I moved in, it was a tiny green spot. It just kept growing."

Tony whistled. "Science fiction."

Bert returned to the kitchen. Fumes rose from the fungus, which was writhing in its death throes from the chemicals John had applied. Huge tentacles opened and closed, like a mouth gasping for breath. The creature peeped faintly, "Help me, help me," as it succumbed to the fungicide.

Jane started screaming, "Stop burning my genitals! I know what you're doing up there! Stop poisoning me! I can't breathe!" She screamed well considering she couldn't breathe.

"What the hell is that?" John peered out the window.

"I have a crazy neighbor. She usually only screams at night. This must be a special occasion."

"Man, she's loud. She scream a lot?" Tony had wandered in.

"Every night."

"I'd slit my throat," John said. "Or hers."

Jane was determined to bring Bert to court, so Evie had found him a lawyer, an old acquaintance at the Bronx County Courthouse. Bert's attorney had talked to Jane's public defender, but even she couldn't shake Jane's resolve to sue him for six hundred thousand dollars. Bert's lawyer wanted him to file a counterclaim for harassment, to spur her into dropping her own suit, but Bert had visions of interminable *Jarndyce v. Jarndyce* proceedings, and so far had refused.

Diana asked him, "Can you imagine the history of literature if Madame Bovary had owned a Visa card?" She had decided she needed a new wardrobe and had just spent a week's salary at Bloomingdale's. Bert had lent Diana a copy of the Flaubert novel a few weeks earlier; he knew she'd like it but had no idea it would inspire her so much.

She said they'd missed him the day before. Harry, Patrick, and she had gone out to lunch together and bitched about the Departments of Sewers, Highways, and Bridges and Tunnels. "We had all of New York covered, Bert. And all of us are miserable. I'm going to grow my hair long. It's time for a change."

Patrick and Kathleen both felt a shake-up looming in Highways. Maybe their boss would be pushed out, maybe Assistant Commissioner Truby would be moved over from Sewers. "Maybe if we're really lucky, we'll all be fired, and we can go on unemployment," Kathleen proposed.

Harry was the most miserable of all. Chuck (it had to be Chuck) had broken into his apartment and stolen his TV and his stereo. "If he needed money, he could have just asked," Harry said dejectedly.

"Did you talk to him?"

"I don't have his number. I'll have to wait till he shows up. Then he's just going to deny it all, the little fucker. I've had it with him."

He told Bert he'd had such a nice day, too, until he got home. Truby had called in sick with a cold, so Harry had taken it easy. He'd bought a pasta salad for lunch, eaten it in the plaza outside the AT&T building, and had a long colloquy with himself about fascist architecture. Afterward he'd joined Patrick and Diana. They'd walked over to City Hall Park, stretched out on the early spring grass, and watched two jugglers pass clubs back and forth.

Patrick had learned to sleep through Jane's screaming, but Bert always woke up. Sometimes he'd watch Patrick sleeping next to him, his chest filling slowly with air, and he'd touch him, to make sure he was real. Sometimes he'd wake Patrick if Jane was screaming, and start making love, since he was up anyway, and since there was something exciting about screwing while she screamed.

"Listen, Bert," Patrick said afterward, lying next to him, an arm slung around Bert's shoulder. "I need to borrow some more money."

Bert didn't say anything.

"You know I'm good for it. You trust me, don't you?"

"I'm not stupid," Bert said. "You keep buying speed. I never even see you take it. When are you taking it?"

"Bert, don't worry. I've got everything under control."

"I think you're doing coke, too. I don't know when. With me it's always downners."

"I'm just having cash flow problems."

"Patrick," Bert said slowly, "it's really becoming a problem for me."

"So what are you saying? You don't want to see me anymore? Fine. I'll leave." He started getting out of bed.

"I'm not saying that, Patrick." He buried his head in his pillow. "I'm saying I'm worried about you."

"Look," Patrick said, pressing his body against Bert's. "I'm in a bind, I admit it. But I need your help." He kissed the back of Bert's neck and his shoulder. "You're my best friend." Bert got hard again. He felt Patrick growing hard behind him. "So you'll help me?" Bert turned around to face Patrick, and put his cock next to Patrick's cock, and kissed Patrick, and rubbed their two cocks together.

The next day, Bert saw an emaciated Latino man standing outside his building, smoking a cigarette nervously. He wore an overcoat with a gray T-shirt underneath. His hair was straggly, his eyes glassy. He spotted Bert and started toward him. Bert thought he was about to be mugged.

"Don' ju worry man, I jes wanna check out ju friends."

"What?"

"Ju friends. I know you got 'em. Ju got some green friends witchew, man."

When Bert looked closer, he saw the man was really quite young, perhaps nineteen or twenty, although his face was ravaged by drugs and exposure.

"Some dudes, man, they ripped me off." He grabbed hold of Bert's arm. "Ju homeboys were there." Bert pulled away forcefully. "Be cool, man, ju gonna stay fresh, okay? I jes want mine back. I didn' light up, okay? Man, some other guys, okay, they ripped me off, man." He was almost crying. "You know who, man."

"I have to go," Bert said.

He ignored Bert. "Hey man, you ain't lookin' at the dude. It was them guys. Ju friends, okay? Ju gotta tell 'em, man, it's ticket time. I saw them. They gotta pay to ride this train. Got to, man."

Jorgen and Luisa came around the corner, and the Latino kid took off.

"You have to give it back," Bert said. He was having a tête-à-tête with Ribsy.

"I didn't know I was getting anyone in trouble."

"Do you think people don't notice when you swipe their drugs?"

"I thought there was so little of it, it wouldn't matter. There couldn't have been more than three, four hundred dollars' worth."

"Four hundred dollars!"

"I couldn't help myself," Ribsy said. "You don't know what it's like. I saw it, just lying on that park bench, this guy was nodding off next to it. It was so white, so beautiful. I just had to have it."

"What are you going to do?" Bert asked Ribsy.

Ribsy reached into malchick's seat and took out a box of tissue to blow malchick's nose. "I don't know."

"Jesus, you have everything in there," Bert marveled. "Like Felix the Cat."

"Fritz the Cat is more like it," Ribsy said.

"I guess you're right. Felix wouldn't swipe someone's nose candy."

" 'Nose candy'?" Ribsy was tickled. "My, we're learning, aren't we."

"About the money," Bert reminded malchick.

"Well, don't look at me," Ribsy said. "How am I supposed to raise that much bread? Moonlight?"

Bert had to take another day off from work to go to city court. He was squandering his vacation on chores. Jane, representing herself in the case, testified that Bert was sneaking into her apartment, stealing her inventions and her toaster oven, taking food from her refrigerator (a meat loaf, three quarts of milk, orange juice, and an Italian salami), tampering with her heart medications, reading her diary, causing her palpitations, poisoning her air, burning her genitals.

"I usually have treated the homosexual community with forbearance," Jane said on the witness stand. "And I have no problem with Bertolt B. Rosenbaum being homosexual, nor with his homosexual lover who stays overnight frequently. His homosexuality is not the problem. As a former high school English teacher, I found many of my best students were latent homosexuals, and while I can't say I encouraged their homosexuality, neither did I ridicule them."

If I weren't sitting here, Bert thought, I wouldn't believe it myself. Patrick had told him that Jane watched him through her window whenever he entered the building, so Bert wasn't exactly surprised by Jane's blithe testimony; but to hear his sex life exposed publicly was horrifying.

"But when his homosexuality manifests itself as hostility to women," Jane continued, "and when that hostility compels him to destroy my life and my health, by shooting his Nazi gas pellets through my air vents, and depriving me of my meat loaf, I think I have no choice but to punish his godless, insane behavior."

Bert testified that he had never broken into her apartment, never stolen her meat loaf, never poisoned her air, never burned her genitals.

The judge, a middle-aged woman with a raspy voice, a tubercular cough, and a Louise Brooks hairdo, said Jane would have to produce independent witnesses to corroborate her charges, or else she would dismiss the case. She set another court date for a month later.

Patrick was supposed to come over right after work, but he arrived quite late. He said that he'd had a bad day at the office, and that Harry and Diana and he had all gone out for drinks afterward. Jane was screaming, at the top of her lungs, "Stop burning my genitals, and not just Bert, all of you!"

"I don't know what I did to deserve this," Bert said.

"Am I keeping you up?" Jane demanded. "Oh, poor baby! You need your beauty sleep, is that it?"

Patrick said maybe he could make Bert forget about Jane. He started unbuttoning Bert's shirt. "Did you get that speed for me?" he asked, kissing Bert's nipples. "Not yet," Bert said. They should smoke some pot, Patrick said. Bert asked if for once they could have sex without any drugs. Patrick said sure, he was just going to get a beer. He came back from the refrigerator and Bert started unbuttoning Patrick's jeans. Patrick said wait a minute, he just had to pee. He put his pants on and went into the bathroom.

Bert waited on his bed. Jane was screaming, "I'm in pain and no one cares! Why don't you do something!"

Patrick came out of the bathroom grinning.

"What'd you take?" Bert asked him.

"What?"

"Uppers, downers, I don't even know what you're doing anymore. What'd you have in your pocket?"

"I'll show you what I have in my pocket." He put his tongue into Bert's ear, then chewed on a lobe. Bert shivered. "The only thing is, Bert" — Patrick was licking Bert's neck — "and I hate to ask this." He was rubbing Bert's ass. "But I need a little favor." Bert was starting to float. "I need to borrow a little more money."

Bert got up from the bed. "Get the fuck out of my apartment."

He couldn't sleep after he threw Patrick out. He tossed and turned on his bed, then finally started reading *The Ambassadors,* convinced the book would put him to sleep. But even Henry James didn't work. In the morning he was so tired, he actually considered going upstairs to Jorgen and asking for some speed.

Steven told him that Truby wanted them to go into the field to interview some workers, and in the afternoon Steven and a barely conscious Bert approached an open manhole. Outside the manhole, and under the late March sunlight, a thin filament of oil on the ground was starting to spread into a slick palette of colors. "I love when that happens," Bert said.

"Me too," Steven said, and for a moment, the two bureaucrats let themselves enjoy the simple pleasure of the rainbow.

Inside the sewer, Bert felt like an idiot: the know-nothing analyst from headquarters wearing a tie and a hard hat. He tripped over something, worried that it was an alligator, then looked down and saw an empty turtle shell. Nervous, he caught up to Steven, who was walking ahead.

"I really appreciate your coming, Bert."

"Don't mention it." Bert decided not to point out that interviewing sewer workers was part of his job.

They walked through the dank caverns. "It's so peaceful here," Steven said.

"Yeah," Bert said. Every echo, the whisper of running water, and any noise that could possibly be mistaken for slithering made his heart race. "Peaceful."

They finally reached the work crew, who were on a late lunch break, eating underground. Bert was surprised they ate down there.

"It's fine, except in April," an old-timer told him. "We're even pushing it this late in March."

"What happens in April?" Bert, excited, got out his notebook and pen.

"Asparagus happens in April," a young man explained. He was maybe nineteen, a big strapping Irish kid. A beam of light from somebody's flashlight sparkled in his bright blue eyes and red hair.

"Ever eat asparagus?" another worker called out.

"Yeah," Bert said.

"Ever pee?"

The sewer workers were laughing.

"If people smelled it down here in April," the old-timer told Bert, "they wouldn't eat so much asparagus."

When he came home, he saw a red BMW parked in front of his apartment building and thought Patrick had driven over in his cousin Kenny's car to apologize. But it wasn't Kenny's car: it was Jorgen's. Jorgen and Luisa, standing on the street, were hissing at each other but managed to smile abruptly when they saw Bert approach.

"You bought a car?" Bert asked them. Jorgen usually borrowed a cab from work when he needed a ride.

"Damn sure, betcha, it's a fine car. I drive it to hell and back so fast the devil don't even wake for breakfast." Jorgen, thin and twitchy, wiped an invisible smudge off the sleek red paint. Luisa, next to him, pinched her lips together and said nothing.

Lars sat behind the wheel of the car, bouncing up and down and pretending to drive. Isabel, in the passenger seat, pulled down the visor, looked at herself in the mirror, rouged her cheeks with imaginary blush, pursed her lips, and applied Chap Stick. "Lars, darling, let's go to the ballet tonight."

"Certainly, my dear."

"And afterward, Sardi's. It'll be glorious."

Luisa watched them, clutched Jorgen's hand, and told Bert, "They're such good kids."

Diana could tell that Bert was upset. She guessed he must have broken up with his girlfriend, whoever she was. "I know I tease you a lot, Bert, but I'm sorry it didn't work out with her. I really am."

She spent a lot of time with Bert, she said she wanted to know more about him. She wanted to know about his friends. She asked questions about Harry, about Patrick, about Alison. "Tell me about high school," Diana said, "where everyone gets high."

Bert told her about King Juan Carlos and the doughnut counter, about playing the *Star Trek* drinking game with Alison.

"Tell me about Princeton, where everyone's a prince."

He told her about his college graduation, outdoors in the rain; how he had never been so wet in all his life; how each senior carried two helium balloons, and when the president of the university conferred their bachelor's degrees, all the seniors had let their balloons go, red and blue and yellow and green balloons, up into the rain, two thousand of them.

Harry said Patrick and he were going out for a drink, did Bert want to come? Bert said no thanks and watched Harry and Patrick step into the elevator together.

Free Men

▾▾▾

BERT HAD ARGUED for months that the best way to reduce turnover at Sewers was simply to increase salaries, especially since the workers hadn't received a raise in two years. Given hiring and training costs, the move would even be cost-efficient. He couldn't push his ideas through the bureaucracy, so he decided to make an end run around it. He drafted a piece for the op-ed page of the *New York Times*.

> Immortalized by Art Carney in *The Honeymooners,* the sewer worker receives scant praise in our society. He serves the city well, yet is scorned for his efforts. He performs vital duties, but his very job title is the subject of ridicule.
>
> Imagine a city without sewer workers, though: imagine permanent gridlock *underground.*

After examining the high turnover rates in the department and mentioning the stench of the sewers in April (without going into details), Bert ended with a stirring exhortation: the public should support the vital tasks of sewer workers and urge their elected officials to approve a long-delayed, much-needed salary increase. "And never, never joke about a sewer worker until you've walked a mile in his or her watertight boots."

He typed the piece at home. While he worked, Jane screamed: "Thirty million monkeys could do what you're doing. What does that make you? A puppeteer!"

Bert sent the article in to the *Times*. You never knew, he thought, it might strike the editors' fancy.

On April 1, Jane screamed, "You're the April fool, not me! You're the one living in a fool's paradise!" On Good Friday, she screamed, "You're crucifying me like you crucified Him!" On Easter Sunday, she screamed, "I'll show you resurrection! I'll resurrect your worst nightmare! Go back to hell, you devils!" On May Day, she screamed, "It's Labor Day, but I'll never be in labor. I'm so alone! Oh God." She cried and screamed at the same time, "I'm a liberal and I'm so tired." Bert visualized her vocal chords (taut, red, angry strings of catgut), and then he imagined numbing them with ice until her voice was reduced to a hoarse whisper, lost in the wind of the air shaft.

The next day, May 2, was Bert's birthday. Isabel gave him a slime mold as a present. "It's a very unusual strain," she told him exultantly. She had forgiven him for removing the fungus in his kitchen without first securing a sample for her.

The aliens had presented him with gifts as well. Herbert gave him a pipe — and permission to call him Harold. Evelyn gave him a Firesign Theater record. And Ribsy gave him a Quaalude. "Happy birthday, you thing from another world, you," Ribsy had greeted him, planting a wet, green, alien kiss on his cheek.

"Can I call you Rivka now?" Bert had asked.

"No," Ribsy said.

Patrick had left a present for him on his desk at work, even though they were generally avoiding each other. Bert unwrapped the gift warily. Inside was a children's book that Patrick had written for him, called *Bert Goes Underground,* about a redheaded boy's trip into the New York City sewer system. The book was full of inside jokes. At one point, the boy puts his ear to a pipe and hears a woman named Jane screaming. A few of the pages were pop-ups, with origami figures of alligators creeping through the subways. He showed the book to the others. Diana couldn't stop laughing as she read it, and she read it dozens of times. Bert loved the present.

*

Bert was walking with Ribsy through Central Park when the nervous Latino man he'd seen before jumped out of the bushes and held a knife to Bert's throat. "Okay, man, it's time to meet ju friends," the kid said. "Ju green friends, man. I know ju got your green friends witchew, man. I see 'em, don' I?"

"Oh, give him the money." Ribsy made dismissive gestures with malchick's hand. "What a pest."

Bert tried to indicate to Ribsy, and to the Latino man, that he didn't have four hundred dollars. He had six dollars. Six fifty, with change. He also tried to indicate that there was a knife against his throat and Ribsy should be a little more conciliatory. Of course, it was hard to indicate anything when he couldn't speak.

"This is tiresome. Just open the envelope Isabel gave you," Ribsy commanded. That morning Isabel had given Bert an envelope for safekeeping. Bert ripped it open. Inside were three crisp one-hundred-dollar bills. The Latino man grabbed the hundred-dollar bills, grabbed Bert's six bucks, and fled.

Isabel explained later that she had developed a new strain of plasmodium and sold it to a biotechnology company. When Bert pressed her, she admitted that although she had written the company, she hadn't heard back yet; she'd taken the three hundred dollars from her father's desk. She said her father had lots of money, he wouldn't miss it. And anyway, she'd pay him back when she sold the slime mold.

Patrick was going to teach Harry how to golf. Bert asked Harry if anything was going on between Patrick and him.

"No. We're just friends."

Bert didn't know whether to believe him.

"I didn't even like him at first," Harry said. "But we're getting really close."

Later, Bert ran into Patrick on the elevator. A few times a week their paths crossed. "Hey," Bert said.

"Hey, yourself. I left a message on your machine. I liked the music."

For his outgoing message, Bert used the TV theme song "Secret Agent Man." This answering machine was the first he had ever owned, and he had bought it precisely to suggest to Patrick, in case Patrick ever called him, that he was fantastically busy and fabulously happy and so pursued by friends and lovers that people had to wait in line to talk to him.

"Yeah. Sorry I didn't get back to you. Thanks again for the book. It's really great."

"I just wanted you to know, I'm doing better. I'm not perfect yet," Patrick acknowledged, "but I'm definitely cutting down."

Bert shrugged. "Pat, come on. Jorgen told me you called him. He said you still wanted speed."

"That was two weeks ago."

"You've been hanging out a lot with Harry."

"Yeah, he's great. You should go out with us some time."

Diana was losing weight. She looked too thin to Bert. She said she'd finally gotten her eating under control. "Now all the boys are going to be after me, Bert."

"They were after you before."

"No," she claimed. "Nobody."

"Me," Bert said. They were in the Xerox room. He placed her hands on top of his hands and started playing slapjack. He pretended to slap her hands. She didn't flinch. He pretended again. She didn't flinch. He went to slap her hands, but she moved away just in time.

"I'm very good at that game, Bert."

"Well, there are other games," Bert said, grabbing her hands and holding them tight.

"Bert, don't."

"Why not?"

"It's just too complicated right now. With Rob."

The next day, Harry came running into the office and handed him a copy of the *Times*. Bert's piece about sewer workers had been published on the op-ed page. Bert was, frankly, astonished. A few hours later a nervous Steven beckoned him.

Steven said the assistant commissioner wanted to see them.

Bert walked into Truby's office, and Truby, his face throbbing scarlet and purple, began screaming at him before Steven managed even to close the door. "What if the union brings up this article during contract negotiations?" Truby pumped his fists up and down, like a speed walker. "You work in personnel. You know things have to be cleared."

Which is precisely why Bert hadn't gone through the proper channels. It took forever to get something approved, and it was always changed into a form that would offend no one, a form that therefore accomplished nothing. "I did this on my own time. I guess I just wasn't thinking."

"It's obvious you weren't thinking," Truby told him. "But you never think, do you. In fact, this is a pattern with you." He opened a file on his desk and passed Bert a few sheets of paper. "Does this look familiar?"

It was the contract with the research firm Bert had signed months before when he couldn't get Truby or Steven to sign. "You were happy with the results of the survey," Bert said. "You told me I did a good job."

"That's not the point!" Truby was screaming again. "You don't have the right to sign contracts without my permission. You don't have the right to sign your name without my permission!" He placed Bert on a week's suspension without pay.

"I know you're worried about your personnel file, but don't take it to heart," Steven said as Bert gathered up some items on his desk before going home. "These things blow over. And I'll always put in a good word for you if you need a recommendation."

Worried about his personnel file? He couldn't wait to get out of this stink hole. He had taken Diana's advice and started looking for another job and had taken Harry's advice and applied to business school. He wanted to get away from Patrick — away from Diana, even — away from all of them.

Barbara was guilt-ridden about the suspension. She blamed

herself for encouraging Bert to sign the contract, and to make amends, she insisted Bert come over for dinner. She lived far out in Queens, in St. Albans, and Bert had to take a long subway ride and then a longer bus ride to her home. He was the only white on the bus, and the West Indian bus driver was protective of him. It turned out he knew Jimmy Giannakopoulos, the husky bus driver–stage director who lived in Bert's building.

Barbara's house was impeccably clean, like her desk at work. Her daughter's paintings covered nearly every wall. The cool, cluttered, oddly ironic studies both embraced and poked gentle fun at black family life. Bert asked if she sold much of her work. Barbara's husband, Ed, snorted, and said, "Niggers can't pay for it, white people don't want it. But you mark *my* words, one day she'll make more money with that brush than James Brown ever made with any kinda tired old song. Poppa's got a brand new bag? Later." Ed, wiry and epicene, spoke with a faint North Carolina accent. He had fine dark features and a pliant, willowy charm. He seemed quite gay to Bert and also quite devoted to his family.

Ed wore a tie, a starched white shirt, a brown blazer, heavy wool pants, and narrow brown and white saddle shoes. Bert was wearing a tie, too, but he still felt underdressed and apologized for wearing khaki pants. Ed whipped off his tie to put Bert at ease. "Free at last," Ed announced. "I hate ties."

"Me too," Bert said. Still, he was glad he was wearing one. Like a boozy ballplayer who wobbled to the plate but heartened himself with the knowledge that at least he was wearing the right uniform, Bert was reassured by the tie. He felt a tie always made him look presentable.

The next night his mother's coworker Tom Helmer took him out to dinner. He had loved Bert's piece in the *Times* and had been outraged when Evie told him about the suspension. Bert didn't want to go, but his mother said Tom's feelings would be hurt if he canceled. Bert arrived at the restaurant twenty minutes late. Tom, sitting on a fire hydrant and reading the new paperback edition of *A Field Guide to Madness,* waited for him.

Bert apologized profusely and explained that the subway had been delayed, but the truth was that he would have been ten minutes late anyway. Dreading the dinner, he couldn't tear himself away from a National Geographic television special on burrowing insects.

"How is that?" Bert pointed at Tom's book.

"Pornographic and insane." Tom stroked his black beard. "I love it. Especially the science fiction elements." Tom said he'd like to prescribe an antipsychotic medication for the author, perhaps a phenothiazine or a butyrophenone — and possibly a monoamine oxidase inhibitor for depression, too. He spoke dryly, and Bert couldn't tell if he was kidding. He told Bert that he was taking a Spanish class so he could communicate better with his patients, and saxophone lessons so he could hang out at smoky jazz clubs, drink whiskey straight, and look vaguely dangerous. "I'm too white bread," Tom complained. "Guys don't go for that." It was the only time he mentioned he was gay, and Bert let the comment pass without offering any confidences of his own.

Tom wasn't so boring as Bert had feared, and he laughed at all of Bert's jokes, meager as they were. But he still seemed too earnest, Bert told his parents, who had him over for dinner later that week.

"You're too hard on people," his mother said.

Joseph said Evie was a surrogate mother to Tom, whose father and stepmother lived in Ohio. Then he wrapped his arms around Evie from behind and kissed her neck. "Baby, you're the greatest."

"You should shave," Evie said, but she was smiling.

Joseph was growing a white mustache, although he insisted it was blond or light red.

Two nights later Diana and Rob made him dinner. He met Diana at Grand Central Station and took the train up to White Plains with her. Bert wondered why everyone thought he was going to starve to death just because he was losing one week's salary; still, he was touched. He could tell that Diana and Rob had had a huge fight in the last few days; their tight politeness to each other was like the aftershock following a major earthquake.

With his free time during the week, Bert jogged around the Central Park reservoir, sunbathed in Sheep Meadow, and took a bus up to the Cloisters, where he practiced his bad college German with a group of middle-aged Austrian tourists. He enjoyed himself and didn't think much about Patrick and Diana, or about Philip. Even the space aliens, busy somewhere, didn't distract him. He ended up reading *The Pickwick Papers,* loved it, and decided he could get used to unemployment. When he got back to the office, a paycheck was waiting for him. Harry explained that the paperwork canceling a week's salary for Bert had arrived through interoffice mail, but Barbara had thrown it out before Steven could sign it.

Bert didn't want Barbara to get into any trouble. "What if someone asks you what you did with it?"

"Did with what?" Barbara asked innocently. When the official reprimand arrived for Bert's file, she threw that out, too.

Truby didn't trust Bert and had ordered Steven to reassign all of Bert's duties to other employees. Steven acquiesced, reluctantly, and begged Bert's pardon. Bert had no work to do. It was awful for him. He wasn't permitted to read at his desk. Instead he just had to sit there and look busy. He was grateful to Harry, Barbara, and Diana, who invented tasks to keep him occupied. "They're on your case like white on rice," Barbara told him.

She stayed late at work every night to practice her word processing. "In this world, you gotta have the skills," she explained simply. She talked about skills all the time, how important it was to have the right skills. Bert felt strangely guilty, hearing her talk. He was going to leave these people behind.

A police car was parked in front of his building with its lights flashing, its siren wailing. The cops had come to arrest Jorgen.

Luisa was crying. The children were crying, too, and clutched at their mother, and clutched at Bert, as the police led their father away in handcuffs. Bert assumed that Jorgen was being arrested for drug trafficking, but the charge turned out to be embezzlement. Somehow Jorgen had stolen money from various airport bank accounts while he was an air traffic controller. In the confusion of the strike, no one had noticed. He probably would have gotten away with it if he hadn't spent so much money, and so publicly. Of course, he might not have spent the money if he wasn't doing drugs. The police were suspicious about the drugs, too, but Jorgen had prescriptions for the hundreds of amphetamine pills and tranquilizers in his possession, and no one expected the drug charges to stick. He was free on bail within a few hours. The excitement soon faded, and the building settled back into its quiet West Side slumber, disturbed only by the bad dream of Jane's screaming.

Bert finally decided to go out with Patrick and Harry, and on a warm day, he joined them on an excursion to the Bronx Zoo. Nervous ferrets scampered in their narrow cages; tigers in the Wild Asia exhibit stalked phantasmal prey; mother bears gruffly nuzzled their cubs; short-nosed fruit bats hung upside down, wrapping their wings around themselves till they were swaddled like patients in straitjackets. Finally the three men stopped to watch Bert's favorites, the penguins. "They're hedonists," Harry proclaimed, watching the birds play. Bert and his brother had gone to the zoo often as children — it was just a bus ride away from their apartment — and Bert still knew his way around the park. He still liked the smell of the zoo: the tang of straw, mud, and manure. Small children dragged balloons and dropped ice cream sandwiches on the ground. Patrick and Harry got stoned in the monkey house when no one was looking. Bert didn't feel like smoking. He was surprised by how much they touched each other, even in public. They never embraced, but rubbed arms together, grabbed each other's waist, slapped asses.

Afterward, they went back to Joseph and Evie's apartment. Evie made iced coffee and served her famous hamburgers. "Do you boys eat well? You're much too thin," she told Patrick. Bert hadn't noticed before, but Patrick had lost weight. Joseph and Patrick talked about the Tigers, and Joseph and Harry talked about foreign languages. Harry wanted to learn another language, either Hindi or Portuguese, so Joseph lent him some of his Listen & Learn tapes.

"You have Hindi?" Bert asked, laughing.

"Of course," his father told him.

Harry wanted to see Bert's old bedroom. The Marx Brothers poster was still up, faded and frayed and peeling off the wall, next to the poster of Reggie Jackson belting a home run for the Yankees (his third that game), which was next to the poster of Jimi Hendrix playing guitar with his teeth, which was next to the Wanted poster of all the Watergate conspirators, which was next to the antiwar poster, which, completing the circle, was next to the Marx Brothers poster.

"You've got so many books." Patrick had moved over to browse through the bookshelves. "Look at these Freddy the Pigs!"

"They're my brother's," Bert told him. "They were always his favorite."

"Mine, too," Patrick said.

Harry put on an old Paul Simon song, "Me and Julio Down by the Schoolyard." Bert's bed was covered with Joseph's magazines and files, so the three of them ended up together on Philip's bed, listening to the music. Bert was uncomfortable on the bed with them. When Evie came into the room, asking if they wanted dessert, he sprang up and led his friends to the kitchen.

Diana said she'd thought about it a lot, but it wasn't right, she didn't want to be unfaithful to her husband. "You'll always be my friend, Bert. That lasts a lot longer. Okay?"

He wanted to do everything all over again and somehow get

it right. He had lost Patrick, he had lost Diana, he wanted to leave his job — he didn't have much to show for the past nine months. His only consolation was that Jane Alley's suit had been thrown out. He had taken another day off from work to go to court, and when Jane couldn't produce any witnesses, the judge dismissed the case. Bert was free.

The Turn of the Screw

▾▾▾

THEY WERE TALKING about his uncle Buddy, and Bert wondered why he had never married. His mother said her brother was very shy.

"Maybe he was gay," Bert suggested.

"He wasn't gay." Evie was furious. "He wasn't. He just needed a very aggressive woman. You don't remember him. I remember him." She retreated to her office and slammed the door shut.

"I remember him," Bert muttered.

"You know she's sensitive about Buddy," Joseph said.

"I didn't mean anything by it."

"I know." Joseph rubbed his shoulders. "It's funny. Both you kids look just like him. And he was a southpaw, too."

"But we got your hair," Bert pointed out. "Hey, how come you shaved your mustache?"

Joseph lowered his voice. "It came in white. Don't tell your mother, or she'll think she's married to an old geezer."

His father was such a sweet, unassuming man. Bert wondered again why they hadn't been closer when he was a child. He asked his father, and to his surprise, his father had an answer. "Well, Philip was always so attached to me. Even as a little boy, he preferred me to your mother — who knows why. I never said anything to her, but when you were born, I kept my distance from you. I figured that way, you'd be closer to her, and it would be fairer. It worked out okay."

"For whom?" Bert felt sick to his stomach.

"Oh, come on, don't make a big deal out of this."

For days afterward, the conversation with his father disturbed Bert. He wondered what kind of man he'd be if his father hadn't pulled away from him — if he'd even be the same Bert at all. It was almost too painful to consider this double, this other, better-adjusted Bert. He willed himself to think less about his father's admission; then he forbade himself to think about it at all; then he forgot it.

Outside his building, the same Latino teenager who had mugged Bert harassed Mr. Watanabe and then the boy with Down's syndrome who lived in the neighborhood. "I wan' ju green friends, man. Okay? I know ju got some green friends, man." Jimmy Giannakopoulos tackled him, and the police took him away.

"The cops are getting very familiar with this building," Jimmy noted. Besides arresting Jorgen and the mugger, the police also made nightly visits to Jane Alley's door because she was still screaming.

Jorgen, meanwhile, had gotten off scot-free. He sold the BMW, returned about half the money he had stolen — the rest was gone — and was put on probation for five years. Bert was happy Jorgen was home for Luisa's and his children's sake.

"If he was black, his ass would still be in jail," Harry harrumphed at lunch. Bert and Harry had gone out together. The office was empty. Barbara had caught a cold, and the virus had swept through the building. Diana had called in sick, and now Patrick was out sick, too.

"So you've been seeing a lot of Patrick." Bert knew he'd said this before, but he was unable to stop.

"Give it a break, Bert."

"I can't help it. Isn't that pathetic?"

"I never even knew you guys were involved. I'm assuming you were."

"He didn't want me to tell anyone."

"Look. Nothing's happened. I mean, maybe something will happen, but nothing's happened so far. He says he's not gay." Harry started laughing. "Oh, really, I'm so bad."

"Does he borrow money?"

"No." Harry seemed surprised. "Did he borrow money from you?"

"Not really."

Kathleen ran into them in the restaurant and asked if she could join them. "Please," Harry said.

Her straight, flat hair was tied back into a ponytail, and she was wearing sneakers. She seemed even tinier than usual. "You look about twelve years old," Bert told her. He was in a bad mood.

"Thanks a lot," Kathleen said.

Bert felt guilty and told them lunch was on him.

There was nothing to do at work anyway, and the weather was beautiful, so Bert had started taking long afternoon walks. After lunch with Harry and Kathleen, he headed east to City Hall Park, and then walked uptown on Broadway. He put his red watchband in his front pants pocket, not wanting to know what time it was; he patted his back pocket, to make sure his wallet was there; and he walked. He'd always loved May, he loved having a birthday in May. He passed Modell's sporting goods store, and the Duane Reade pharmacy; examined the coral ducks hanging in a window on Canal Street, and debated about buying jeans at Canal Jeans; ambled through Soho, watching the yellow cabs cruise by; walked up to the Village, dipping west into the green of Washington Square Park, where three different people tried to sell him drugs; walked back to Broadway, past the barber shop on Astor Place; rested on the steps outside Grace Church; looked in the window of Forbidden Planet, a science fiction store, and leafed through some paperbacks outside the Strand; skirted the vague danger of Union Square Park and took the N train to Macy's, where he bought a silk tie patterned with blue crescent moons and heard a deranged Jamaican man with dreadlocks outside the store shouting, "There's a reason they're putting all of us in prison, mon!"; continued up the odd, vague stretch between Thirty-fourth and Forty-second streets (an elderly female chef, still wearing a stiff cap, stepped into the street from a restaurant, smiled at him, and said "*Bonjour,*" to which Bert replied, "*Sei gesund.*"); approached the neon lights and pornography shops of Times Square, then headed east along Forty-second Street toward Fifth Avenue, past the newspaper kiosks alongside the public library; east, past the electronic shops selling compact disc players; east, past the street vendors outside Grand Central Station; east, toward the Grand Hyatt Hotel.

Coming out of the Grand Hyatt, he saw a man and a woman, holding each other and laughing. And he knew who the man was, even from the back; it was Patrick. But Patrick was blocking the woman's face, and Bert couldn't see her. And then she swung around into the sunshine, and Bert saw Diana. And he knew two things, from the way they were holding each other and laughing with each other: neither one of them had a cold, and this wasn't the first time they'd gone to a hotel. Bert had the strangest feeling of déjà vu, as if he'd lived through this exact moment before, or read about it somewhere.

Diana saw him, but Patrick had his back to Bert. She said something to Patrick: Bert thought she was telling him not to turn around. They were deciding if he'd seen them, what he'd seen, how much he'd seen. Then Patrick faced him, too, to see what Bert would do. And Bert waved feverishly at them — and even this, even this wave, he'd lived through before — pretended to have spotted them just then, pretended to be happy to see them, because it was so much less awkward, so much easier for all of them. Really, all he had to do was give in.

"We just decided to play hooky and go see a movie," Diana told him when he trotted up.

Bert didn't ask what movie in case they hadn't agreed on a story. But there wasn't even a movie theater nearby. Surely they could have done better than that.

"I thought I had a cold this morning," Patrick said, speaking too quickly, "but I started feeling better around lunchtime. And I called Diana to see how she was doing, and she was feeling better too, so we decided to meet midway between Queens and White Plains."

Keep it simple, Bert wanted to advise him.

Stupidly, Bert began to apologize for meeting them, for taking a walk, for the absurd coincidence of bumping into them. Diana said, forget about the movie, they should all go out for a snack, so they went into the Oyster Bar in Grand Central and ordered oyster pan roasts.

And he knew it didn't make sense, but the thing that bothered him the most was that Patrick and Diana had gone to a hotel. And to the Grand Hyatt, where Muzak versions of "Mood Indigo" wafted through the lobby. It was so, well, bourgeois. And Bert knew Patrick, the polite midwesterner, would have insisted on paying for the hotel, which meant that Bert, with all the money he'd lent Patrick, had actually paid.

They ate oysters, and drank beer, and cleared their palates with Choward's violet mints, which Diana always kept in her pocketbook. Patrick's leg twitched nervously, and Bert thought about the first time he'd met Diana's husband, in the bar and how awkward he'd felt.

"I had lunch with Harry and Kathleen," Bert told them.

"She's great," Diana said. "Don't you think she's great?"

"Yeah, Kathleen's really great," Patrick agreed quickly.

"We have to find a good man for her. Maybe Bert."

Just then, Bert hated both of them so very much.

Harry wanted to make a change in his life — either travel abroad, or go to grad school in clinical psychology. "But I just don't know if I could be a therapist," Harry said. "I wouldn't be able to deal with white patients. If I had a white patient, I'd fuck with his mind."

"Uh, in that case, I vote for traveling."

Chuck wasn't coming back, and Harry wasn't waiting for

him anymore. He made Bert keep him company while he went to the Luscious Lollipop, a shop that specialized in sexual aids and paraphernalia. Harry bought a dildo, and Bert eyed the blow-up dolls. "You know," Bert said, "these things are looking better and better."

Is It True?

▾▾▾

JUNE. Harry was dragging him to the sleaziest bar in all Manhattan, he promised, a place called The Manacle, down by the piers. It was a cool evening for June, and Bert had worn a sweater, but as they walked to the bar, he got nervous and started sweating, so he wrapped the pullover around his waist.

"I just hope we're not disappointed," Harry said.

"What do you mean?"

"I'll consider the evening a success if I go home with a cute guy," Harry said.

"I'll consider the evening a success if I don't lose my sweater." Bert tightened it around his waist.

He walked behind Harry into the smoky club. A single dull light bulb throbbed overhead; parts of the room were cast into pitch-blackness. Men moved slowly in a circle around the bar. Bert caught sight of his old boss Juan Carlos on the other side of the room, looking a little older, a little thinner, but still the King. He was giving a hand job to someone. It depressed Bert to see Juan in these squalid surroundings. Of course, Bert was there too. Harry faded into the crowd, and Bert left the bar.

A few doors down from the Manacle was a quiet country and western bar. Bert was too shy to start a conversation with anyone, but a friendly, husky man with fair skin, wavy dark brown hair, and very blue eyes began talking to him. Bert ordered a beer; the man ordered a bottle of Calistoga water. His name was Scott, and he'd moved to New York a week earlier. He was rooming with the bartender — they had a mutual friend in San Francisco. Scott had a pleasant, forthright goofiness that reminded Bert of his brother, Philip. He was twenty-six and had been in Alcoholics Anonymous for six years. After joining AA, Scott had become a Catholic and now went to Mass every week. He took Communion but said the wine wasn't a problem. Bert asked him why he'd finally joined AA.

"I was living in Seattle, and I'd been trying to cut down on my drinking and my drugs for so long," Scott told him. "Every day I'd say, okay, I'm not going to drink, but by seven at night, I'd always be at the liquor store. I rotated between different liquor stores, so no one would know how much I was really drinking. That last night, my friend Darryl was going to Atlanta on business and wanted some cocaine for the trip. I went out hunting for him. One friend didn't have cocaine, but he gave me some crank."

"Crank?"

"Crystal meth. Then I went to another friend, he didn't have cocaine either, but he gave me a hit of acid. Finally, I found some coke. I brought it back to Darryl, and we ended up doing half of it right there — maybe a quarter gram each, maybe half a gram each. I took a Valium to cut the high. My doctor had given me a prescription for Valium because I was having really bad anxiety attacks every morning when I woke up. Very typical of late-stage alcoholism, but I didn't tell him why I was anxious. Okay, so now I drive home from Darryl's, and the LSD starts kicking in, so I pull over at a bar. It was Valentine's Day. They had doubles for the price of singles. I loved gin and tonic, that was my favorite drink. I ordered eight double gin and tonics. And with each gin and tonic, I took a Valium. Then I met this guy at the bar. I don't think I looked very appealing by that point, but I told him I had some MDA at home, so he was willing to go home with me. We split a quarter gram of MDA between the two of us. I don't remember having sex with him, but I know I did. I think I threw up, too.

"The first miracle is that I woke up the next day," Scott went on. "And I realized it was a miracle. I kicked the guy out of my apartment. I said, you have to go now, I need help. I called work — I worked for the phone company — and said I needed a vacation day. I had one Valium left, and I took it, and then I called my group health plan to make an appointment to see a drug counselor. The counselor didn't have any time that day, but I begged her, and she said, okay, come in at four. Somehow I made it through the day, and I went to see her. She wanted me to go to a drug treatment center right away. I said absolutely not. Then she said I had to go into AA. I said absolutely not. She said, well, what do you want me to do, then? I said, I want you to give me medicine." Scott smiled at Bert. "I actually wanted her to give me a pill so I wouldn't be an alcoholic anymore. Finally I agreed to go to an AA meeting. There was one about a block away. Except for Communion, I haven't had any alcohol since. And once I had gallstones, and they gave me painkillers. But I've been drug-free for six years. It's a gift," he told Bert. "That's what people don't understand. It's a blessing."

Bert was moved by the story, inspired by anyone who had sunk so low and pulled himself up by his own bootstraps. He believed people could change, he believed that wholeheartedly. Then, too, Scott's tale of drink, drugs, anonymous sex, and near suicide had, strangely, turned him on. Scott touched his leg, and Bert touched Scott's arm, and then they were touching more and more, and then they were talking about leaving the bar.

Scott was fascinated when he learned Bert was Jewish. "Well, I know one thing about you," he told Bert. "I know you're cut."

Bert told him the sex wouldn't be very exciting. (A friend of Harry's had just died of AIDS. Bert was being very careful.) Scott said, "No expectations." They went back to the bartender's apartment, and right away Scott took off his shirt and pants. He was wearing blue Jockey shorts. A tattoo of a falcon wound around his upper arm. They started kissing.

"Is it true," Scott broke off, "that if you have a tattoo, you can't be buried in a Jewish cemetery?"

"I don't know. Maybe."

They started kissing again.

"Is it true," Scott inquired, "that frogs aren't kosher because they live both on land and in water?"

"I don't know."

They started kissing again.

"Is it true," Scott wanted to know, "that Paul Newman's Jewish?"

"Yes."

Bert took off his pants and then Scott helped him off with his underpants before he took off his own. "You've got red pubic hair. Do all Jews have red pubic hair?"

"Yes," Bert told him, but then he worried Scott would believe him. "No, of course they don't."

Bert wouldn't put the tip of Scott's penis in his mouth. He'd lick only the sides. Scott didn't seem to mind.

"Do you want to hear a joke?" Scott asked him.

"Sure."

"Jesus said, 'Surely I come quickly,' " Scott recited. "Well, big deal, who doesn't."

Scott gave Bert a blow job, and Bert jerked Scott off until Scott came too.

"Can I see you again?" Scott wanted to know.

Bert was surprised. He thought Scott would have felt cheated. But he didn't want to date Scott. After Patrick and Diana, he didn't want to date anyone. "You're such a nice guy, but I don't want to go out with someone right now. I'm really sorry."

"I understand."

He gave Bert a little smile, and Bert sank. "But the good news is, I'm not the only Jew in New York City. I promise."

He took the subway home. Someone had scrawled on the wall of the car, "THE MOUSE THE CAT THE DOG CHASED DIED." Bert felt proud of himself — his first pickup. He got out at the Ninety-sixth Street station and saw Jane Alley sitting on a bench on the subway platform, smoking a cigarette under a NO SMOKING sign. It was three in the morning. "My, my," she said. "Look what the cat dragged in."

Nice

▾▾▾

JULY. Bert had dinner with an old high school friend, Peter Fortunato, who had come back to New York to work at Blithedale Brothers Publishing for the summer. Afterward they went to a bar on Second Avenue. Peter started chatting up a girl, and Bert felt left out. Then he ran into Kathleen, who was there with friends. He bought her a drink, they talked about work, he bought her another drink, they talked about Kathleen's old boyfriend, he bought her a third drink, he got her to invite him home. He was pretending to be a little drunk himself, so he could have an excuse in case she wasn't interested. But he knew she'd be interested, he knew she liked him, and he already felt guilty.

The apartment was very neat and a little bare. On her white walls Kathleen had hung a beautiful Romare Bearden poster, an overly familiar print of the unicorn from the Cloisters, and a small line drawing of two horses galloping down a beach. She had a collection of W. J. Jacobs short stories on her chiffonier, and on her nightstand, the inevitable copy of *Sonnets From the Portuguese*.

He was nervous with her, he didn't know why. "This is a nice couch. This is a nice table. You've got a nice apartment," Bert said idiotically.

"You like it?"

"It's nice."

They lay on their backs at first, next to each other on her bed. Overhead, on the ceiling, Kathleen had hung an E.T. mobile. "I was never sure you liked me," Kathleen said.

"Of course I liked you."

"And" — she still wasn't looking at him — "I thought maybe you were gay."

"No." He turned to her and they started kissing, and then undressing each other.

"Bert, this is awkward . . ."

Bert understood: she wanted him to use a condom. She had a packet in her nightstand.

She had small breasts, but they were very pretty, prettier than Bert had expected. And she was so small, so light, Bert had an urge to pick her up, just to feel how light she was. He wished she had more edge. He liked women with an edge. He wished she excited him more.

"You've got red pubic hair," she told him. "It looks nice."

"I dye it."

They fucked for a very long time before Bert could come. Somehow he couldn't come, so he just kept fucking. She had an orgasm quickly, but didn't want him to stop. Finally Bert started fantasizing about Patrick, and then he came.

"Oh, that was so nice," Kathleen told him afterward. She made him a midnight snack, a turkey sandwich on crisp French bread, with onions, tomatoes, and olives. She wanted him to stay the night and said she'd make him breakfast. She said she made killer French toast. But Bert felt itchy. He wanted to leave. He made some excuse about going up to the Bronx in the morning and kissed her goodbye. "You're so nice," she told him.

"You are too."

Nice going, he thought. What a perfect shit he was. On the subway home, he saw couples. Everywhere he looked he saw couples.

Havana-Lied

▼▼▼

AUGUST. Steaming streets, oppressive air, his shirt wet from sweat before he'd even walked the two blocks to the subway, people packed tight in the one car with air conditioning. A chilly movie theater, by himself, then back into the heavy, sultry streets and a slight breeze that teased more than it cooled. A bar called Hades, a man named Hendrick Santiago. Cute, slim, cocoa-colored, preppy. His mother was Dutch, his father was Cuban. "Real Cuban. Big trunks." He said he'd lived in Holland, and he was the only Santiago, and he'd lived in Miami, and he was the only Hendrick.

"You've got red pubic hair," Hendrick told him in bed.

"No I don't." Bert looked down at himself. "Oh my God!"

Steamy, sweaty sex, terrific sex (unexpectedly).

Afterward, on the subway, no air conditioning, smelling of sweat and sex. And a homeless man, without shoes, his feet purple and swollen and fetid and cracked, stinking, angrily smacking his forehead, talking to himself. "Thy will be done, Thy will be done," rapidly, over and over again. And people laughing, people actually laughing at the sight of the man.

"Many Who Have a Notion of Their Possibilities and Needs Still Accept the Prevailing Order by Their Actions, and by Doing So, Strengthen and Confirm It."

— R. W. FASSBINDER

▾▾▾

SEPTEMBER. He avoided Patrick and Diana at work. He avoided Kathleen, too. He'd sent her flowers with a note saying that he'd been drunk and regretted what had happened but wanted to remain friends.

His whole office was breaking up. Harry was moving for a year or two to India of all places. As part of an exchange program, he'd be advising the Bombay Sewer Department on budget matters and capital allocation plans, while Bombay sent an analyst to New York City to learn about New York's financial control systems (or lack thereof, Harry suggested). Barbara, who hated Assistant Commissioner Truby more and more, was trying to get transferred to Transportation or Bridges and Tunnels. And Bert was leaving because he'd been accepted by Columbia University's business school. An admissions officer told him she had been impressed particularly by his op-ed piece, which he had included in his application.

Since his mother worked at Columbia-Presbyterian Medical Center, he'd get a big break on his tuition as part of her benefits package. It was too good an opportunity to pass up, although somehow, in a million years, Bert had never expected to get an M.B.A. He felt like a class traitor. "These are the eighties, Bert, get used to it," Harry told him.

He'd be losing his apartment, too. The building was finally

going co-op, and Bert had to move out. Attending school full-time, he wouldn't be able to afford his own place, so he was moving back home with his parents.

Bert packed up his things. He was exhausted — awake and overtired and, oh God, horny too, all at the same time. Even now, lying on his bed, he had just to think about the possibility of sexual excitement to become sexually excited. Talk about theory into practice. "The materialist doctrine that men are products of circumstances and education, that changed men are therefore products of other circumstances of a different education, forgets that circumstances are in fact changed by men — and that the educator himself needs educating . . .

"The coincidence of the changing of circumstances and of human activity can be conceived and rationally understood only as *revolutionizing practice.*"

God, he missed dick!

"Men make circumstances just as much as circumstances make men . . ."

Part of him hated himself, thought himself weak, but it didn't make sense; only he, only Bertolt was weak. He held no man or woman low for being gay or bisexual; he held only himself low. And he wanted to hold himself high, he wanted to so badly: he got up from bed and went out for a walk, and as he sauntered past The Columbia, a huge luxury condominium being constructed on Broadway, he listened on his Walkman as Bruce Springsteen sang "So walk tall or baby don't walk at all" on *The Wild, the Innocent, and the E Street Shuffle,* and he vowed that he *would* walk tall.

Harry said they — "they" — would probably try to put gays in the oven, and Bert expected they'd put Jews there too. Well, if it happened again, and it probably would, he would go down fighting. He swore he would. He'd defend himself and his comrades and take a few of those fucking Nazis down with him. He was by no means a pacifist.

He passed an aging hippie, a heavy woman who was graying at the temples and handing out flyers about nuclear disarmament. A dog frolicked at the woman's heels, then ran up ahead to sniff strangers, only to return joyfully to his mistress every few moments. A red and black bandana was tied around the dog's neck. The woman, handing out the last of her sheets, called to the dog, whose name was Rainbow.

Bert went back to his apartment to finish packing. Outside his building, Jane Alley sat on an easy chair, right on the street, calmly smoking a cigarette. The city marshall was starting to move all of her possessions out of her apartment; the nuisance case had finally been decided, and she was being evicted. Boxes, lamps, chairs, bookcases, books, shopping bags, radios, clocks, were piled up around her. She was waiting for a bus from a woman's shelter to pick her up.

"Well, you win," Jane told Bert.

He wondered if he should tell her that he was moving too. "I'm so sorry," Bert said.

"Yes, yes, very sorry. Well, it's time for my benediction." She raised her hands and waved them in the air three times.

"Don't do this —"

"Don't worry, you'll like it. Ready?"

"Please don't do this," Bert begged her.

"May all your wishes come true," Jane said. "Isn't that nice? Read 'The Monkey's Paw.' My students always loved it." She smoked her cigarette, leaned back in her easy chair, and blew out a smoke ring. "Fuck you, you faggot."

ON TURTLE ISLAND

(It's Just Like) Starting Over

▾▾▾

IT WAS STRANGE being home again, in his old bedroom. Bert took down the Watergate and antiwar posters, replaced the Reggie Jackson with a Dave Winfield, kept the Marx Brothers up on the wall (first making some repairs with Scotch tape), added a long-necked, redheaded Modigliani and a van Gogh, *The Bridge at Trinquetaille*. He moved the two old twin beds into the storage room in the basement of the apartment building so his double bed could fit.

Two weeks after Bert moved back, Philip's roommate called from California and told Joseph and Evie he was putting Philip on a plane to New York. The roommate said he couldn't stand taking care of Philip anymore: Philip played electric guitar in the garage at four in the morning, antagonizing the neighbors; Philip's behavior was so unpredictable that the roommate was afraid to bring guests back to the house; Philip stood outside on the lawn, on the edge of Watts, and screamed that blacks needed to seize their own history, their own surplus labor, because whites and the Japanese would never cede it to them without a struggle. Joseph and Bert awaited Philip's return with apprehension, while Evie, to Bert's surprise, seemed the calmest. "If he's sick, if he's really sick, we'll take care of him," she said. "He's family."

When Philip showed up at the apartment with his guitars and his thick duffel bags, he trembled, but was coherent. Philip said he liked the new posters, especially the van Gogh. He admitted that he was tired, he needed a break. Working two jobs had finally caught up with him. He was happy to be home. Bert and Philip carried the double bed down to the basement and brought the two twin beds back upstairs. After all this time, they were sharing a bedroom again.

Philip told Bert about a girl he liked in Los Angeles, Lee-Anne, who didn't like him. "I'm twenty-five. I'm too old for a crush, but man, it hurts." Bert told him he'd feel better soon. It was good that he was living in New York. He'd forget about her. "Meet any nice women?" Philip asked Bert.

Philip looked over the books on the shelves. Bert had organized them by subject: fiction, science, psychology, the occult. "Did you know Carl Gustav Jung was a great percussionist?" Philip asked his brother.

"Really?"

"That's why he wrote *Man and His Cymbals.*"

They sat together on the sofa in the living room, studying old family photos. Bert and Philip, in matching cowboy hats, astride matching hobbyhorses, pretended to giddyap. Brandishing oversized boxing gloves, the two brothers boxed on Joseph and Evie's bed. Inside gorilla outfits, the boys growled at the camera before going trick-or-treating. Joseph carried Philip on his shoulders at the 1964 World's Fair. Evie and Bert danced together at Bert's bar mitzvah. Philip, wearing a greasepaint mustache, twittered a cigar in his best Groucho imitation. King Kong, in a fuzzy close-up taken off the television screen, climbed the Empire State Building. Bert graduated from Princeton, in the rain. A shot of Van Cortlandt Park revealed, on closer inspection, a mound of packed dirt, marking the grave of their old wood turtle.

"Whatever happened to your snapping turtle?"

"Ma gave it away. I was in college, and she got tired of feeding it. A kid on the second floor got it."

"That's good. That's really good," Philip said earnestly. "We couldn't take care of it anymore. We weren't around."

Philip got a job as a cashier in a neighborhood liquor store but said it was a pathetic job for someone whose brother had attended Princeton. "Hey, I used to work for Sewers," Bert reminded him. Philip decided he was going to go back to college ("this time I really mean it, Bert") and finish his degree. He'd get a big tuition break at Columbia, just as Bert had, but if he didn't get in, he'd go to one of the city colleges, maybe Lehman. "By the time I graduate, I'll probably need a cane. Maybe some of the freshmen girls will like older men."

Bert and Philip caught the last few ball games of the season, rooting for Winfield, admiring a rookie named Don Mattingly, who had quite a knack for covering first base (he was a lefty, naturally), going to the Loews Paradise and then sneaking into a second film while they were there (the glorious Paradise had been subdivided into smaller movie theaters), sharing an ice cream soda at Jahn's on Valentine Avenue, making a pilgrimage back to the Bronx Zoo.

In his spare time, Philip went to the music library at Columbia. While doing research at UCLA, he told Bert, he had learned that Bob Dylan and Louis Armstrong had met in 1966 or 1967, in West Saugerties, New York, while Dylan was recovering from his motorcycle accident, and had collaborated on a song entitled "On Turtle Island." The song had never been released, although bootleg copies apparently surfaced now and again. He was determined to track down any leads and at least get the song published if he couldn't get a single released.

"Phil," Bert said nervously, "are you sure about this?"

"I know it sounds crazy," Philip told him. "And I know you think I'm being weird about Dylan again. But it's really true. The two of them sat around and scribbled some words, and Dylan played his harmonica, and Louis played the trumpet, and they came up with a little two-minute song. I met a guy in Santa Monica who heard it." Philip's hand trembled while he drank some coffee. "I did."

Connect the Dots

▼▼▼

BERT ANSWERED a job posting at Columbia and started making extra money typing for the writer Ezekiel Eisenberg. Eisenberg was born in a small town in Poland in 1930. After the Germans invaded, his parents hid him with Christian friends in Warsaw, hoping his life would be spared. Separated from his sponsors, he lived on the streets of the capital, and as an eleven-year-old perfected a false foreskin constructed of wax which is still called "the Eisenberg hood" in Poland. Later he was captured by the Nazis and sent to a series of concentration camps, finally arriving at Auschwitz, where he met up with his parents shortly before his father's death from typhus and his mother's death in the gas chambers. After the war, Eisenberg wandered Europe as a refugee and suffered from a form of hysterical blindness on and off for four years. Later he worked as a journalist in Paris and then London before coming to the United States.

His book about Auschwitz had been translated into a dozen languages. He had become something of a social darling: he attended lavish parties, polo games (he played polo well), fashion shows. A frequent voyeur at after-hours clubs, he had documented the sordid world of sex clubs in New York in a series of articles for *Playboy.*

For many years Eisenberg had been a professor of Human Suffering at Yale University. He continued to write best-selling accounts of the plights of Jews. Indeed, he'd turned suffering into something of a cottage industry. He lived on Fifth Avenue in a long, elegant, L-shaped apartment and had remarried several years earlier after a bitter divorce, but his wife spent most of the year in Rome and maintained *pieds-à-terre* in Paris and Jerusalem. Bert had heard that Eisenberg had commissioned his friends to write letters championing him for the Nobel Peace Prize. It was said he wanted the prize very badly. He was apt to be snappish at times, and occasionally he insisted on modeling his new polo outfits for Bert. But he paid well, two dollars a page, so Bert didn't mind the job.

A tremendous film buff, Eisenberg was starting to build a videotape collection: *Night and Fog, Victor/Victoria,* the second *Star Trek* movie (with that wrathful old Khan), *The Birds,* Peter Brook's *King Lear, Apocalypse Now.* Bert assumed that *Star Trek* was a favorite of Eisenberg's daughter from his first marriage, who was away at college, or of his young son, who lived most of the year with his mother in Rome. Mrs. Eisenberg came from a patrician Italian-Jewish family. Judging from her portrait in the living room, she was a beautiful woman. Eisenberg himself stood over six feet tall. He was extremely thin, and his face looked like a death mask. Bert wouldn't call him a warm sort of fellow, certainly not the type to like *Victor/Victoria.* Now *The Birds,* that was more Eisenberg's speed: the inexplicable violence, the sudden descent into chaos, pain, and humiliation. Yes, Bert thought, Eisenberg must be a great fan of Hitchcock.

Bert typed in Eisenberg's daughter's room. Sometimes the writer, lost in thought and agonizing over a difficult passage, would walk into the room and react with surprise when he found Bert there. Once the shower in the bathroom near Eisenberg's bedroom was broken, so he used the shower in his daughter's bathroom. He emerged, dripping wet, with a towel wrapped around his thin waist and another towel twisted into a turban atop his head, doing a Marlene Dietrich impression. "See what the boys in the back room will have," Eisenberg sang, dancing a little, "and give them the poison they name."

Uris Hall, the home of the business school, was a dark, ugly building on the north side of the campus, near the gymnasium — darker still because the building wore plywood and scaffolding like a carapace. A new extension was being built above and behind the school, and asbestos was being removed from the ceilings within. The planks and metalwork shut out the sunlight, and shadows flooded the offices and halls. The cafeteria, the only area for socializing, was the darkest room of all. The people seemed dark, too, dressed in dark suits for humorless job interviews, or calculating the gloomy net present value of grandiose revenue streams. Bert would never forget seeing the brutal, patronizing, infinitely dismissive smile on a Chilean student's face when a teacher mentioned socialism — the only time in his four terms that Bert would ever hear the "s" word uttered in class. A humor piece circulated at the school, proclaiming, "Unions have been compared with roaches. Describe the union motel. Design an ad campaign with Muhammad Ali: 'De workers punch in, but they dasn't punch out.'" The problem sets in one of his textbooks, Miller's *Intermediate Microeconomics,* invariably "demonstrated" the inefficiencies of unions, unemployment compensation, and guaranteed minimum incomes. The climax of the book was Miller's economic defense of capital punishment. The text subscribed, Bert argued in tortuous bull sessions in the bleak cafeteria, to the John Birch School of Economics. He hated business school but felt he had no one to blame but himself: a Marxist shouldn't get an M.B.A. unless he's a masochist too.

He didn't make many friends; probably he didn't want to. He spent a lot of time alone, going to movies or bowling at Amsterdam Lanes or burrowing through the stacks of Butler Library. His closest friend at school was a black woman named Lisa Prescott. She had studied physics and engineering at Penn State and wanted to work in marketing for a high tech firm. Almost too thin, Lisa exercised compulsively. She said she'd been chubby as a teenager and never wanted to be heavy again. Intense, driven, and highly competent, she was also self-destructive: going on crash diets, staying up all night on coffee, biting and tearing at her fingernails all day long, leaving her cuticles raw and angry-looking.

She was attractive but not beautiful. She had light brown

eyes with little flecks of gold in them and smooth brown skin, but her teeth were crooked and her jaw jutted forward, upsetting the balance of her features. Her dentist had recommended orthodontia when she was young, but her parents hadn't wanted to pay for it. She was embarrassed by her teeth and tried not to smile too broadly. Sometimes Bert thought she had a crush on him, although in those endless cafeteria debates, she had been his most strident opponent. Bert was more attracted to men now than to women, but he liked her, very much, and hoped over time her crush would fade.

Lisa was obsessed by Zeno's paradoxes. She tormented Bert with them. "Now, either space and time are infinitely divisible, or else they consist of indivisible, tiny components. Correct?"

"Please don't do this to me," he beseeched her. He hated paradoxes. They made him feel unsteady.

Lisa ignored him. "It's an either-or proposition. One of the two has to be true. Let's assume space and time are infinitely divisible. That means that motion is smooth and continuous. Like a curve. You follow?"

"Lisa, I have a headache." Bert hated math. This whole line of reasoning smacked of math. Bert knew it was math, cleverly concealed.

"Okay, so we're assuming it's divisible. But let's say Achilles and a tortoise are in a race. Achilles gives the tortoise a head start. Then he can never overtake the tortoise. Because when Achilles reaches the point where the tortoise starts, the tortoise has already moved on to another point. And when Achilles reaches that point, the tortoise has inched ahead to still another point. And when Achilles reaches *that* point —"

"This is like Abbott and Costello," Bert said. Perhaps she wouldn't notice the divagation. "Abbott tells Costello, suppose you're forty years old and you love a girl who's ten years old. You're four times older than her. You wait five years. You're forty-five, she's fifteen. Now you're only three times older than her. You wait fifteen years more. You're sixty, she's thirty. You're only twice as old as the girl. How long do you have to wait until you and the girl are the same age?"

"That's brilliant!"

"Aw, shucks."

"So assuming infinite divisibility means Achilles never beats the tortoise at a race. Now, we know that's not true," Lisa plowed ahead. "If we make an assumption and it leads to a contradiction, then we know the assumption must be incorrect. So space and time aren't smooth, continuous functions. Instead, we're saying space and time consist of indivisible components. That means motion proceeds by a series of tiny connections of this minimum unit. Kind of like connect the dots."

"So what's the problem?"

"But Bert! This assumption leads us to another series of paradoxes!"

"I'm so excited."

"Now, these are a little more difficult, so bear with me."

"Some other time," Bert said plaintively. "Please, Lisa."

"You're no fun." Lisa was disappointed. "Oh well."

Lisa loved Madonna, especially "Holiday," which they played at her health club. She watched MTV obsessively and noted approvingly that Madonna "danced pretty well for a white girl." She was a musician herself: she had studied the cello for years, although she was reluctant to play for Bert. She had perfect pitch and, after hearing a song even once, could sing it note for note or play it by ear on the battered piano they found in a corner of Ferris Booth Hall.

"How come you'll play the piano for me, but you won't play the cello?" Bert asked her.

"I don't know. The cello's more private."

"But you've given concerts," Bert pointed out.

"Not anymore." They were working on a problem set together in the Uris Hall library. Lisa used her Hewlett-Packard 12C calculator to figure out an internal rate of return and smiled to herself because the answer was a perfect square. Then she covered her lips with her index and middle fingers. "When I was at Penn State, my father came to one of my concerts and said I played pretty well for a beginner."

"And that made you stop? Because your father's a dick?"

"I stopped because I thought my father was right." She smiled down at the numbers on the page, her fingers rubbing her lips. She liked numbers. "Hey, are you going to the party?" The business school was throwing a costume party for Halloween.

"Yeah, I guess." Bert hadn't really thought about it.

"Do you want to go together?"

"Sure."

Lisa ended up going as Harriet the Spy (Harriet the Black Spy, she insisted), wearing a pair of round tortoise-shell glasses, sporting binoculars around her neck, carrying a small notebook and a Bic pen, nibbling on a supply of tomato sandwiches. Bert considered going as Trotsky — he loved the idea of Trotsky appearing in Uris Hall and beheading business students left and right with a stroke of his sharpened, unbuttoned foil (somehow, in Bert's mind, Trotsky always seemed to be one of the three Musketeers, perhaps Athos) — or as Bela Lugosi (he could do a good imitation of Dracula's "children of the night" speech and also excelled at "To diiie, to be reeeally dead, that might be glawwwrious") but decided in the end to buy a bushy mustache at a novelty shop and go as Mark Twain.

There were a few men in drag at the party, one of them shockingly pretty with his red dress, powdered décolletage, pearl necklace, and red high-heel shoes. The wink and yet absolute fidelity of transvestism always made Bert feel squeamish. To Bert, drag didn't parody sexuality so much as make it overt. Sometimes Ribsy had a similar effect on him: malchick jeered sex, flaunted sex, loved sex. Malchick held a mirror up to Bert and said, This shape, this thing, is you.

They stayed at the party late, and Lisa asked him if he wanted to sleep on her couch — she lived in a dorm at International House on Riverside Drive, a few blocks from the campus — instead of going all the way back to the Bronx. He didn't want to sleep over; it seemed too intimate to him. He always felt uncomfortable in her apartment, even during the day. He thanked her but said he wanted to go home. She pressed him again to stay and then pressed him a third time. He told her he slept best in his own bed, and he never really minded the subway at night anyway. He actually found it more civilized then. He walked her to her building and didn't speak much. She gave him a quick peck on his cheek before running upstairs. He knew she was disappointed. He was disappointed with himself, too, disappointed because he always needed to stay so aloof. Even pursuing someone was a way of remaining aloof, of remaining in control. But being pursued, and responding, required him to let someone in, required him to let go. And letting go terrified him. Because where would it end?

His father was still up when he got home, lying on the living room floor in the dark, watching a movie on HBO. He had told his parents he might be home late, but his father had worried nonetheless.

"Dad, I'm getting a little old for you to wait up for me." But he was moved by his father's devotion. "It's sweet of you," he said.

"What makes you think I was waiting up? I just got hooked on this shit."

"So what are you watching?"

"Who knows." Joseph said he was tired, shut off the television set, and went to bed. "Go to sleep," he called to his son. Bert turned on a small lamp in a corner of the dark room and read the newspaper, then went to his bedroom and got undressed. A new purple bong sat on Philip's bureau. His brother was smoking too much pot. Philip was whimpering, "No, no," in his sleep. He clutched his pillow and moaned, then whimpered louder, "No, no." Bert woke him up.

"What?" Philip said. "What's the matter?"

"You were having a bad dream." Bert felt tears welling up in his eyes. He wasn't sure why. He patted the blankets over Philip's shoulders. "Go back to sleep. I love you, Phil."

"I love you, Bert," Philip muttered, and fell back into a dream.

*

Ribsy had a whole garbage bag full of pot and was rolling huge joints out of newspapers to celebrate Halloween. All the while Ribsy was doing an imitation of Herbert trying to be cool about drugs: "Looks like good shit. Where did you buy that shit? How much did that shit cost? Who sells it to you? Where can I buy some?"

Bert couldn't help laughing.

Ribsy went on, "What does that shit do to your system? Imagine what that shit does to your blood pressure." The imitation was really very good. Nasty, but good. "I'm not sure that shit's good for you. Do you think you should be smoking that shit? That shit's expensive."

Later, they went to a coffee shop. Ribsy had swallowed two or three 'ludes, and spittle hung down from malchick's lips. It gathered in a little pool on Ribsy's side of the table. While Ribsy remained invisible, evidently the spittle could be detected, for the waitress kept swabbing the table with a rag, grinning nervously at Bert. Bert grinned back.

Later still, against his better judgment, Bert agreed to swipe one of his brother's Thorazines for Ribsy. Ribsy accepted the gift greedily. They went bowling. They were dressed alike, both in khaki pants and white tops — an old, comfortable Oxford shirt for Bert, a new silk blouse for Ribsy. Ribsy also wore a strand of fake pearls. Malchick bowled well, a strike, a nine, and two spares, until the Thorazine hit. Then malchick bowled a two, a four, a one, and eight gutter balls. On the last throw, Ribsy became disoriented and forgot to detach malchick-self from the ball. Bert watched helplessly as Ribsy traveled down the gutter, going round and round, wrapped around the ball, disappearing behind the pins. Ribsy crawled back up a quarter of an hour later, with large, black grease stains across malchick's white silk shirt. Plastered to the floor, malchick launched into another imitation of Herbert: "That looks like good shit. How much did this beauty cost? Where can I get some of that shit?"

Gee, but It's Great to Be Back Home

▾▾▾

AT FIRST Philip worked hard at the liquor store, but then found he couldn't concentrate. He lost interest, gave the wrong change, grew absentminded. He started having strange thoughts and giggling to himself. He made the customers nervous, and the owner too, and so the owner fired him.

Next he took part-time work as a stockboy in a supermarket. "Bert, I'm a textbook example of downward mobility." He found it extremely difficult to get up in the morning. Some days it took him three hours to gather enough strength to get out of bed, so invariably he showed up late to work. The manager of the supermarket let Philip slide for a few days but then fired him.

"I'm just not feeling so great," he'd tell Bert, lying in bed. "I don't know. I just don't feel right." He'd throw an old Spalding ball up in the air, catch it, throw it, catch it, throw it. "I got a bluesy feeling," he'd growl, imitating Louis Armstrong. Between his naps in bed, he'd rest on the sofa in the living room, listening to all of Joseph's Listen & Learn foreign language tapes. He wanted to learn Hebrew and live on a kibbutz, or learn Portuguese and move to Lisbon. "You can live for three thousand dollars a year in Lisbon," he told Bert.

If Philip took his medicine and didn't smoke pot, he was more or less okay. If he didn't take his medicine, or he smoked pot, his behavior deteriorated. And if he didn't take his medicine *and* he smoked pot — a strategy Philip especially relished — he grew incoherent.

"God wants me to smoke marijuana," Philip said.

"I don't need these pills," Philip said. "I'm not sick."

"You don't know how good pot is for me," Philip said.

Joseph was continually surprised by the things Philip did. He tried always to glean the significance of the scraps of paper Philip wrote on, the import of the Dylan songs, the secret meanings Philip imparted to everything. "There *is* no significance," Bert tried to explain. "He's crazy." But it didn't seem to sink in with Joseph the way it did with Evie.

Joseph confided his sorrow only falteringly: "I feel so bad for the kid." That's what he called Philip, the kid. "I feel so bad for him," Joseph said, smoking a pipe as he took a walk with Bert. "I just wish I could do something for the kid."

Evie also wished she could help Philip, but she remained distant from him. She had expected Philip to be sicker when he arrived. She told Bert she could take care of him when he was acutely ill, and she could enjoy his company when he was healthy, but this in-between state was destroying her because she never knew what to expect. She worried what Philip would do next, what he'd throw out, whether he'd be violent. She still cooked for him; she still washed his laundry; she simply wanted him out of the house. She told Bert it was too much for her. She said she'd take an extra job to support him, but when she came home from work, she needed to relax. And she couldn't relax with him home.

There didn't seem to be anything that anyone could do. Philip didn't stay on his medication. He got a little better; he got a little worse; he got a little better; he got a lot worse. And on and on and on.

"I just wish I could do something for the kid."

And his father said other things, patently ridiculous things, but felt compelled to say them nevertheless. "If I had owned my own business, then Phil could have gone into it. There wouldn't have been so much pressure on him."

Yeah, Bert thought, and if you weren't you, you wouldn't be you. And I wouldn't be me. And Philip wouldn't be Philip.

"If Philip had had a girlfriend," Joseph mused sometimes, snacking on some food. He ate when he was nervous, and he was gaining weight. "If he'd just had a girlfriend, he would have been happier."

If he'd had a girlfriend, he would have been a different Philip, he wouldn't have been Philip.

"If I had just gotten him better summer jobs," his father said. "I got you good summer jobs, but I could never get Philip good summer jobs."

Philip went crazy because he didn't have good summer jobs? His father was grasping at straws — grasping, Bert knew, because there was nothing else to do, nothing else to hold onto.

"If I could just do something for the kid." His father looked older, his sandy red hair was turning sandy gray.

"If I could just get him out of the house, I'd be a happy woman," his mother said. "If I could get him out of *bed*."

"I feel so bad for him," his mother said. "But what can I do?"

"I can't take much more of this," his mother said, biting her nails. "I try to be good to him, I really do. I just . . ."

"Your father will let Philip stay here till he drives us both crazy," Evie told him. "I feel like I'm slipping. I used to have such a good memory. I can't remember anything anymore." It took her longer to finish a crossword puzzle, and even coffee didn't help. She was still thin, still in good shape, but her face looked older, worn. Her stomach was giving her problems. She had to avoid almost all foods with a high fat content. For Thanksgiving, she ate a few slices of turkey and a plain baked potato. "This year — it's just gone, a big hole."

Bert thought, Just let him get well.

Bert thought, Phil will never get well.

Bert thought, God, why can't you just let him get well?

Bert thought, I'm sharing my room with a crazy person.

*

Philip said he'd finally collected the lyrics to the Armstrong-Dylan collaboration, although he was still waiting for the music. But he had a contact who worked at ASCAP who had a friend at BMI who knew someone at Columbia Records who knew Sarah Dylan, so maybe he'd get the music, too. He showed Bert the lyrics to the song:

On Turtle Island

I live a life of ease
On Turtle Island.
Got a girl I can please
On Turtle Island.
Eat some feta cheese
On Turtle Island.
No disease
On Turtle Island.
Study Portuguese
On Turtle Island.
Watch out for the bees
On Turtle Island.
Where you get change back from your dollar.

"Did they write these lyrics, or did you, Phil?" Bert asked softly.

"I'm not really sure," Philip finally admitted. "I wish I were sure." He whispered to Bert, "I think I did."

"Prominence to the Prominent, Concisiveness of Expression for the Benefit of the Masses, and Distinctiveness in Shades."

— CHAIRMAN MAO

▾▾▾

LISA WAS so conservative in her politics. She hated Reagan because he was stupid and a racist, she said, not because he was right-wing. Bert didn't understand her. How could you study quantum mechanics, the statistical interdependency of all things, and not be a socialist? "I don't see why I should work my ass off to pay taxes so some junkie can get on welfare," Lisa told him. "Basically, I just don't want to have to worry about money. Ever again. I worried too long. And I'm not going to worry anymore. You don't know what it's like."

"I didn't exactly grow up rich."

"You don't know what it's like," she repeated. "Your mother helps you out. Your father helps you out. My father never helped me out," she said bitterly. Lisa hated her father. Her father had doted on one of Lisa's sisters and paid for all of her college tuition but hadn't given Lisa a penny. Lisa loved her mother but criticized her for being too passive, for kowtowing to all her father's demands. "You have role models," Lisa told him. "What role model do I have? My father's nasty, and my mother lets him walk all over her. Nice people have nice parents. I don't have nice parents. Maybe I won't be nice."

"But you are nice," Bert told her. "You are."

She smiled a little, forgetting to cover up her teeth.

"You know what we should do?" Lisa asked him.

"What?"

"We should assume that time and motion *aren't* infinitely divisible," Lisa told him. "That they're built of tiny little jerks."

"Oh God. Connect the dots," Bert remembered, resigned to the discussion. "Why do I have the feeling something awful's about to happen?"

And he was right. The paradoxes that arose given this latest assumption were impenetrable. Bert simply took Lisa's word for it: motion was impossible. But maybe there was a solution, Bert proposed. What if space and time weren't composed of a cinematographic series of dots and weren't continuous either. What if somehow they were simultaneous? Waves *and* particles.

"Oh, Bert," Lisa said mournfully, "how are you going to prove it?" She seemed so forlorn that Bert had to laugh, and then she laughed because he was laughing, and then she nervously covered her mouth with her hand. Sometimes she seemed so vulnerable to Bert, he just wanted to take care of her. Other times she kept herself in a shell, as though she were protected by armor plating. Bert never knew how she'd react, whether she'd fly into a rage if a shopkeeper slighted her, or burst into tears if a fellow classmate didn't want to study together.

As Bert expected, the class that gave him the most trouble was statistics. He didn't understand his fear of mathematics. He was a reasonably intelligent person. But when it came to math, he panicked. His statistics professor was named Mr. Maurice, and Mr. Maurice promised the class two things: first, that at least once during the term he would wear his infamous maroon suit (a promise he made good on), and second, that he would try to tone down his habitual insulting of students because the dean of Academic Affairs had asked him to (a promise he had a harder time keeping).

"Degrees of freedom are the capabilities of a statistic for variation," Mr. Maurice informed the class. And how many of them are there? "Jeez, can't you get this through your thick skulls? As many as the number of unrestricted and independent variables determining its value." Huh? If someone could explain to Bert what degrees of freedom meant, explain in perfectly comprehensible English, he was sure he could understand. But no one seemed able to help.

Bert studied hard for the final and walked into class mildly confident. If he got something about degrees of freedom wrong, or if there were a question about "significant figures," another term he couldn't quite grasp, well, he'd get partial credit at least. Mr. Maurice passed out the test, smiled at the class, and watched them get to work. Get to work, Bert told himself. He looked at the first question, the second, the third, the fourth. His mind was a blank. He didn't know how to answer a single question on the test.

He panicked. A horrible nausea came over him. He looked down at the test questions again, and the print seemed to swirl together. Bert went out to get a drink of water, then came back. He tried answering the simplest question, a small regression analysis, but he had to divide by the number of degrees of freedom. He just couldn't do it. He couldn't concentrate; his thoughts were whirling; his hands were shaking.

He failed the exam.

During his office hours, Mr. Maurice handed back the tests and told the students the class mean, median, mode, and the standard deviation. Everyone had done badly, but few had done as badly as Bert had. "See me," Mr. Maurice had scrawled atop his paper. Bert suddenly felt like a very little boy. He was required to repeat the class and placated Mr. Maurice by promising to get Lisa to tutor him.

Bert found a copy of W. J. Jacobs's *A Field Guide to Madness* on Ezekiel Eisenberg's couch. "A vulgar writer," Eisenberg pronounced. "But it's selling well." He cracked open a peanut with one hand and popped the meat into his mouth. "I hear there's going to be a sequel," he added caustically. Bert asked if he could borrow it. "Be my guest, Mr. Rosenboym."

The book was a highly erotic first novel about a twenty-five-year-old investment banker and his tempestuous, obsessive relationship with his redheaded girlfriend, a sexually confused, rising young editor at a major New York publishing house. Complicating the picture was a lesbian succubus, possibly imaginary, who competed with the man for the woman's affection. The book jacket promised "an urban tale of love, loss, and redemption set against the glitter and glitz of the go-go eighties." Bert couldn't put it down. It was like candy.

He finally finished typing the English translation of Eisenberg's latest manuscript, a six-hundred-page account of a Polish-Jewish Communist party bureaucrat who must wrestle with his conscience and choose between Solidarity and the party line, knowing the defeat of the party might spark renewed anti-Semitism. It was all terribly earnest. When Lech Walesa won the Nobel Peace Prize in December, Eisenberg spent the day on the phone, telling everyone how much Walesa deserved it and how happy he was for him.

He invited Bert to a reading he was giving at the Ninety-second Street Y, and Bert watched as Eisenberg wept, reciting an old Hasidic tale. "They are such bewteefill stories, such sad stories," he told his audience. Bert loved Eisenberg's Polish-Yiddish-French accent. Eisenberg spoke English superbly but had trouble with a few select words: "beautiful," "love," and "Rosenbaum," among others.

Once he asked Bert which he liked better, the Armani suit or the Hugo Boss. He held each one up on a clothes hanger. Eisenberg was going to a cocktail party at Felix Rohatyn's house and wanted to look his best: "That cute Jane Pauley is going to be there!" Bert voted for the Armani, which he thought had a classic beauty. "Thank you, Mr. Rosenboym, I *shall* wear the Armani."

The next day, Eisenberg's wife and son, Daniel, returned from Italy to spend Chanukah with him. Bert was there when Eisenberg answered the door and swept Daniel up into his arms. He saw the look on Eisenberg's face. It was a look of love, certainly, but also of surprise, of disbelief that he had somehow managed to father a son who was wealthy and well fed. Eisenberg began singing "Papir iz Doch Weiss."

Bert had hoped that after Jane Alley was evicted, Jorgen and Luisa might get back together again. But the marriage was still foundering, and Jorgen had finally moved out to a small apartment in Queens. The children spent every weekend with him, but they missed having their parents together. "You're not blaming yourselves, are you?" Bert worried. "Because it's not your fault."

"We know whose fault it is," Isabel told him icily. "Jane Alley's."

"I hate her," Lars said.

"It's not her fault either," Bert said. "She was sick."

But Lars swore one day he'd get even with her. His parents' separation seemed to hit him harder than it did Isabel. He withdrew into himself and into his insect collection. "We're going to get married, Isabel and me," he told Bert. "You don't believe us because we're brother and sister, but it's true."

Bert tried to see them every week or two because they were going through a rough time. They played Chutes and Ladders or Monopoly and talked a great deal about the aliens: after Bert described the holograms he had seen of their children, Isabel wondered if they would ever have another baby.

Bert told the children that the Bureau of Air Traffic Control had mailed him a lengthy questionnaire, asking about possible contact with extraterrestrial life forms, which he had thrown in the garbage. Later, he said, he had received letters from the bureau, asking for lengthy, Maoist-style "self-criticisms," again concerning his involvement with space aliens. Isabel and Lars said they had received the letters, too. Ribsy completed Isabel's for her, confessing to a multitude of sins: chocolate addiction, consorting with lower life forms, beating up malchick's younger brother, transporting cottage cheese across galaxy lines, stealing money. Then he began a list of his own. "Oh, and one time

I kissed a hominoid on Cygnus 3, on a bed of Betelgeuse lettuce," Ribsy told them. "He was really stacked, I remember."

"The hominoid?" Bert asked.

"The lettuce," Ribsy said.

As a joke, Isabel wanted to send Ribsy's confession to Air Traffic Control under her own name, but Bert wouldn't let her.

Tom Helmer called him out of the blue and asked him to a small dinner party he was hosting. Bert thought it was generous of Tom to include him. And he was pleased that he'd been invited: he thought he might meet someone interesting at the party. Tom lived with two roommates in a large apartment in Washington Heights. He showed Bert his room. His desk, cluttered with books and papers and dozens of snow globes, was messier than Bert had expected. Bert shook one of the globes and watched snow descend on the Eiffel Tower. "People think I collect them, so they keep giving me them," Tom said. "Everyone's so happy because they always know what to buy me. I don't even want them anymore. But if I told people that, they'd be disappointed." Tom shook a globe and started laughing. "I hate these stupid things!" Above the desk, Tom had shelves and shelves of compact discs, neatly arrayed. Bert found three loose discs on top of the stereo system: Tom Waits, Graham Parker, George Clinton.

"Wow, I like all these guys," Bert told him.

"Great. It only took me two hours to decide which ones to leave out."

Tom sat next to Bert at dinner. Most of the other guests seemed to be couples. After the meal, over coffee, Tom told Bert that his union drive at Columbia-Presbyterian had ended dismally. Now he was going to pharmacists all around the city to gather signatures for two petitions: the first advocated national health insurance, the second called for an end to the death penalty. One of the other guests, overhearing the conversation, asked why pharmacists cared about health insurance — they were paid no matter what. Tom said that nowadays pharmacists, particularly at the chain drugstores, had no incentive to provide nondispensing services because they were reimbursed only for selling a product. As a result, pharmacists were being deprofessionalized, converted into technicians, salesmen, pill counters. But under a national health system, Tom argued, pharmacists could be encouraged once again to answer questions about drugs, help patients make informed choices about their health care, even counsel clients about preventive medicine. In fact, Tom said with growing enthusiasm, in addition to prescriptions and over-the-counter products, the government could create a new, intermediate class of medications, which would be available at drugstores but could be sold only under the auspices of pharmacists. Bert wanted to reach out and touch the funny bump on Tom's nose.

The idea that pharmacists alone might bring about universal health coverage seemed sweet but foolish, Bert told his parents at breakfast the next morning. But the idea that pharmacists alone could abolish capital punishment seemed absolutely insane.

"You know, here's a guy who stands for everything you believe in. And you're still not satisfied," Joseph said. "What do you want?"

Bert considered the question for a moment. "Socialism with a sense of humor."

"Deliver me," his mother said.

Evelyn had finally finished her dissertation, "Modes of American Jewish Humor," and she let Bert read it while she worked on a crossword puzzle. The paper began with a comparison of moneylending and comedy. Like many other scholars, she argued that Jews had ended up working as moneylenders because almost all other occupations were closed to them in the Middle Ages. Similarly, Jewish immigrants in the twentieth century had gravitated toward show business, seizing whatever opportunities to advance they could find. Now, both moneylending and comedy had this in common, Evelyn proposed: while accepted, licensed, and even encouraged by the State, they also challenged the hegemony of State power; and wherever moneylenders and comedians got too powerful and posed a true threat to the State, they were inevitably and summarily crushed (e.g., the expulsion of the Jews from Spain in 1492 and the government's legal assault on Lenny Bruce). In the second section of the dissertation, Evelyn provided a close reading of Bruce's work, citing two images as essential to his comedy: the Jew as outsider and the wise fool. She then compared Bruce's use of these images with Shakespeare's in *The Merchant of Venice* and in *Lear.* In the final section, she called for a specifically Jewish, antifascist reading of Shakespeare, which would combine Shylock, Lear's Fool, and Lenny Bruce into a single character. She suggested casting Jeff Goldblum in the role, "although Dustin Hoffman would probably leap at the chance, and might have more box office clout."

With the dissertation finished, Evelyn began work on another monograph, on the sociopathology of certain children's board games: Candyland, Mousetrap, Trouble, Operation, and Battleship. Herbert, meanwhile, was making occasional road trips to Pittsburgh, to write a report on a bitter strike by steelworkers, and to Nashville, to do research on Hank Williams. Ribsy was still spending almost all of malchick's time doing drugs. Ribsy looked terrible.

"The highs you get as an addict are so much more intense than the highs you get anytime else," Ribsy told Bert. "Of course, the lows are lower, too."

In time, the alcohol seemed more of a problem than even the cocaine, though Ribsy could rarely be found without traces of white powder on malchick's lips and chin. Malchick stopped eating, grew thinner and thinner, lied. Malchick's thinking grew distorted. Drugs came first, everything else a distant second. One day Bert found malchick fiddling with the dial of a transistor radio. "What are you looking for?" he asked.

"Space aliens," Ribsy said. "You think we're the only ones

here." Then malchick laughed, tee hee hee. "Listen to me, I'm getting crazier and crazier."

Evelyn and Herbert's other work was forgotten. The two spent all their time and energy trying to get Ribsy into treatment. They outlined a program of immediate abstinence, hypnotic training at the ship's Reich-Eisenstein console, eavesdropping at AA meetings, and counseling with Herbert (who was a certified psychotherapist on the planet Debbie). Ribsy agreed to consider the idea, then began shooting up heroin. Bert, Lars, and Isabel found Ribsy in the back yard of the children's building. Malchick was sitting on the ground with the same young, weather-beaten man whom malchick had previously stolen cocaine from, the one who'd held a knife to Bert's throat.

"What are you doing?" Lars asked Ribsy.

Ribsy looked up, mute, holding a syringe. Bert began backing the children out of the yard.

Ribsy stole money. Ribsy missed appointments. Ribsy was drowning and they seemed powerless to help.

Lisa had finally agreed to play the cello for Bert. Bert went back to her dorm room with her. Her room was always meticulously clean: the bed was made with perfect hospital corners, the bedspread was smooth, a small vase on her nightstand was filled with fresh, trimmed flowers. The walls were bare, except for one poster over her bed, a print of Jacob Lawrence's "Other Rooms," a highly geometric study of northern blacks. The stainless steel frame was crooked when they walked in, and Lisa, looking embarrassed, straightened it before she unpacked her cello from its hard brown case. Bert sat across from her, nervous as always in her apartment. She rosined her bow vigorously, smiled at him without opening her lips, and began playing the Bach Suite number 3 in C Major. She played very well, missing a few notes at the beginning because of nerves, then settling down and becoming increasingly passionate and expressive as she went on.

"I loved the fourth one," Bert told her afterward.

"You didn't like the others?"

"Of course I did. I just liked the fourth best."

"Oh well." She seemed disappointed.

"I liked the last one a lot, too."

"The gigue . . . I guess if you liked the fourth and last ones best, it means you liked the others less."

"I told you, I liked them all."

"But, Bert," she was insistent, "if you liked two of them more, then you had to like the other ones less."

Bert agreed that, logically speaking, she had a point. "But I'm not going to argue mathematics with you. You're always going to win."

She picked at her cuticles. "I missed notes."

"Pablo Casals missed notes."

"No he didn't." She laughed out loud, and Bert caught sight of her crooked teeth. He thought he'd be more attracted to her if her teeth were straighter and if she didn't have an overbite, and then he hated himself for being petty. It wasn't as though he looked like Robert Redford. She snuggled next to him. "Bert, we should go away for a weekend."

"Where would we go?"

"Anywhere. It's getting cold. We could go to the Bahamas for three days."

"Lisa, I can't afford that." He got up and walked to the other side of the room.

"But there are some great student deals. Didn't you see the flyers on the bulletin boards?"

"I still can't afford it."

"I can pay for it."

"I don't think so."

"Why not? I've got money." Lisa was consulting for a software company and making a decent salary even while going to school. "I can work on my tan," she joked.

She busied herself cleaning up the already clean apartment, and dusted her desk with a tissue, and suddenly she was crying.

"Lisa, I'm gay," Bert told her, and not for the first time. It was the truth, more or less. Diana was the last woman he had been really attracted to.

"I just think we have a special connection," Lisa was saying, wiping her eyes. "I just think. . . . Oh God, listen to me, I'm such an idiot, such a stupid idiot, chasing after a gay man. It's like a bad joke. But I can't seem to stop." She bit her nails, ferociously, until one of her fingers started bleeding. Bert washed her finger with soap and water and put a bandage on it. "Oh well." Lisa smiled at him and covered her lips with her bandaged finger. "At least we'll always have first aid."

He invited her to his house one weekend for brunch. He had told her about his brother and warned her about what Philip might do, but Philip, quiet and shy, said hello nervously, and then stayed in their bedroom most of the time. Evie was gracious to Lisa, and Joseph was grateful to her for shaking Philip's hand so warmly.

Over brunch, Evie talked about her work. Columbia-Presbyterian had asked her to write a training primer for all the pharmacists at the hospital. Joseph said they'd asked her because she was the best pharmacist and the best writer. Evie said they'd asked her because they wanted someone to type it for free, but she was determined to do a good job, anyway. Organizing the manual was tricky, though. She wondered whether professionalism should be included under ethics, or whether ethics should be included under professionalism.

Lisa told them it reminded her about a paradox in set theory.

"Oh God no," Bert said, but Evie wanted to hear it.

"It's called the barber paradox," Lisa said. "Bertrand Russell was interested in it. Let's say the Barber of Seville shaves all the men who live in Seville, except for those who shave themselves."

"Well, that seems easy enough," Joseph said.

"Just wait," Bert warned his father.

"The question is," Lisa said, "who shaves the barber? You see, if he shaves himself, then he's not supposed to be shaved by the Barber of Seville. And if he doesn't shave himself, then he's one of the men in Seville who is supposed to be shaved by the Barber of Seville. Either way, it doesn't make sense."

Evie and Bert were stumped, but Joseph had an answer: "I know who shaves him," he declared.

"Who?" they all asked.

"His wife."

Sweet Limitation

▼▼▼

WHENEVER PHILIP left the bedroom, he went through an elaborate series of motions. He never deviated from the ritual. First he checked the stereo. He turned the volume knob all the way to the left. If it was already all the way to the left, he turned it to the right first, and then back again to the left. Then he turned off the power switch. If the power switch was already off, he turned it on, then back off again. Then he put the treble and bass knobs to the center notch. He moved over to the alarm clock and made sure the alarm wasn't set. He ran his hand over the albums in the cabinet and smoothed them out, so they lined up evenly. He turned the light switch off. Then he turned it on again, surveyed the room, then turned it off again. Then he turned the light on and began the whole process again, with the stereo, the alarm clock, the albums, and the light switch. And then he left the room.

Bert found it exhausting just to watch.

Philip started writing poems, most of which he never finished, and almost all of which he threw out. Bert started filching the more complete examples out of the wastepaper basket. He wanted to save them. He didn't know why.

"Hey Grandma"

I said, "Hey Grandma make me a vest"
she did and you know:
it was the best.

You know my Grandma
  she's just a cut above the rest,
  She's my grandma,
You know she's the best.

Hey Grandma, you cook such fine stuff
Tell me, Grandma, do I pass the test:
  Could I ever really love you enough?

Twice a week Philip saw a psychiatrist in Manhattan. The psychiatrist's first name was Phillip. Philip was fascinated by this congruence. He detested the psychiatrist but flatly refused to see another. Sometimes he called the psychiatrist "Phillip Traum." Sometimes he called himself Philip Traum. He often missed his sessions. Occasionally he'd grow wild, and wildly impatient, and blow up into rages. Then he'd grow silent, and sink into himself, and lie down on his bed for days at a time, barely eating.

Sometimes, when he went off his medication for several days and smoked too much dope, he talked nonsense at a feverish pitch. The patter went on and on with bits of sense mixed in. "If I open up this textbook, I know on page thirty-five I'll find the names of two of my friends, the first names only, and if I turn to page seventy I'll find their last names. I think that on page fifty-six, no, fifty-seven, I can find the names of three psychiatrists, two psychologists, and one psychiatric social worker. The hobos communicated by a system of signs painted on boards, on railroad tracks, and on homes. They rarely went hungry. True or false, Lou Brock hit better from thirty-three to thirty-eight years old than from twenty-eight to thirty-three years old. If I open this book I can read what's on the page following each page without turning the page."

He still regaled Bert with sports trivia. Besides the Lou Brock question (a perennial favorite), he hounded Bert to name a player who wasn't on the Yankees who had probably hit the longest home run in Yankee Stadium. (Joseph finally supplied

Bert with the answer: Josh Gibson, who had played in the Negro Leagues.) That this astonishing command of trivia, ephemerals, facts, and figures could coexist in a mind so confused and disoriented never ceased to amaze Bert.

Philip argued with them all. He argued when they begged him to get out of bed. He argued when they criticized him for missing his sessions with the psychiatrist.

He practiced on his acoustic guitar every day — and loud, penetrating, screeching sounds shot out of the electric guitar every night. Philip insisted it was a new kind of music. The neighbors complained.

Buried underneath a pile of papers on his desk, Bert found a few diary entries Philip had prepared. He felt guilty, reading them, but he read them anyway:

1/3/84
Life is empty for me because I have no female companion to share my life with. It just goes on and on.

I've just got to get better on the guitar so I can get into a band and impress women.

1/16
I think I've had my last psychotic episode and my last anxiety attack. I'm really sure of it. January 23rd will be the fifth and a half anniversary of my being admitted into the psychotic ward.

1/18
Someone threw a rock at my bedroom window. I must have been playing too loud. Or too bad. Or too good for some people to take. Maybe it was just too late to play that loud. Maybe someone was a little jealous. No one yelled up to ask if I would turn it lower. I would have turned it lower if someone asked.

All colors I see seem more alive
Soon I'll cease be immoralized
immoralized

1/19
I had a dream a man was chasing me.

Sweet Limitation on I Ching.

*

Philip kept asking Bert for his interpretations of Dylan songs. Philip believed that "A Hard Rain's A-Gonna Fall" contained a secret or prophetic message about nuclear war, underneath the more general message, a secret message that was intended for him and only a few others.

"Phil, why are you so important that you get to hear the private message?"

Philip didn't answer. "Just listen," he told his brother. "Really listen." He put on the song. Bert listened as hard as he could, straining to find the message that Philip heard. "Do you hear it?"

"What am I supposed to hear?"

"The thunder that roars out a warning, that's Hiroshima. And the wave that can drown the whole world, that's the last wave. And it's coming."

"Maybe not, Phil. And not this minute, anyway."

"*Any* minute," Philip countered. "And you don't know when. But here's the secret: it's happening right now. That's what Dylan is telling us, that there won't be any witnesses left. That's why it's like a ballad: he's talking about a future event as if it were the past, because if he doesn't do it now, he'd never get the chance."

Eddie

Eddie lays a fart on
  his father's jaw
Loses said 'ginity with
  Puerto Rican whore

Despritly needing girl
  to suck him raw
Dreams of openin' up
  some comic book store.

Eddie saw "King Kong"
  bout hunrid fifty times
Bawt a nickel pot with
  uncirculated dimes.
  (and they was valuable ones, too!)

After reading "Eddie," Bert realized that Philip had indeed used his collection of uncirculated dimes to buy marijuana. Bert didn't have the heart to tell his father, who had built up the collection with Philip over a period of years. But things were forever disappearing from the apartment. Bert continued to lose albums and books, and took to storing valuable items at the homes of friends.

Joseph and Evie looked dazed, like two punch-drunk boxers. (Bert spent as much time as possible at school, at Eisenberg's, with Lisa, with Isabel and Lars.) None of them was sleeping well. Joseph was averaging only four or five hours a night. Evie slept, but she said her sleep was restless. Sometimes Philip muttered so much at night that Bert couldn't sleep in the same room with him. Then he'd repair to the living room, put the stereo on low volume, listen to one of the inevitable foreign language tapes, start conjugating verbs, and nod off.

Creative Concept Liaison Delight

Some girls are like robots
they just want to dance
Six hundred army cots
Shall send them to France

I feel as if doomed
And want to know better
Been wombed to tombed
Bet that's light as feather

Dig Creative Concept
Then Liaison Delight
Needs latent like respect
Would they could live all night

So truly be made known:
The Brave & the Bold
Vanilla Ice Cream Cone
Same Way I was Told

Philip had affixed some private liner notes to Bert's copy of *Bob Dylan's Greatest Hits, Volume II:* "This fine record album, destined for fame, *real*eased in 1972. listen. then listen again. the apostrophe is present *Giving Prescience.* If only he woulda — and he did!"

Bert had to admit (and it was foolish of him, he knew) that what bothered him most was simply that his brother had written on one of his records. Let Philip write on his own record. "Phil, don't write on my record."

"Record *album,*" Philip corrected.

"What difference does it make? The point is —"

"I've told you time and time again, adult men should say record *album.*"

"All right, record *album.* But why did you write on it?"

"I didn't think you'd notice," Philip said.

"How could I not notice? It's plastered on the cover. And Philip," he added more gently, "what you wrote doesn't make sense."

"Doesn't make sense," Philip aped Bert.

"Are you taking your medication?" Bert asked.

"Taking your medication?" Philip repeated with a sneer.

"Don't do this, Philip."

"Don't do this, Philip."

"Phil, I'm trying to help you —"

"I do not need help!" Philip exploded. "You're the one who needs help, you're the one who's crazy. Can't you see you're hurting me?" He began to bang his fist against his head, again and again. "Can't you see that?"

Bert was almost crying. "Stop it, stop it." He wrestled with Philip, trying to get him to stop hitting himself. "Please stop. I'm sorry, I'm so sorry." He apologized like crazy.

Wobbly

HIS PARENTS' BEDROOM was decorated with Danish modern furniture, a dark armoire, an antique wall clock that always ran a few minutes slow, and a digital clock radio that ran a few minutes fast (Joseph and Evie would average the two to get an accurate estimate of the time). On his bureau, Joseph kept a photograph of his mother, who had abandoned her children and her husband and moved back to Russia for two years in the 1930s, and another photograph of his boyhood dog, Farfel.

"I loved that little doggie," Joseph said.

"I always wanted a dog," Evie said. "I'm sorry you boys never had one. There was just no room in the apartment." She had so many regrets. She said she should have become a pharmacist sooner. She would have made good money and had her own store by now; they could have afforded a house; they could have afforded lots of things.

"We did okay," Philip told her. "We did the best we could."

Bert watched his mother's face soften, and then she kissed Philip. "You're a good boy." She didn't kiss him often. "So tell me," Evie addressed all of them, "who's making dinner?"

"I thought you were," Philip said in a worried tone.

"Sweetheart, I was kidding." Evie hurried to the kitchen.

II

Ezekiel Eisenberg had a beautiful chess set, made in Spain in the sixteenth century. The chessboard was balanced on the back of a bronze tortoise, one of whose legs was partly missing, so that the whole structure wobbled. The chess pieces were actually ivory tiles with pictures of rooks, knights, bishops, queens, kings, and pawns painted on them. Eisenberg turned the tiles over for Bert: on the underside of most of them were Hebrew letters. Eisenberg explained that the chess set had been made by Marrano Jews in Spain who had outwardly converted to Christianity but who continued to practice their Judaism secretly. Whoever had built the set had been a follower of the Kabbalist Abraham Abulafia, who believed that higher states of consciousness could be induced by contemplating the Hebrew alphabet and the individual words of scripture. By combining Hebrew letters into words, even into made-up words, and "jumping" from one word to another, the meditator would leave the crass, sensual world, untie the knots of the soul, and enter another realm, where the individual and the divine were joined in prophetic ecstasy.

One day two of the tiles were missing, a queen, with the letter *"chet"* underneath and a rook with the letter *"yud."* Together the letters spelled the Hebrew word *"chai." "Chai"* means "life," and an incensed Eisenberg accused Bert of stealing the tiles in a weird, Kabbalistic attempt to pilfer Eisenberg's life force. Bert said he hadn't stolen anything. Eisenberg said he was going to call the police. Bert said, go ahead, and started to leave. Eisenberg told him to wait, he wanted Bert to finish typing his article for *Commentary.* A little later, Eisenberg came into his daughter's room, where Bert was typing, and apologized abruptly: he'd found the tiles on the kitchen floor, where his cat had been playing with them.

A few weeks later, Bert accidentally jostled the chess set, and the unsteady board tipped over, flinging the tiles to the floor.

Bert picked them up hastily, checking carefully to make sure all thirty-two were accounted for.

"I'm so sorry," he apologized again and again.

"My dear Mr. Rosenboym," Eisenberg told him. "It's just a chess set."

III

"I'm not asking for anything. All I'm asking is to be with you. What's wrong with that? Why can't I just be with you?"

"I don't want you to get too attached to me. We've been through this before." Bert was getting angry and frustrated. He resented Lisa for making him feel so uncomfortable. "Why do we have to keep going through this?"

Tears welled up in her eyes, and she looked down at her fingers. "I must be really repulsive if you don't even want to be with me."

Now Bert felt awful. He took her hand and spoke softly. "I want to be your friend. That's what I want to be."

"But we can be more. It could be nice, Bert. I'm lonely. I think you're lonely too."

He just shook his head. What she was asking from him, he couldn't give her.

"You told me you've slept with women. Didn't you tell me that?" Lisa asked him.

"I don't know what you want me to say."

"It's your stupid smile," Lisa said. "If it wasn't for your stupid smile I wouldn't have any problems." And then she smiled at him, and cried at the same time, showing all her crooked teeth. Bert was mesmerized by her teeth, he couldn't stop looking. "Oh well." She blew her nose. "Let's have dinner."

"Can I buy you a pizza?" Bert offered lamely.

"Yeah, but I'm warning you, I'm ordering everything on it. It's going to be the most expensive pizza you've ever seen in your life."

"We'll have to stop at my cash machine."

"Good."

"One, one, two, three, five, eight." He listed his secret bank code to cheer Lisa up, for it had been Lisa who had persuaded him to adopt the Fibonacci sequence as his personal identification number. She rewarded him with another crooked smile.

Which Side Are You On?

▼▼▼

THE ROSENBAUMS fought daily with Philip about his medication. Every time he swallowed his medicine, they felt a small sense of victory. Philip claimed the drugs dampened his sex drive and made him feel woozy. Joseph said he should talk to the psychiatrist, who could modify the drug regimen and monitor his blood levels. But Philip was missing more than half of his sessions. The Rosenbaums began to fear that the psychiatrist was incompetent and cold and grubbing for their money, as Philip had insisted all along. But they still thought he was better than nothing.

Philip had lost all of his friends. One of them told Bert, "It's just too hard to be with him." Bert could understand their embarrassment, but he still thought they could spend an hour or two with him, even if only once or twice a year.

The Rosenbaums began trying to get Philip the Social Security disability payments for which he was eligible. They faced the most massive bureaucratic obstacles. To think that a mentally ill person could manage alone the paths and byways, the obscure turns, the doublethink and doubling back, of the Social Security Administration — the very idea that a mentally ill person could handle such strain and stress without going crazy again — well, Joseph and Evie concluded, it was just idiotic. But Bert thought it was more than idiotic: it was deliberate. The system was *designed* to keep people off the Social Security ranks because the government didn't want to pay. And this was money Philip was entitled to. He was disabled. He couldn't work. He was a diagnosed schizophrenic. That's what the program was for.

The Rosenbaums filled out forms and filled them out again, made appointments with social workers and psychiatric social workers and Social Security administrators and psychiatrists and then social workers again. And the paperwork was difficult, the forms were, well, crazy. Tell me, Evie asked everyone, tell me, how can a mentally ill person possibly do this?

The disability program rejected Philip's application initially. The Rosenbaums had to appeal. Joseph waited with Philip for hours in a dim, yellow government office while the appeal was processed desultorily. Philip grew increasingly anxious as the time passed. Joseph put an arm around his son and paced back and forth with him, in front of the rows of sick, indigent, uneasy, and hopeless castaways. One of the appellants, an elderly, toothless woman shaking from fear, illness, or the D.T.s, picked soggy, begrimed newspapers off the floor and threw them in the garbage. Another appellant objected: he wanted to read the papers. How did they expect a mentally ill person to wait for hours, Joseph demanded of a bored bureaucrat while Philip got a drink of water. How did they expect a mentally ill person to have the wherewithal to file an appeal in the first place?

This was a system, Bert decided, that not only feared the mentally ill, that not only derided them, but actively punished them. New York State had deinstitutionalized tens of thousands of mentally ill patients in the 1960s and 1970s — but not in response to civil libertarians, Bert was sure. Oh no. That was the front. New York State had discharged them because it was cheaper. What madman would release these patients, cheering wildly about community-based housing — *and then not provide any*? You think this was an accident? This was no accident. This was conspiracy.

Philip told Bert how often he had to walk through bad neighborhoods to reach various social service agencies in the Bronx. "Before, I would have been really scared," Philip said, lying in bed, looking up at the ceiling. "Now I don't think twice about it." He threw his Spalding ball up and down, threw it, caught it, threw it, caught it. "On Turtle Island, all the neighborhoods are good."

What would it be like if Philip got well? What would that be like? "You've got to understand, your brother has a chronic condition and will never get better," the psychiatrist told Bert. Bert was furious. It was all right for him to despair about his brother's prognosis, but a psychiatrist had to have hope.

When Lee-Anne Is Eighteen, Part One

When Lee-Anne is 18
all sealy ships go past
        the front wheel drive of my love

nor my loves depression
        shall have access to
        this nowhere near virgin

all together two words now:
        and under my underware —
in those olden times —
when I was despondent

Lay Down Sally (Junior Mints)
Shes got Hendrix trains in Blue
Bobby simmers (Gale Force Winds)
I got comics: dice leagues too

Philip's social worker said a state medical examiner had to sign a certain form before she could. The examiner said the social worker had to sign first. Finally, by chance, Evie met them both, at the same time, walking through the Bronx County Courthouse. (She was delivering some papers she had typed to make extra money to pay for Philip's psychiatrist.) Evie shouted, collared them both, and forced them to sign the document simultaneously, so that neither could object. This was synchronism indeed. Or serendipity. Or something. "That's how the *I*

Ching works," Philip told Bert. "Things are always connecting, working themselves out on different levels, at the same time."

Philip kept Bert awake nights with his masturbation. It was fine with Bert if Philip wanted to masturbate, but why when Bert was trying to sleep? Just as Bert was beginning to nod off, he'd hear a noise, the rustling of sheets, a few murmured words — and then he'd be wide awake. He didn't like being confronted with Philip's sex drive, didn't like that the sex instinct, throbbing like the stalwart heart of a Mongol warrior, or coiling energetically like a snake, overpowered mental illness, marijuana, indolence, poverty, despair. Sex broke through Philip's insanity, but sanity itself couldn't break through — which meant sex was stronger than sanity. Or was sexual hunger itself a kind of disease? Bert remembered his own ardor for Patrick and Diana. The next time, Bert swore, his partner would have to come to him. The next time his partner would be addled first.

Philip talked to himself. Walking down the street, he'd enter into impassioned conversations with imaginary companions and smack his hands together angrily. His face would contort into a grotesque snarl. Or he'd laugh to himself and smile broadly when the fantasy was good. The sheer *annoyance* of Philip. Because few could be so annoying as a schizophrenic. Bert came home from school to find his microeconomics textbook gone. "God told me to throw it out," Philip said. "God doesn't like capitalism." True, probably, Bert thought, but it was a thirty-dollar book. God also told Philip to throw out all the plants in the house, the toilet plunger, and Bert's Nikon camera. Dylan albums were savored or thrown out, then bought and savored and thrown out all over again.

When Lee-Anne Is Eighteen, Part Two

I'm getting a little tired of having to say
Due on the horizon
One look at me and then she's free
die-hard lotion

You don't need maps
to know thats
Lee-Anne's Subtle Stare
(and) Lee-Anne's lazy pair

Somewhere in this fabled fan
dig this mystyfying horror —
and all those once-and-for-all-wise Mayans

When Lee-Anne is 18, man
there is no excuse for
she hurries when shes cryin'

With the masturbation, with the fights over taking medication, with the wild conversations, with the crazy poetry Bert found all over the room on scraps of paper — Bert was tense all the time. To relax, he watched *Taxi* reruns. Every night at eleven, Philip, Bert, and Joseph gathered in front of the television set (Evie was usually in bed already) for *Taxi,* the one sure moment of respite in Bert's day.

"It must be so hard for you," Philip told him.

"I don't know what you mean."

"It must be so hard for you to have a brother who's mentally ill."

Redhead Blues

▾▾▾

DURING BERT'S SECOND TERM at business school, there was a good-looking student in his marketing class, Derek Potts, with smooth, fair skin and a tangle of dark hair, a thin, sharp nose, and a playful mouth that always seemed to be smiling at some private irony. Sometimes Bert would sit at the opposite side of the U-shaped classroom, just to get a better look at him. It was a while before they became friends.

Derek's father owned a small mineral-processing company with headquarters in St. Louis and had sent him to São Paolo for a year after college to work in the firm's office there. Derek spoke fluent Brazilian Portuguese. He said he missed St. Louis when he was in São Paolo, and he still missed it now that he was in New York. But New York was an "inneresting" city, he acknowledged. He always dropped the first "t" but pronounced all four syllables very distinctly.

He had gone to Catholic school through twelfth grade and then lived at home his first two years at Washington University. Derek said São Paolo had opened his eyes quite a bit, and New York was opening them even more.

Lisa knew about Derek right away, before Bert even knew. She pouted. "You like him more than you like me."

"What are you talking about? I hardly even know him."

Bert and Derek exchanged compact discs (Bert had finally made the plunge and bought a CD player, at Derek's urging), clipped articles for each other from newspapers and magazines (they were both magazine addicts), and went to an abortion rally together (Derek confided that he'd gotten a girl pregnant once, and he told Bert how scared he'd been that she'd wanted to keep the child).

Bert liked looking at Derek, at his long nose that was out of proportion to his other, more delicate features but that prevented his face from seeming too pretty, at his incredible skin, and at his thick, dark, almost blue-black hair.

Lisa felt left out. They went to a movie together on a Saturday night, and she asked him, "So, did Derek cancel on you tonight?"

"Of course not." But the sour truth was, he had. Bert's elbow was resting next to Lisa's on the armrest in the movie theater, and before the lights went out he looked down and saw the fine brown hairs on her brown skin and suddenly realized that every part of her, every single part, had hair on it. It gave him the willies.

Kathleen had a party at the beginning of March. Bert knew he had to go, but he was dreading it. He asked Lisa to go with him. "But I'm so fat," Lisa complained. "I have to get in shape for a party."

"You look great." She did.

"Just tell me. Am I going to be the only black there?"

"Of course not," Bert assured her. "There'll be two."

Actually, Barbara was the only one he really looked forward to seeing. He'd studiously avoided Kathleen, Patrick, and Diana. He missed Harry, but Harry was still in India; he'd joined one of the communist parties there and sent Bert postcards excoriating the ruling class or extolling the sexual prowess of Indian men.

Kathleen was happy to see him, kissed him immediately, and shook Lisa's hand warmly. Lisa saw the Romare Bearden poster on the wall, and the two women started talking about the artist. Bert made his way past the white furniture to the heavily spiked punch and took a big glass.

"Hello, sailor." It was Diana. She'd gained back some of the weight she had lost, Bert noticed.

"Hi." Bert waved shyly to her husband, Rob, across the room.

"Kathleen said you were coming, but I didn't believe her. Who's your date?"

"Her name's Lisa."

"She's cute." Then she told him she was four months pregnant. He wanted to ask who the father was, but he managed to resist the temptation. "Things are great with Rob now," she said softly. "I guess that was just a rough patch we had to go through." She was going to stay at Bridges and Tunnels until she had the baby, then she would stay home for a year or two. She and Rob had found a house to buy. Bert talked to her about work, talked to her about business school, and then Diana joined her husband on the other side of the room.

Patrick came to the party late, but he came up to Bert right away and gave him a big hug. "You don't answer my phone calls, you goof."

"I've just been real busy."

Patrick said he wasn't dating anyone, but he looked relaxed and happy. He'd started working out at a gym; his neck and arms and chest now fit his broad shoulders. "I'm a little obsessive about it," Patrick admitted. "But I guess if you have to be obsessive about something, it might as well be exercise." Later Patrick said Lisa seemed very nice.

Barbara and Lisa were talking and sipping punch when Bert joined them. "They say Jews like money, they say Scottish people like money," Barbara remarked. "You know who likes money? Black people like money, that's right. They say the Irish like to drink. You know who likes to drink? Black people like to drink." Barbara had been drinking a little herself. "They say Italians like to eat. You know who likes to eat?"

"Let me guess," Bert broke in.

"Black people like to eat," Barbara concluded.

Before he left the party, Kathleen asked him if he was dating Lisa. "Yeah," Bert told her, "I am." It just seemed much easier all around.

"I think she's great, Bert." Kathleen was such a sweet girl, such a sweet, dull girl.

*

Eisenberg handed Bert a portfolio and told him there was a sheet in it listing the addresses and phone numbers of London hotels. He wanted all the information entered into his computer. Bert typed the entire list, put the original back in the portfolio, and then showed a hard copy to Eisenberg. Bert was trying to play a game, Eisenberg said. He went through the portfolio, pulled out a list of hotels, and indeed it was a different list from the one Bert had typed. Bert shuffled quickly through all the papers, looking for the list he had copied, but he couldn't find it.

"You see?" Eisenberg told him. "You made it up. A silly joke. Strange boy."

Bert shuffled again and again through the papers.

"I think you're a little crazy, Mr. Rosenboym. A little bit nuts in the head."

"I don't think so, Mr. Eisenberg." Bert tried to control his temper. He hated when Eisenberg said he was crazy. He kept searching for the original paper. Finally Bert found the list he had typed from. It turned out that there were two separate lists in the portfolio.

"I wanted the other one," Eisenberg told him sharply.

"Sorry."

Whatever Bert typed, Eisenberg found fault with it. "Are you in luff?" Eisenberg asked him. "Have you found a girl to luff? Your head is spinning. I know that feeling, oh yes, Mr. Rosenboym."

Eisenberg's daughter was staying in the apartment over her spring break. So was her boyfriend. Bert did all his work at the dining room table. "Dat boy's a munster," Eisenberg told Bert. "No job, no edoocation, nothink." His accent got worse when he was upset. "She should find zomeone like you, a nice Jewish boy like you, who could luff her."

Derek and Bert would go walking through Central Park whenever the snow melted, looking at the rock formations. Derek knew a lot about geology, his father had taught him. He said he wanted to go skiing with Bert for a weekend; they needed to get away from New York.

Bert and Lisa were having lunch together in the dreary Uris Hall cafeteria, sharing a sandwich, when Bert told her about the weekend plans. "You know, there's a little problem," Lisa said.

"Yeah?"

"He's straight."

"I don't know," Bert said. "I think he's interested in me." He smiled to himself. "Innerested."

"Bert, he's not interested."

"How do you know? People change."

She shook her head and took a bite of her sandwich.

When he got home, Dr. Ruth was on the radio, promising to answer anyone's questions about orgasms. Philip dared him to call her up and ask when he'd have his next one.

"We're going to have so much fun when we go skiing," Derek said. "It's going to be a blast."

"We never have enough time to talk," Derek said. "I just want to sit down and really have a heart-to-heart."

"You're my best friend," Derek said, and Bert's heart skipped a beat.

"Don't say that," Bert cautioned him.

"Why not? In St. Louis it's not generally perceived as an insult. In New York, I guess you never know."

"It makes me nervous. Never mind."

On Saint Patrick's Day, Bert and Derek went out for a drink at the West End, across from Columbia, and listened to a band play Van Morrison covers. Derek was wearing a dyed green carnation through one of the buttonholes in his green shirt. A waitress came up to them and took their orders. "Sure, and I'm sorry for everyone that's not Irish. But God bless those that are, present company included," she said, looking at Bert, and speaking with a soft Irish lilt. "Red hair is a great miracle, a sign from God to let us know we're in the presence of one of His chosen, a true Irishman."

"Begorra," Bert replied.

Derek's mother was Irish, and he said she always threw a party on St. Patrick's Day and got drunk. She was very religious — she went to Mass every day, Derek told him — but the lady liked to drink.

"Confession must be great," Bert said. "I mean, to have everything forgiven, just like that."

"I hated it," Derek said. "I used to make up things to confess, much worse than the things I actually did." He grinned into his beer. "I was a strange kid."

Outside the bar, an old man folding green balloons into animals offered Bert and Derek a giraffe and then a dachshund, each for a buck. "Go ahead," Derek urged. "Buy one." Bert finally decided to buy the dachshund for Lars and Isabel. "I think you overpaid," Derek teased him, squeezing Bert's arm. He wasn't imagining it, Bert told himself. Derek was always touching him. But he would wait, Bert thought, he would wait for Derek to come to him. This time he would get it right. He wouldn't be greedy. But oh, it would be nice to be greedy again. He felt an old, familiar longing and hollowness in his throat and chest.

Ribsy wouldn't stop drinking. Yes, Ribsy said, malchick was an alcoholic. Yes, Ribsy admitted, the drugs would probably kill malchick. Yes, malchick was disintegrating. No, Ribsy insisted, malchick wouldn't stop.

Malchick told Bert a story: "There was a very rich man who couldn't stop drinking. He lived in a beautiful house, and one day he was drinking his expensive brandy, and he went over to his cupboard to look at his silverware. And he said to himself, Well, if I'm ever down on my luck, I can always sell the silverware. And then he thinks, Oh my God! Listen to me! I must be an alcoholic. And he goes to an AA meeting.

"Then there was a man who had lost everything. He was living on the street, lying in a doorway in the rain, drinking cheap wine. But he still had a nice pair of warm boots. And the man says to himself, Well, I've still got a pair of nice boots. I can't be an alcoholic." Ribsy was smoking some crack. "Guess which one I am."

Bert took the subway downtown from Columbia and got out at Times Square to switch to the N train. Walking through the tunnel to the BMT, Bert saw a faded Keith Haring chalk drawing of cupid, left over from Valentine's Day, and then passed a large, bulky homeless woman, in rotting clothes and high-heeled shoes, dozing on a blanket smeared with mud (or worse), leaning back against the wall of the tunnel. He stopped short, looked again, and realized it was Jane Alley. He inched closer to get a better look. She'd aged a good deal in the past seven months. Her skin was an unhealthy, pasty color, and flaking; the mustache over her upper lip was thicker; coarse hair was growing out of her chin. He moved closer still, took out a dollar bill, and was about to put it in the little tin cup she was holding in her hands. Then he reconsidered, put the dollar back in his wallet, took out a five instead, and pushed it down into the can so no one would see it and steal it while she slept. She woke and looked at him through eyes covered by mucus. The effect was like that of a large cat's half-closed nictitating membrane. She didn't seem to know him. Then Bert thought he saw a glimmer of recognition register on her cloudy pupils. Then the glimmer faded too.

It snowed again at the end of March, and Derek said it was probably their last chance to go skiing. They rented a car so they could drive up to Vermont. Derek had bought some new ski clothes (he loved to shop for clothes) and the car was packed tight, even though they were going away for only a weekend.

They left on a Friday morning. During the car ride up, Bert told Derek he was gay. He thought Derek knew, but he wanted to get it out into the open. It was one of the first times he had ever called himself gay without qualifying the description in any way — a gay man who sometimes liked women, a gay man who occasionally liked women, whatever. His legs trembled slightly, so he knew he must be nervous. Derek took the news calmly and told him his roommate in college had been gay. They got to the ski lodge by nightfall. They put their bags in the semidetached cabin they were renting, then went over to the ski lodge to eat dinner. The lodge was crowded and they ended up sharing a table with two young women from Brussels, one a short, sly, sloe-eyed brunette smoking a cigarette, with a gap between her two front teeth, the other a slim redhead who liked strong coffee. Bert and Derek sat next to each other, but because Bert was left-handed and Derek was right-handed, their elbows kept bumping. The Belgian women were amused. Derek hit it off right away with Simone, the prettier of the two women and the redhead. They arranged to meet on the slopes in the morning.

Derek and Bert stayed up late drinking Molsons and arguing about music. Bert was in an argumentative mood. Derek touched Bert's shoulder or knee whenever he wanted to make a point. So now Derek knew he was gay and was touching him anyway, Bert thought to himself. He considered it a good sign. He wanted to touch Derek too, but he didn't know how to do it naturally. And he still wanted Derek to make the first move.

They met the Belgian women in the morning and went skiing together. Bert wasn't a great skier, but he wasn't bad either. He'd skied in college with one of his roommates. Derek was just a beginner, and Bert was supposed to give him lessons — Bert was looking forward to it, actually — but somehow Simone took over. Derek and Simone spent most of the day together, disappearing periodically into the lodge. Sometimes Bert skied with the other Belgian, sometimes he skied alone. They all had dinner together, and then Derek and Simone disappeared again. Bert went back to his cabin. The couple in the cabin next door was having sex. Bert could hear them through the walls. He'd met the couple briefly — two social studies teachers from Greenwood Lake, in New York. The bed creaked, back and forth, occasionally slamming into the wall that separated the two cabins. The creaking continued for a long time, and the man kept moaning, but the woman made no noise at all. Finally the man stopped moaning and the bed stopped creaking.

Derek came back about two in the morning. Bert was surprised to see him at all. "Sorry about that, Bert." Derek patted Bert manfully on the back.

"You like redheads." Bert hazarded a guess.

"Yeah." Derek smiled. He seemed embarrassed. "I guess I do. She's inneresting."

They skied with the Belgians again on Sunday, then they all exchanged addresses and telephone numbers, and then Bert and Derek started the long drive back to New York. "I never get bored when I'm with you," Derek told Bert. "You're such good company." He squeezed Bert's thigh and said they'd have to go away for a weekend again, it was nice getting out of the city.

Vertigo had finally been released on videocassette, and Ezekiel Eisenberg watched the tape over and over again. "Oy, is this sick," Eisenberg muttered each time. "Oy, this part's even sicker. Bert, come watch this part. It's so sick." Bert still hadn't bought a VCR. Eisenberg's was the first he'd ever used. When Eisenberg went on a tour of the United States and Europe, lecturing about the evils of exploiting the Holocaust for commercial gain, Bert would stop by the apartment, let himself in with the key Eisenberg had given him, and watch a movie or two. Eisenberg said it was okay with him. "I'm paying enough rent on this place. Somebody should enjoy it." His daughter was back in school and had started dating someone new. He was Jewish, so Eisenberg was relieved.

"*A sach kinder, a sach tsurris,*" he told Bert. "Do you know what that means?"

"Yes."

"It means, 'Many children, many troubles.' "

His wife and his son were coming back to New York for Passover. Eisenberg could hardly restrain his excitement. He made his black housekeeper, Martina, dust and vacuum the apartment every day — all the books, all the objets d'art, all the furniture. He even made her vacuum the cat. His son had developed asthma, and Eisenberg worried that cat hair would bother him. "He's losing his Polish. I'll have to learn Italian," Eisenberg told Bert, but somehow he seemed pleased that the boy was forgetting the language.

Bert had read that Eisenberg was about to publish another novel in France, and he congratulated the writer. "I don't have another novel," Eisenberg lied. He could be quite cagey sometimes, not admitting to anything unless he absolutely had to. "What makes you say that? Where did you read that?"

He gave Bert another article to type on the computer and heaped abuse on Bert's word processing abilities. "So many typos I have to correct, so many! You're a terrible typist. I don't know why I pay you."

"One typo," Bert countered. "In a twenty-page article, I made one typo."

"That's one too many."

"It happens. I'm sorry."

"I thought there was a spelling program on the computer."

"There is. It didn't catch it."

"You didn't use it, did you. You forgot to use it, didn't you. You're in luff, aren't you."

"I used it," Bert insisted. He had misspelled "goal" as "gaol." The computer recognized "gaol" as a word, and so it hadn't caught the error.

"You're a little crazy in luff, aren't you." Eisenberg smiled to himself. "It happens to the best of us. Even Jews."

Bert complained to Herbert and Evelyn about Eisenberg. Ribsy wasn't around — malchick was probably getting drunk somewhere. "He says I'm a lousy typist."

"Nonsense," Evelyn said. "You're an excellent typist."

"It's weird. In a month, I'm going to be twenty-four. But here I am, typing to make some extra cash, just like when I was a kid."

"When Bruce Springsteen was twenty-four," Herbert reminded him, "he recorded *Born to Run.*"

Bert said, "Why don't you just drive a stake through my heart."

You couldn't exactly say that Bert applied himself at business school. Most days he cut class early and ran over to the journalism school, where one of the TV sets was hooked up to get cable, so he could watch *Leave It to Beaver* reruns on TBS. But now Bert studied five or six hours a day for his statistics final. He even began dreaming about statistics. He dreamed he was running to his statistics exam, and he looked everywhere for the room, but he couldn't find it. He looked in every hallway, his feet sprinting soundlessly. He climbed stairs till he was exhausted. The minutes ticked away, the test had already started, Bert had broken into a sweat, but no matter how hard he tried, he couldn't find the exam room.

The actual class, though, and the final, were easier the second time around, but the math still gave him trouble. He emerged from the exam shaking. He thought he had passed. The next day, he walked up the stairs to the second floor of Uris Hall, where the school posted examination grades by Social Security number. He found his number and he looked in the next column to find his grade. H.

H meant Honors.

He felt happy, insanely happy. He hated business school, he hated tests, he hated statistics, he didn't believe in grades (for that matter, he didn't believe in capitalism), so why should a stupid test score give him so much pleasure? And yet it did.

Bert's father hated math as much as Bert did. If any math problem was put before Joseph to solve, his whole body would tense; a look of pain would flit over his face; then suddenly he'd burst out with the words "inverse proportion!" and wrestle with the problem till he had it in the form of a ratio, whether that was the way to solve it or not.

*

Derek liked going to comedy clubs. One Friday night they went down to Caroline's at the South Street Seaport to see a comic from St. Louis whom Derek knew slightly. Bert had lived in New York his whole life, but he'd never been to the Seaport. Thousands of M.B.A.s in yellow power ties gathered on the plaza, drinking beers, shouting as they were pushed together by the crowd, shouting again as they were pulled apart, looking to Bert like nothing so much as a heaving sea.

"That's going to be us in another nine months," Derek told him.

"Uch."

They went inside Caroline's and watched a few comics perform. Their elbows banged into each other as they drank a couple of beers. Derek's leg brushed against Bert's leg under the table. Bert wasn't sure Derek knew what he was doing—but maybe he did.

"I think he's teasing me."

"You sound happy about it." Lisa blew on her tea to cool it down.

Actually, Bert was. Derek's teasing seemed to him like a kind of flirtation, a kind of foreplay.

"I don't think he's teasing you," Lisa went on. "I think he just gets off on attention. That's what I don't like about him."

"Why does he bother you so much?"

"I don't know, he just does." Lisa, chary, took a small sip of the hot tea. "He's taking advantage of you. For God's sake, date somebody else. It'll take your mind off him."

"Well, there's this girl in my finance class who's pretty cute. Rochelle. She's married, though."

Lisa had started dating Roger, a tall, thin, plain, but amiable black student in the school, so Bert felt more comfortable talking to her about his crushes. Although only in his second term, Roger was already vice president of the Black Business Students Organization, vice president of the Marketing Club, and treasurer of the Class Council. He was regarded as highly dependable but slightly geeky by most of the black students, Lisa told Bert, and Bert did find him overly earnest and ridiculously filled with school spirit; but he was kind to Lisa and never seemed threatened by her friendship with Bert, so Bert liked him. Besides, he'd grown up in the Bronx and hated George Steinbrenner. Bert was prepared to make allowances.

"You know, if you go after married women and straight men," Lisa told him, "that's a good way to keep yourself alone."

"Blah blah blah," Bert said.

"What is it, Bert? You want to punish yourself? You think since your brother's not happy, you don't deserve to be happy either?"

"Thank you, Dr. Freud, for that brilliant capsule summary of my entire personality."

"I once saw a movie about Freud, and I guess he wrote someone a letter about, quote, 'the greater independence that comes from having overcome my homosexuality.' "

"Overcome *this,* Siggy." Bert grabbed his crotch.

"Oh, that's lovely, Bert."

Bert did an imitation of the murderer in Alfred Hitchcock's *Frenzy,* contorting his face and crying out in a strangled voice, "Love-ly. Love-ly. Love-ly." Lisa looked at him quizzically. "It's spring," Bert explained. "My sap's rising."

"You know, you're getting crazier and crazier." Horrified by what she had said, Lisa put down her cup of tea and put her hand over her mouth. "I didn't mean that. You know I didn't mean that."

Bert was amused. "It's okay. I think you're right."

I'll Be Your Mirror

▾▾▾

When Philip masturbated at night, keeping Bert awake, Bert felt ashamed for getting angry. He thought he had no right to deny Philip pleasure. How could Bert complain about the one activity that undoubtedly gave Philip satisfaction? But some nights were very bad. The sheets rustled, Philip muttered loudly, it was uncomfortable to be in the same room with him. Bert was embarrassed. He wished Philip would do it privately, in the bathroom, away. Philip's public masturbation seemed to indict Bert, made him feel guilty for ever having a relationship or ever wanting one, when his brother was always alone.

"You're keeping me up, Phil," Bert said one night.

"I'm writing poems."

"Can't you do that in the morning?"

"It's more real at night," Philip told him. "The poems are more real."

"Just be quiet, Phil." Bert was exhausted. "Be quiet about it."

"I'm so tired," Bert told Derek the next morning. "I'm always so tired."

"You know, people can get psychotic from sleep deprivation," Derek said.

"People can get psychotic without it, too," Bert rejoined.

Their room was a mess. Philip strewed his things about, and Bert and Evie both lacked the energy to pick up after him. In fact, Philip had so consistently overwhelmed Bert's attempts to maintain some semblance of order that Bert had finally given in and thrown his things around pell-mell, too. Sometimes Bert would look at the jumble on the floor and be reminded of the shredded litter at the bottom of a parakeet cage.

Bert still found Philip's poems scattered around the disarray of the room or in the nearly empty, tin wastepaper pail, the one that featured a picture of Charlie Brown, to whose mouth Philip had attached, with Magic Marker, a word balloon proclaiming "Suck my dick, Snoopy." The poems were written on scraps of paper covered with complicated multiplication and long division problems. Underneath them and, if he ran out of room, along the margins and then around to the top, Philip wrote his crazy quilt of poetry.

T.K.O.

She can make your
  sensitive knees
Just like the Bees
  all go for honey.

She went out and
  Found herself a man.
Well I thought that
  that's just not right.

And I knew her right away
so —
  I said —
"No technical knockouts
  till the third round."

Oh oh,
  etc. etc. OOOOHH.

Evie made a cake for Bert's birthday and put twenty-five candles on it (one for good luck), and Bert blew them all out and made a wish: for Philip to get well.

"We should have asked Lisa to come," Evie decided.

"So, uh, are you and Lisa going out?" Joseph asked, cutting himself a nice-sized slice of cake. "Dating, I mean?"

"No. We're just friends."

"I've never had a girlfriend," Philip announced. "I'm twenty-six years old, and I've never had a girlfriend."

"Well, maybe you will soon," Bert said hopelessly.

"On Turtle Island, I've got a girlfriend."

"Where's Turtle Island?" Joseph asked his son. "Where is that, Phil?" Evie and Bert looked at each other. Once again, Joseph was trying to find logic in one of Philip's delusions.

"You take the lost highway all the way to the end," Philip directed. "You make a right at Medgar Evers Stadium, a left at the Ho Chi Minh Masonic Temple, and then you're right there."

Breasts

Got to have em
need em every day
wish I was one
nearly all the way

See em bobbin'
in da wind
sorta suckin'
unner dem

Make two big ones
if you dare
total justice
she beware

"I can make this room turn just by the force of my mind," Philip told Bert. "I can make space bend. I believe in eternal life, I know it can be done. Bob Dylan knows about me, don't you know that?"

"I know you think he does, but I think you're mistaken," Bert responded carefully.

"He knows who I am. He's a Zen master. A Zen master can bend time and space. He has lost his ego. He's not stuck. He defeats the Empire of cause and effect. It's important for you to know this. God told me it's important for me to tell you."

His parents argued, quietly, about Philip. His mother insisted that they begin legal proceedings to get him committed. His father said they should wait. Maybe Philip would improve spontaneously. It didn't seem likely to Bert. Philip talked all the time about unchaining himself from his ego, escaping from his ego, and taking flight. Brother, Bert thought, you've already escaped.

"If you looked at each individual thing, let's say under a microscope, you'd see it's composed of thousands of identical things, but smaller." Philip had been smoking a lot of pot. "And each of those things can be broken down in a thousand bits, and each of those bits would be identical, too, but smaller. I can look at this magazine and know that the word "premature" occurs four times and the word "water" seven times. Bob Dylan knows who I am. Bob Dylan loves me. Bob Dylan's my best friend. Some problems don't have answers. Inside each problem you'd find another problem, exactly identical to the first problem, but smaller, inside it. It's like that with space too. Everything around us can be folded up, folded into a ball, or into a circle. But you don't get anywhere. That's why a circle's the saddest shape. Tomorrow we'll have pot roast and peas for dinner. I know this for a fact."

Mentally Phil

Therapy is such a thrill
especially with Phil
Just sixty-five bucks a session
and my mind learns the days lesson

I told him a dream I had
I had it on Saturday knight
It made me really sad

But Phil made me feel almost right:
Said, "I want to hear one from tonight."

My medication is running low
I just got to contemplate prescription
Or else I'd suffer infinitygo —
and that is sure not a cool condition

Hey kids, I want you to know
(having been there sold-out show)
Ontogony recapitulates Philogony
Dizzy Dean could conduct pytchofyfotherapy

Phil, of course, was both the patient's name, and the psychiatrist's. Bert could trace the progress of Philip's disease through the poems, which became progressively more incoherent, filled with the arcane language Philip was developing and the secret fantasy life he still harbored.

One day Bert was lying in bed, reading one of his textbooks. He sat up, and Philip sat up too. Bert stood up, and then Philip stood up. Bert yawned, and Philip mimicked his yawn. Bert stretched and Philip stretched. Bert turned toward Philip. Philip turned toward Bert. Bert took a step closer. Philip took a step closer. Bert was grinning by now, and Philip matched his grin. Bert tugged at his ears. Philip tugged at his ears. Bert opened his mouth and hooted like an Indian. Philip did the same thing. Bert stopped hooting suddenly. Philip stopped hooting at the same moment. Bert did a little Indian dance, turning round and round, chanting "Ai-ai-ai-ai." Philip danced and chanted in perfect unison.

"Like Harpo and Groucho," Bert said.

"Like Harpo and Groucho," Philip repeated, doubling Bert as best he could. Finally he released Bert from the exercise. "We look alike," he told his brother.

"Yeah, we do."

"Except I wear glasses."

"And you're hairier," Bert told him. He knew Philip was very proud of his chest hair.

"Yeah," Philip said happily, rubbing his chest. "I am."

Silent Thighs

Student Nurses
in a row
at Larrys Bakery

Just the way she
took the ticket
I knew shed go out with me

So why do I feel so lousy?
I even know what
I am Gonnaram wear
Re-entry wharf rat
is utterly unclear.

The Rosenbaums and the psychiatrist began urging Philip to check himself into a hospital. Philip still refused. Every day was an adventure. One day Bert came home to find that Philip had thrown out his new glasses. "Uncle Buddy told me not to wear glasses," Philip said.

"But Uncle Buddy is dead," Bert said.

"Before he died. He told me."

Philip was convinced he could improve his eyesight if he stopped wearing his glasses. Maybe so, Bert thought, but in the meantime Philip was bumping into walls.

Then Philip began insisting that various people owed him money. Juan Carlos, from their Bronx Science days, owed him money, he claimed. "He promised to give me twenty thousand dollars," Philip said. Their neighbor Nina owed him money (and he asked her for it, too). Evie's mother owed him money, Philip told them.

"I'm keeping Grandma and Grandpa alive. That's why they should give me money." Philip was truly convinced he was keeping them alive. He wanted fifty thousand dollars from them in payment for his services.

"But Philip, even if what you said made sense, they just don't have that kind of money," Evie told him.

"They have so much money. You have no idea how much

money they have," Philip said angrily. "They're rich. They have three hundred thousand dollars and twenty-four cents."

Occasionally Philip would venture to Manhattan without enough money to return home. Bert would have to take a subway to Manhattan just to give Philip a token. Philip would call collect from Manhattan. "You mean you don't even have twenty cents?" Bert demanded once over the phone. "You have to call collect for a local call?"

"I didn't have any money."

"But you must have known you'd have to get back, honey," his mother said on the extension.

"Don't call me honey. Call me Philip. I object to your hypocorism."

So Bert went downtown to give him the token (first looking up "hypocorism" in the dictionary, to see if it was a real word). All the way downtown just to give him a token. . . . When Bert was low on cash, Philip advised him: "Budget your money better."

Philip put a personal ad on the back page of the *Village Voice,* asking for the whereabouts of two friends he had made when he'd stayed at Mount Sinai Hospital six years earlier. The ad quoted a line from Bob Dylan, and the Rosenbaums received hundreds of calls from Dylan fans but none from the friends Philip was trying to contact.

Bob Dylan, incidentally, owed Philip money as well.

"He hurt me, he hurt me so much," Philip told them. "He promised to give me money and he didn't."

"When, when did he promise?" Joseph wanted to know.

"At a concert."

Philip continued to lose interest in the things around him, retreating to the secret world inside his head. The fights grew more strident over his medication. He went for weeks at a time without taking it. He stopped combing or brushing his hair. It grew long and greasy and unkempt. He refused to get it cut because Dylan wore his hair long. Philip said it was more masculine to wear his hair long. He was bored, he said. Some days he spent entirely in bed. He grew so depressed he couldn't eat. He lost weight, becoming very thin.

"Do you know why you're depressed?" Bert asked.

"The loneliness, I guess," Philip replied simply.

Philip began drawing up Topps-style baseball cards for imaginary players and imaginary teams.

579. Brad Riley Tatum Dover Brown Metucheon

B: August 3, 1964 BRTL
Height 6′1⅜″ Weight 179
Drafted: Oct 18, 1983 (Please!!)
Acq: Trade Nov 30 1983 Home: Where He Lives

COMPLETE MINOR LEAGUE RECORD

YR	CLUB	G	AB	H	AVG.
1980	Albany Bios	113	387		
1981	Stony Brook Psychs	127		203	
1982	Plattsburgh Tigers	133	533	232	.440
1983	Canoga Park Moons	141	561	257	.460

Hit for the Cycle May 2 and Sept 2, 1981 vs. Potsdam Eggrolls
Hit 4 homers in game May 23, 1982 vs. Purchase Furies
Hit 9 homers in Doubleheader vs. Binghamton Bings July 1, 1983 including 3 grand-slams
Knows Good Girls Make Good Women March 21, 1983

True or False: Lou Brock hit much better when he was 33–38 years old than when he was 28–33 years old.

Philip was obsessed with being drafted. He claimed that the draft was still on and that he'd be forced to serve soon. Joseph tried reasoning with him. "Philip, even if there was a draft, you wouldn't have to serve because you've been ill."

"Oh yeah, that's right," Philip said. For a few days he felt safe.

Total Breakdown

Standard Fare
for the modern man
is something almost
taken for Grantheard

Last stop on the subway
Sundays almost here
Everybody knows
Simpsons Season
was better than mine

Ratiocination
albeit recalcitrant
Dont you ever get confused
(I'm so green with envy —
even down to my own shoes)

Socially replete
status what I seek
dog gone incomplete

Research data
is now on my mind
Get down funky
on da udder side

Philip became crafty, hiding his obsessions and fantasies and beliefs. "What are you laughing about?" Bert asked his brother after catching him cackling to himself.

"I'm laughing about the time I told you to let your balloon go, so it could keep my balloon company." Bert could tell Philip was lying, but he had to give him credit for some quick thinking.

"Are you having those bad thoughts again?" his mother would ask when he angrily banged his fist into his hand, lost in some violent reverie.

"No, no. I'm not, really. I'm just thinking about how Ronald Reagan screws poor people. It gets me mad."

Philip told them he had a son.

"A son? You don't mean that," Joseph said.

"Well, maybe not," Philip wavered.

"I need a woman," Philip told Bert. "I'm just so lonely."

"Remember the Tholian Web episode of *Star Trek*?" Philip asked him. "I feel like that."

"What do you mean?" In the Tholian Web episode, inter-spatial mental illness broke out on the *Enterprise,* while aliens surrounded and paralyzed the starship with a cone of energy.

"I'm being wrapped up. And I can't get out." Philip said this with great resignation.

Degrees of Freedom

▾▾▾

RIBSY LOOKED TERRIBLE. Thin. Drawn. Wasted. Malchick was wasting away. "His malchick-mother killed malchick-self, you know," Evelyn confided. "It's very unusual. Malchicks are by far the most stable gender, emotionally. You should see our malchick-child. Like a rock. It's tearing me up inside to see Ribsy like this." She blinked away tears. "You don't know how hard Harold's taken it. He hides it, but I can tell."

Bert went for a walk with Ribsy down Broadway. Ribsy had binged on cocaine the night before and then had drunk gin and tonics to bring malchick-self down. Teetering a bit, malchick had to hold on to Bert for support. They caught sight of their reflections in the window of a camera shop. Ribsy stopped for a moment to study malchick's image in the window. Ribsy was astonished by the yellow of malchick's eyes and the bags under them.

"I didn't know I looked so bad. I'll be dead in two weeks," malchick said flatly. They walked a few steps more. Ribsy stopped again. "I don't know if I even have the strength to fight."

"Fight," Bert said.

They spent much of June together, buying the new Springsteen album as soon as it came out, seeing *Purple Rain* on opening night, going to Yankees games or to Mets games if the Mets were playing St. Louis (Bert liked Gooden, Derek liked Andujar), taking the same seminar in business ethics, campaigning joylessly for Mondale, shopping.

Derek insisted that Bert come with him to look for a pair of new shoes. They went to Columbus Avenue together, but Derek's narrow feet were hard to fit and he didn't buy anything. Bert ended up with an expensive pair of black leather lace-ups made by a company called To Boot.

"You know, you've got really good taste." Derek stood back and admired Bert in the shoes.

"You mean I like the same things you do."

Derek laughed at himself. "That's inneresting."

They went into another clothing store on Columbus, and Bert tried on a pair of slacks. "I think they look good on you, Bert. Turn around," Derek directed. Bert turned around. "Oh yeah, they look great. Get 'em."

Bert went back into the changing room to take off the pants.

"Do you wear boxers or Jockeys?" Derek called to him from the other side of the curtain.

Another good sign, Bert thought. "Jockeys," Bert said.

"I wear boxers," Derek said.

Bert decided to buy a pair of boxer shorts along with the jeans. Upon Derek's urging, he ended up buying a forest green silk shirt as well. "Man, with that shirt, and those pants, and those shoes, you're going to be the best-looking guy in business school," Derek told him.

"I'm not even the best-looking overeducated gay Jewish socialist in business school."

"Hey, don't cut yourself down like that," Derek said. "I think you're good-looking." Bert smiled to himself.

Walking with Derek through Central Park on a hot summer day, Bert bumped into Tom Helmer, who was riding his bike and wearing a T-shirt covered with Neil Young concert dates. Bert introduced him to Derek — "Tom works with my mother" — then added, "So you like Neil Young, too."

"He's a genius," Tom said.

"How are your petitions going?"

"Don't ask," Tom replied, and began to laugh. As Tom laughed, his lips opened wide, and Bert caught sight of the pharmacist's discolored teeth. He wondered why imperfect teeth always bothered him so much.

Derek left to buy some ice cream from a vendor in the park and started flirting with a young woman buying a cone. Tom asked Bert what other music he liked — if he liked Bronski Beat, the Smiths, Malcolm McLaren's "Madam Butterfly"; asked what clubs he went to; asked if he'd seen *Rope* or *Rumble Fish,* or if he'd read Burroughs. Now both of them were laughing. They knew where the conversation was heading.

"Are you gay?" Tom finally asked.

"Mostly," Bert said, still laughing. "Sometimes I'm a little wobbly."

"Does your Mom know?"

"No. I haven't told my parents. Does my mother know about you?"

"No. But I was thinking, maybe we could go out together. Why don't you give me a call sometime."

Derek had returned with an ice cream sandwich in time to hear Tom ask Bert out.

"Sure," Bert said.

"Are you going to go out with him?" Derek asked after Tom had left. Maybe he was jealous, Bert hoped.

"I don't know," Bert told him. "Probably not." He remembered the old, overly quoted Groucho Marx line — that he never wanted to join a club that would have him for a member — and decided it was overly quoted because it was true. The very fact that Tom was interested in him made Tom less appealing in Bert's eyes.

"I think he's handsome," Derek said.

"He's okay," Bert said.

Bert called up Lars and Isabel to see if he could take them to *Pinocchio,* which Disney had rereleased. Luisa thanked him but said Lars wasn't feeling well, and anyway, she didn't think the children would be interested. Bert ended up going with Evelyn and Herbert.

Ribsy had confounded all their predictions, and some of Ribsy's own, by staying alive. Periodically, Ribsy would stop drinking or snorting coke, until malchick got strong enough to start binging all over again. Then, one day, Ribsy woke up in the gutter — literally, in the gutter — covered with vomit and dog piss, outside Poe Cottage on the Grand Concourse, in the Bronx. Ribsy had no memory of how malchick had even gotten there. It scared malchick. "That's it. I've hit rock bottom," Ribsy said, "and now there's no place to go but up."

Ribsy's recovery began. Abstinence was hard, incredibly hard, but little by little, Ribsy improved. Maybe the hypnotic tapes on the spaceship's Reich-Eisenstein console helped. Mostly, Bert thought, it was the AA meetings Ribsy was sneaking into. Ribsy credited malchick's recovery entirely to the Higher Power. Bert credited Ribsy's own willpower and the prodigious quantities of chocolate Ribsy was eating.

"On some sections of Enoch, chocolate is still illegal," Evelyn told him.

"They don't know what they're missing," Ribsy said, stuffing another bar of bittersweet chocolate with hazelnuts into malchick's face.

But Ribsy still *talked* about drugs so much. Malchick reminisced about polyscene with Bert. "Once I traveled back in time and saw the creation of the galaxy out of primordial fire and vapor. It was a gas." Bert and Ribsy laughed together. Tee hee hee.

"But you're not going to do polyscene anymore, are you?" Bert worried.

"No, that wouldn't be a good idea. But I miss it," Ribsy said. "I have to admit, I miss it. A glass of wine with dinner, a few tokes of grass when you're making love, half a hit of acid at a Grateful Dead concert — that's a lot to give up. But," malchick reminded malchick-self, "I have a world to win."

Eisenberg shook his head sadly. "She says she's in luff, but this boyfriend's even more of a munster than the last one."

"I thought you liked him more."

"I told you that because he was Jewish," Eisenberg said, "but now I think he's a psychopath. My daughter likes dangerous men. She likes them. She likes to be hurt. Even physically, I think."

"I'm sorry."

"It's none of your business, really."

Bert was typing the translation of Eisenberg's new novel, which had appeared miraculously on the typing table in his daughter's room. "Is this the one they just published in France?" Bert couldn't resist asking.

Eisenberg shrugged. "I don't keep up with these things. My agent handles it all for me." He began singing a Marlene Dietrich song. "*Ich bin von Kopf bis Fuss auf Liebe eingestellt . . .*" He turned to Bert. "A luff song, Bert, for my friend who's always in luff, and makes so many mistakes."

"Do you know 'Lili Marleen'? My dad keeps asking me to get him the words."

"Yes, I know the song." Eisenberg was cracking peanuts again. "The guards used to sing it at the camps. I don't want to sing it."

Derek wanted to go to a dog show at the Kingsbridge Armory in the Bronx. Bert thought he was kidding, but Derek kept asking about it, and they ended up going together. They walked up and down the rows of dogs, talking to the breeders, patting the friendlier animals, playing with the puppies. In the center of the armory, obedience trials were taking place. The Shetland sheepdogs always won, but to Bert they seemed like little fascist dogs, blindly following their masters. He admired the retrievers most, especially the handsome, friendly Labradors. They weren't the most obedient, but they had the best personalities. Derek had grown up with a springer spaniel, and he liked spaniels more. But they both agreed they hated cats. Derek said he didn't know if he could marry a woman who had a lot of cats.

"Derek, I've been wondering. How come you never talk about dating anyone?"

Derek shrugged. "I don't know. I haven't met any women who interest me lately."

After they left the armory, Bert showed Derek around his old neighborhood. It was awkward: he was sure Derek would want to see his apartment, but Philip was home, and he didn't want Derek to see Philip. Now that Bert was sharing a room with Philip, he had reverted to his old secrecy. Finally he told Derek about Philip's illness.

"Why did you wait this long to tell me?"

"I don't know. It's a little hard to talk about."

"I'm glad you told me," Derek said, putting an arm around Bert, like a boy consoling his kid brother after a costly fielding error. "Does Lisa know?"

"Yeah."

"You told her first." Derek was disappointed.

"Well, she's got a messed-up family anyway. Your family's too perfect."

"Oh yeah, perfect. Mom's a drunk, and Dad cheats on Mom."

With Ribsy's recovery proceeding nicely, Evelyn and Herbert returned to their own work. Herbert was writing a chapter about the homoerotics of grief in Hank Williams songs, and Evelyn was finishing up her monograph on American board games. Evelyn claimed that the games were actually sustained exercises in sadomasochism. She saw sadism in the sudden chaotic descents in Chutes and Ladders, the Rube-Goldberg-Meets-Franz-Kafka torture device of Mousetrap, the bodily mutilations of Operation, and the rent-gouging of the aptly titled Monopoly. On the other hand, she saw masochism in the various fetishes (Park Place, the triple word score in Scrabble), in the sense of oppression, suspense, and reversal, and most importantly, in the way a child's natural aggressive/sexual impulses and instincts were turned against the child's own self; so that children were taught to identify with the winner, even when (or more precisely, *because*) they were losers. Like the sadist, the child delighted in endless mechanical repetition, in his or her feelings of omnipotence. Like the masochist, the child playing a game entered into a contract, creating through his or her fantasy a private world with rigorous rules and no clemency.

"I'll never think of a Pop-o-Matic the same way again," said Bert, recalling the dice popper at the center of the Trouble game board.

Evelyn found this same sexual ambiguity in word games. Crossword puzzles, cryptograms, and the like, fought against an imaginary opponent (the creator of the puzzle, or the newspaper editor, or the published solution), or more precisely, fought against the self, combined elements of both sadism and masochism, and so were especially loved by a rainbow coalition of Jews, women, African-Americans, gays and lesbians, addicts, the disabled, Supreme Court justices, and pre-Batista Cuban businessmen.

Bert called up Lars and Isabel to challenge them to a game of Candyland. He wanted to see if Evelyn knew what she was talking about. But Luisa said that Lars had a doctor's appointment, and that Isabel was busy getting a slime mold ready for a science fair. She didn't think Bert could see them anytime soon. Bert asked if he could talk to them on the phone, but she said they were both out. Bert had the feeling she was lying, and it worried him.

Bert proofread everything he typed for Eisenberg a half dozen times so Eisenberg would have no reason to complain. Bert could tell that Eisenberg was stewing, waiting for an opportunity to yell at him. It was a little game they played. One day, Bert missed a mistake: he transposed the vowels in the word "dais."

"Did you go to a party last night? Did you get drunk and meet a girl and fall in luff? Is that why you make so many mistakes?"

"No."

"Maybe you're a little crazy, like my daughter."

"I don't appreciate your calling me crazy, Mr. Eisenberg."

"Very well, I'll stop," Eisenberg said, donning Persol sunglasses. "You're fired. Just leave the keys on your way out."

Bert knew he was going to have to say something to Derek. It was getting to be too much. He wished Harry were around because Harry would know what to do. Derek kept touching him, making eye contact, giving him little presents: a Cardinals mug, after he went home to St. Louis for Labor Day; a tape of superbly chosen, bad seventies music; a Partridge Family novel he picked up at a flea market. He talked about how good-looking men in their class were but insisted he was straight. Bert knew he should date other people, but he didn't want to. Derek interested (innerested) him more than anyone else. Certainly, no one else knew as much about seventies culture. Derek demonstrated the hustle for Bert, humming the song while he danced. He had a nice-sized basket in his faded jeans, Bert couldn't help noticing. "Van McCoy, avant-garde composer or idiot savant, you be the judge," Derek intoned.

"Hey, there's a gay film festival at the Bleecker," Bert told him. Maybe if Derek saw what gay men actually did with each other, he'd be inspired. "Do you want to go with me?"

"Sure," Derek said, "I'll go. But I'll have to get some new clothes. That's a tough audience."

Udder Despara

▾▾▾

SOMETIMES PHILIP would mutter to himself on nights when Bert was tired and frazzled, when he fell in and out of half sleep and was thinking the strange, disoriented thoughts characteristic of such stages of sleep. Then Bert would feel himself influenced by Philip's muttering. He imagined that Philip's distorted brain wave patterns were emanating from his head, surrounding him, enmeshing him. And he felt as though the waves were seeping into his own brain, so that his brain waves were beginning to synchronize with Philip's — so that Bert, in his disoriented half sleep, began to fear that he was thinking like Philip, trapped in his brother's psychosis.

Riding on a Sled with a Faggot Named Glen

Da da Dada Da
Riding on a sled
with a faggot named Glen

Eddie Murphy: I ate an
eggroll wif Arnol'
Suddenly (Dot Dot Dot)
sullenly

All the women: Submissively
like a doo (ooh) deee
Tayste me
Hayste me

*

Philip turned on the TV, then turned it off immediately, ten or fifteen times a day. He listened to the radio and searched for signals from homosexuals, from other planets, from Bob Dylan. The only thing that gave him any pleasure was music. Music could still thrill him. He paced back and forth through the apartment. He lied about taking his medication. He said he'd taken it when he hadn't. He pretended to swallow it and then spat it out. It wasn't that his behavior was so much better when he took his medication but that it was always terribly disturbed when he didn't. Later he became more open about not taking his medicine.

"Are you taking your pills?" his mother asked anxiously.

"God doesn't want me to," Philip replied. God didn't want him to do lots of things: clean up their room, get out of bed, take a shower, give up pot.

Phil asked them for money, promising them, "I'll never ask for another penny again."

He said he was thinking of going to Amsterdam, later Israel. He would stand silently in front of them, watching them, and then suddenly say, "I love you, Mom." Or, "I love you, Dad." Or, "I love you, Bert." He always spoke in a plaintive but flattened tone, sending chills up and down their spine. Meanwhile, the battles with bureaucrats continued: an unending stream of appointments with doctors and Social Security administrators.

Diros Sos Glare

Remiss a'kitten
Dos papos nylarera
Seeming dense two for
  only o virginaire

Sedgwick dependence
    Seymour and Clare
Simptoms repentance
    Diros sos Glare

Stupendous Reduction
Moon is Aware

I don't know
An' You Don't Care

Godawful Brought Silought
Kankakees aint square
Why Earpal Why ought
Bamambo sweat rare

Philip wasn't eating well, he wasn't sleeping much. He refused to see the psychiatrist any longer. He was nervous around the apartment. He picked up the phone quickly, listened to it for a moment, then put it back down. "They're tapping our phone line."

The whole family ate together in an Italian restaurant on Arthur Avenue for Joseph and Evie's anniversary in October. Supposedly the restaurant was owned by the Mob. The food was superb, but Philip was too ill to enjoy it. He rocked back and forth on his chair. He was depressed, he couldn't sit still, he couldn't eat. His eyes looked so full of pain — Bert had never seen so much pain in someone's eyes.

Bert suggested that Philip see the psychiatrist again. Philip was incensed. "I don't need a psychiatrist!" he shouted. "I don't need a doctor! I need a woman! I need a woman to suck my cock!"

There were titters throughout the restaurant. Bert remained very calm (though he did have a momentary vision of enraged Mafiosi gunning down his entire family). In a way, he much preferred Philip's anger. At least when he was enraged he didn't seem so lost in pain and despair.

"Just tell me one thing," Philip said tearfully. "Do I have a son named Trent? Just tell me." He really didn't know.

"No, Philip, you don't," Bert assured him. "Really."

They begged him to go to a hospital. He still refused. Evie wasn't sleeping well. Late at night, Bert would find her in the kitchen solving crossword puzzles. Joseph paced sadly up and down the living room. Bert listened to music, the Velvet Underground and Roy Orbison singing for the lonely; watched *Taxi;* was depressed.

Diculous

Udder despara
Anoga Monair
Phiby Koten Noto
Saturday eglare

Phoistas Los Lumnos
Gamarra Revenge
Stoby Die Faggots
Noosmyna Komstenge

"Diculous" was Philip's final poem. He was too disoriented to write any more, although, as Lisa observed when Bert showed her the poem, Philip still had a pretty good sense of meter.

Bert was walking down Amsterdam Avenue, near Columbia University, on a cool autumn day when he saw his old friend Juan Carlos in front of St. Luke's–Roosevelt Hospital. The King looked extremely thin. Bert could see the bones of his face under his skin, and his eyes looked haunted, and he was leaning on a cane, and Bert knew, he knew without asking.

"Hi, Bert."

Bert hugged Juan tight. "How are you doing?"

"Not so great, kiddo. Not so great."

Bert took Juan out to lunch at a restaurant called The Restaurant, under street level, opposite the law school. Juan itemized his recent health problems: thrush, pneumocystis, Kaposi's sarcoma. When he had the pneumocystis, he'd gone into a coma. Now he was getting chemotherapy for the cancer because it was starting to spread into his mouth. He said the chemo took a lot out of him and caused neuropathy in his legs. He admitted he was down in the dumps. His own sister wouldn't let him see his nephew and his niece. A neighbor thought she could get AIDS if they took the elevator together. Bert kept telling the King he had to think positively and hated himself for sounding so banal and knew there was nothing else to say but banalities.

Juan Carlos lived nearby. Bert walked him to his apartment building and then took the elevator upstairs with him. He had never seen Juan's apartment before. He found it dusty and sad, filled with shelves of Tito Gobbi albums and disintegrating piles of *Opera News*. Juan told Bert he had inspired him to shave — for days now he had been too depressed to bother. Bert stood in the doorway of the bathroom while Juan lathered his face. His hand shook while he worked the razor.

"Do you want me to do that for you?" Bert offered, although he was afraid of cutting Juan, and afraid also of Juan's blood.

"No, I'll manage," Juan said. "But thanks. You know, I read the *Quixote* again last month. In English, this time. It's like a different book in English. Cervantes says, 'It is an office of more trust to shave a man's beard than to saddle a horse.' What do you think of that?"

Dejected after seeing Juan, Bert went for a walk and ended up fifteen blocks downtown in front of his old building. He buzzed the Heibergs to see if Isabel and Lars were home from school. Luisa came down to the lobby and stood at the door without letting him in.

"I don't want you seeing the children anymore," Luisa told him.

"What?"

"Lars is having some emotional problems. I think you're a bad influence."

Bert was stunned. "Luisa, I'm so fond of your kids. I would never do anything to hurt them."

"I'm sorry." She was starting to cry. "You can't see them anymore." She shut the door and ran through the lobby and then up the stairs. Bert felt shaky. He sat on a bench on one of the islands on Broadway, next to some elderly black men drinking cheap wine and playing dominos.

Lisa was trying to cheer him up in the Uris Hall library. The library was built directly above the underground university swimming pool, and beneath them they could feel the rhythmic plashing of swimmers doing laps. Bert felt lousy. He didn't even want to be at school, but he couldn't go to Eisenberg's anymore, and Philip was home, and *Leave It to Beaver* wasn't on yet, so there was nowhere else to go.

"You can't let it get to you," Lisa told him.

"People really think if you're gay, you're bound to be a child molester."

"She didn't say that."

"What else could Luisa mean? She was crying. I'm surprised the cops don't show up to arrest me. If Lars is having emotional problems, maybe it's because his parents are getting divorced and his father's a speed freak and a felon."

"Bert, I don't think it's because you're gay. There's some other explanation."

But that made Bert worry more. He was afraid that the time he had spent with the children — their conversations and fantastic games — had indeed damaged them. The idea that he had hurt them, even unintentionally, made him feel sick.

Lisa was eating a stalk of celery. She was happy. She'd fallen in love with Roger, her boyfriend at the business school. Now that she was so attached to him, Bert was jealous. He wondered if he'd made a terrible mistake with Lisa, if he should have tried to pursue a relationship with her. He might have, he reasoned, if he hadn't been fucked up about Derek, and if she'd had straighter teeth.

"Maybe this'll take your mind off things. We're ready to progress in our studies."

Bert's joy knew no bounds. "What is it this time?"

"Skolem's paradox."

"Does it have to be a paradox?"

"This one's a cutie."

Lisa's reasoning was abstruse, but basically she proved, by applying something called the Lowenheim-Skolem theorem, that real numbers, which consisted of all the integers and all the fractions and everything in between, were nevertheless denumerable. "Denumerable" meant they could be counted, one, two, three, and so on. But, of course, she said, real numbers were *not* denumerable: there were too many of them to be counted in this way. Hence the paradox.

Bert was, as usual, and at best, barely following. But he understood the horrible import: real numbers weren't real. He felt like the rug had been pulled out from under him. Even numbers weren't safe. Even numbers were unstable. "This is really creepy, Lisa."

"You know," Lisa mused, "this isn't having quite the effect I'd hoped for. What's the matter?"

"I don't know." Bert rubbed his knuckles. His fingers felt puffy from the salt he had eaten. In the morning, he had come to Uris Hall famished, but the cafeteria kitchen was closed for asbestos removal. He had decided to buy something from one of the vending machines, but the bill changer was broken, throwing him into a vile mood. Because he had only two quarters in his pocket, all he could afford for breakfast was a bag of potato chips. He had eaten the snack greedily, but with vast, quiet resentment. "I guess it's that you can't depend on anything."

"You can depend on me," Lisa assured him.

"But how can you tell if anything's real? Even numbers lie."

"I guess ultimately it comes down to perception," Lisa said. "Don't you think?"

"Perception?"

"It is so, if you think so."

"But what if you're mistaken?" Bert demanded. "What if you see something, but you know you're imagining it. Or what if you don't know you're imagining it, but you are." Because those were always possibilities.

"Like Philip," Lisa said. "Interesting. Philip actually sees his hallucinations, so doesn't that make them real?"

"It's not just Philip . . ."

"You know, Bert, you're not your brother," Lisa said sharply. "You can depend on your eyes and ears and mind. If you see something, if you think something, it's real."

*

They went to a double bill at the gay film festival. The first film was a documentary about two elderly lesbians, both excommunicated Mennonites. The women talked about their lovemaking (apparently very passionate and fulfilling) while they quilted; they were very funny and brutally honest. The second movie was a fictional look at two gay men in Montreal, one French-Canadian, the other from Ottawa. The movie showed some scenes of their lovemaking, nothing too explicit, but Derek shifted uncomfortably next to Bert in the movie theater.

After the movie, they walked down to a restaurant in Little Italy. Bert loved the checkered red-and-white tablecloth, the dim lighting, the candles in fat, wax-stained glasses on the tables, the smell of garlic and fresh bread. They ordered espresso with dessert. Bert wondered what he should say, how he should say it. But he was determined to say something.

"Look, Bert, I think we should talk," Derek began.

"Okay," Bert said, and waited for his heart to begin pounding. Yup: there it went.

"This is hard for me. I don't know how to say this exactly. Maybe I should just say it." Derek glanced at the tables on either side of them, then leaned toward Bert and started speaking so softly that Bert couldn't hear him over the din of the restaurant.

"What?"

Derek spoke up a bit. "I've never had a homosexual experience. But I'm attracted to you."

"Well, good," Bert said, excited and happy. "Because I'm attracted to you, too." Derek looked nervous. Bert was nervous, too, but he forced himself to appear calm. If he wasn't calm, he'd scare Derek away. "Don't worry. We can take this really slowly."

"Take it slowly?"

"Yeah. I mean, at first we can just hold hands. You know, something like that."

"Bert, I can't do that."

"What do you mean?" Bert asked, dreading the answer.

"I can't get involved with you. Physically, I mean."

"I don't understand." Or rather, he hoped he didn't understand. He wasn't feeling calm anymore. He was beginning to panic.

"I just can't do it, Bert. I can't get involved with a man. I can't do it."

Bert started laughing nervously.

"What are you laughing about?"

"I don't know," Bert said. "I feel really shitty."

"I'm sorry."

"What do you want, Derek? Why did you bring this up if you weren't going to act on it?"

"I just had to get it off my chest."

"I bet you're feeling better now."

"Yeah, I am."

Bert was laughing hard. "You're such a fuckhead."

Derek was laughing now, too. "Are you mad at me?"

"Yeah," Bert said. "I am."

"Real mad?"

"Yeah." He wasn't laughing anymore. "Real mad."

"We can talk about it."

"Go fuck yourself." He stood up at the table, dazed, furious, trembling, insane. "You're a cocksucker," he shouted. "What do you think of that?"

His hands were still shaking as he ran out of the restaurant. Almost immediately, he wanted to go back and apologize. He stopped, paralyzed, on the sidewalk, wondering what to do. He had wanted everything to go right this time, and nothing had gone right. It wasn't Derek's fault. It wasn't anybody's fault except his own, his own stupid fault. He started walking. He would apologize, but not now. If he apologized now, he'd start crying. He hadn't cried since he was fifteen, since before Philip got sick.

Confused and unnerved, he walked blindly through the Village and ended up at a gay bar. He didn't look at the other customers, didn't care about anything. His thoughts were reeling like an out-of-kilter carousel. Somehow he kept making the same mistakes. Somehow he seemed drawn toward making them. Still trembling, and feeling stupid for trembling, he ordered a double gin and tonic. He'd never ordered a double in his life. Then he recognized the bartender.

"Hey, you were that guy's roommate," Bert said.

"What guy?"

"That Catholic guy. Scott." Bert remembered his name, then smiled, thinking of all of Scott's questions about Judaism. "Whatever happened to him?"

The bartender swabbed the bar in front of Bert. "He died. A couple of months ago. Pneumonia."

"Yeah," Bert said. "Yeah yeah yeah."

He was drunk when he left the bar, and he was drunk on the subway, and he was drunk when he missed his stop. He was still drunk when he finally got home. Evie and Joseph were asleep. Philip was awake, on the couch, playing Bob Dylan softly on the stereo.

Little rooster crowin', there must be something on his mind
Little rooster crowin', there must be something on his mind
Well, I feel just like that rooster
Honey, ya treat me so unkind.

Well, I struggled through barbed wire, felt the hail fall
from above
Well, I struggled through barbed wire, felt the hail fall
from above
Well, you know I even outran the hound dogs
Honey, you know I've earned your love.

Look at the sun sinkin' like a ship
Look at the sun sinkin' like a ship
Ain't that just like my heart, babe
When you kissed my lips?

Bert went into the bathroom, looking for some Tylenol but found Philip's bottle of Thorazine instead. He swallowed two of the pills, then went back to the living room and squeezed in beside Philip on the couch. They lay there in silence, next to each other, nestled like two spoons, and listened to the music.

"It's beautiful," Philip said.

"Yeah."

"I wish it was still the sixties. It was so easy then. Everyone loved music. And the more you loved music, the cooler you were."

"Yeah."

Soon Bert started feeling the Thorazine. The whole room was spinning. It was nice just to lie back and enjoy it. It seemed to him as though he were floating on a bed of compressed air a few inches over the sofa. A magician could have passed a hoop over the levitating Bert and amazed his audience.

"Tomorrow I'm going to Turtle Island," Philip told him.

"I know how to get there," Bert said, still floating.

"You do?"

"You take the lost highway all the way to the end —"

Philip smiled his beautiful smile. "Make a left at Medgar Evers Stadium —"

"Then a right at the Ho Chi Minh Masonic Temple." Bert giggled up in the air.

"And you're right there."

"Philip," said Bert, who was now floating at an angle, so that his head was grazing the chandelier in the middle of the ceiling, his feet hovering just above the couch. "Maybe I could go with you?" It had been such a rotten couple of weeks.

"Sure. You can come," Philip said generously.

Bert turned around in the air. Now his feet were on the ceiling. He wrapped his arms around himself and hung upside down like a bat. Then he blew out, hard, and started to descend. He caught his head in the crook of the sofa and pulled himself down. He hung on tightly to the couch so he wouldn't become airborne again, and nestled once more next to Philip.

"I live a life of ease," Philip started reciting, "on Turtle Island."

"Got a girl I can please," Bert continued, "on Turtle Island."

"Eat some feta cheese on Turtle Island."

"No disease on Turtle Island."

"Study Portuguese on Turtle Island."

"Watch out for the bees on Turtle Island," Bert cautioned.

"Where you get change back from your dollar," they sang out in unison. They woke up Joseph, who walked into the living room a few moments later, saw them lying on the couch together, and smiled warmly at them. And Bert and Philip felt warm, to be smiled at so warmly, and then Joseph told them, did they know what time it was? and that they should go to bed, come on, scoot.

I Hate to Leave You Now

▼▼▼

BERT WOKE UP in the morning, and he had a hangover, but he was not crazy, no matter how much he tried, and he looked at Philip, asleep in the bed across from him, and he saw the banner Philip had posted to his wall that trumpeted, "MENTALLY PHIL, GENTLY PHIL, ACCIDENTALLY PHIL, PROPIGLANDISTICALLY PHIL" (the last written in smaller letters, so it would fit), and he loved his brother very much, and he thought: Bert Rosenbaum is not Philip Rosenbaum. Bert Rosenbaum is not Philip Rosenbaum. Bert Rosenbaum is not Philip Rosenbaum.

Alison had sent Bert an article on Feynman diagrams. Bert thought he understood most of it. Feynman believed that subatomic particles moved freely through space and time, even *backward* in time if they so desired, in such a way that their paths through space-time were always the sum histories of all the possible paths they might ever have taken. It clicked for Bert: subatomic particles as tiny existentialists. That meant that space and time were woven together out of the mathematics of experience. Feynman must believe that, Bert thought. Bert believed it too. "People like us, who believe in physics," Einstein once wrote, "know that the distinction between past, present, and future is only a stubbornly persistent illusion." He was the Bert who was Bert the night before and the Bert who was Bert the morning after; the same Bert who would be Bert a moment later, and then the moment after that; he was always the same Bert. By his bootstraps, Bert thought. He would lift himself by his bootstraps.

*

The aliens told him they were leaving.

"But I thought you were going to stay a couple of years."

"We're pregnant," Evelyn said bashfully.

Herbert coughed, and knocked his pipe into the palm of his armrest to clean it. "It was an accident."

"As soon as I was sober for a month, my period started. And as soon as my period started, we got pregnant. I guess it was safer when I was drinking." Ribsy smiled to malchick-self. "Of course, when I was really drinking, I couldn't even get it up."

"These organs of yours confuse me," Bert said.

"Use it or lose it, I always say. Use it or lose it."

"How long do your pregnancies last?"

"Two years," Evelyn said. "Like an elephant. And that's what I'll look like, an elephant."

"We both will," Ribsy reminded her.

"So we've got some time yet," Herbert told Bert. "We'll leave for Debbie on Christmas Day."

"Why then?"

"No reason, really, it just seems so wonderfully theatrical," Evelyn answered.

"Well, congratulations! I'm really happy for you."

"I'll just be so glad to see all the kids," Ribsy said.

"Yes." Evelyn flushed dark green. "That will be very nice."

"It will." Herbert, taciturn, puffed at his pipe, then went into the spaceship, cranked up the stereo loud, and sang along to Paul Simon's "Mother and Child Reunion."

Lisa had urged Bert to take a higher-level statistics course his last term in school, and Bert, still cocky over his final grade in statistics, foolhardily agreed. "It'll be a snap," Lisa promised. "I'll help you."

The first day of class, the instructor, a Professor Lewitt, told them, "We'll be studying the Box-Jenkins methodology here, and let me tell you, Box-Jenkins is perfectly simple to understand — so long as you're Box, or Jenkins."

The class tittered. Tee hee hee.

"I'm going to be sick," Bert told Lisa, sotto voce.

The Box-Jenkins methodology was a means of time-series analysis. For example, Box-Jenkins gave you a way to compute monthly sales figures as a function of monthly advertising expenditures. There was no final in the course. Instead, each student had to build a model for an actual business and then report on the results. Bert's friend Peter Fortunato had put him in touch with the marketing research department of Blithedale Brothers magazine division, and Bert was going to investigate what factors affected the sales of Blithedale's crossword puzzle magazines.

One day Philip opened the window in his room and poured out all his belongings: his books, his wallet, his sheets, his blankets, his pillow, his radio, his turntable, his records, his comic books, his clock.

Evie, Joseph, and Bert scampered outside, gathering the belongings, as passersby watched curiously. It was humiliating. The next day Philip threw everything out again. They gathered the items up one more time and locked them in closets. They begged him to enter a hospital. He still refused. He stopped eating. They told him that if he didn't go to a hospital, they would force him to go. He still refused.

Finally, Joseph called the police and reported that Philip had been violent. Two policemen came to take Philip away for a psychiatric evaluation. Bert answered the door, and the policemen smiled at him, thinking he was Philip. Evie called for Philip. Philip saw the policemen. The cops took out a straitjacket.

Evie became hysterical. "Never, never!" she screamed. "Don't you dare!"

The cops put away the straitjacket and took out handcuffs.

"I'll go," Philip said sullenly. "You don't need the handcuffs."

"Please don't use the handcuffs," Evie begged the policemen, crying.

"You don't need them," Joseph said.

The policemen insisted on using them. "I never thought I'd

live to see policemen take my son away in handcuffs," Evie said after they had left. "It's like a piece of my heart is being torn out."

The police took Philip to the Bronx State Psychiatric Center. Evie and Joseph followed in a cab and told Philip they would have him committed if he didn't sign himself into the hospital. Philip agreed and signed himself in. He started getting better with regular medication. Bert talked to one of the nurses, a Filipino woman, and told her that he always had mixed feelings about the drugs, even though he knew how much they helped Philip.

"I've been a psychiatric nurse for fifteen years," the woman said. "I got over my mixed feelings a long time ago. Sure there are problems. But I think it's much, much worse to hallucinate twenty-four hours a day."

And Bert thought: Philip went crazy so I wouldn't have to.

The smell of vomit and urine permeated Philip's ward at Bronx State. The snake pit, Joseph called it. The light was harsh. In the corners, patients cackled. Off to the sides, a few were weeping. Everywhere people talked to themselves. The better-adjusted patients played cards for hours at a time. People drank coffee in voluminous quantities.

Some of the patients were violent. Bert saw one man bang his head with all his might against the wall ten, fifteen times before the staff could stop him. Women stood in the middle of the ward and shrieked belligerently till the nurses' aides succeeded in hushing them.

It was ugly in the ward. The light was ugly. The walls were a filthy yellow color, the floor was sticky yellow, the ceiling was spotted with yellow stains. Patients laughed and wept, stood up and screamed at God or the devil. Usually the devil. The devil was everywhere in the ward. Patients could see the devil. Patients said they were possessed by the devil.

Once, Bert was leaving the ward and the guards stopped

him for a moment and wouldn't let him out — they thought he was Philip. This happened before, Bert thought. Everything had happened before. He was continually mistaken for Philip by the staff. The patients could always tell them apart.

Philip looked lost and lonely and afraid in the ward. (They were all afraid.) Sometimes he talked to himself. Sometimes he played cards. Sometimes he stared off vacantly. Much of the time he watched TV.

A protracted period of bureaucratic wrangling began anew as the Rosenbaums attempted to get Philip transferred to a better ward. They had never succeeded in getting him disability payments, but they were determined to get him out of the ward. They made dozens of phone calls. They wrote letters. They made great nuisances of themselves at the hospital. Nothing could be done. Finally, Joseph managed to contact a union shop steward at the hospital — they had some acquaintances in common — and the steward got Philip transferred. So something *could* be done.

"Even in a mental hospital, you've got to have connections." Bert was appalled.

Philip was transferred to an experimental ward. The experiment seemed to consist of having fewer patients, more staff, a cleaner common room. The ward stank of ammonia instead of piss or shit or vomit or cum, and it was quieter. Philip liked it better. People still talked to themselves, still laughed or cried on the sides of the lounge. Philip still watched TV. But he improved. He didn't talk to himself so much. He talked to the other patients. He played some pool and Ping-Pong. He started making friends. Philip was closest to a gray-haired black woman named Nancy and a black man in his early forties named Lawrence, who said he had once played guitar with Jimi Hendrix. There were very few whites on the ward, or for that matter anywhere in the hospital.

At first, when Bert asked Philip a question, Philip took a long time to respond, as though his mind had to travel through yards and yards of fog. The medicine, which blocked the delusions and hallucinations, also made it difficult for Philip to concentrate. But the dosage was decreased, and Philip adjusted, and usually he was glad to see his family. Often when Bert visited, Philip would grin broadly when he first caught sight of his brother — a healthy, rational, normal smile.

The hospital was shoved into an inaccessible section of the Bronx. The buildings were either ancient, creaking, cold, and cruel, or sparkling new, cold, cruel, and empty. Bert found it difficult to convey to friends (for he was being more open again about Philip's illness) the spookiness, the surreal quality of the facility. The grounds were vast, the buildings separated by blocks. It was easy to get lost. One of the new buildings, evidently a dormitory for the mentally retarded, was so empty, so scary (a ghastly fluorescent light spread through the glass building, but there were never any people around), that Bert had nightmares about it. If you weren't crazy already, the Bronx State Psychiatric Center would make you that way.

Visiting was a Herculean task. First the Number 1 or Number 2 bus to Fordham Road. Then the cross-town bus down Fordham. Then a bus across Eastchester Road, to the hospital. Then a long, long walk from the bus stop to the ward. Three buses. It took an hour and a half, each way. Once he just missed the Number 1 bus, and then just missed the bus down Fordham, and then just missed the bus across Eastchester, and each time he had to wait a long time for the next bus. It took him three hours to get to the hospital, and by the time he arrived, visiting hours were over. He went back outside to the bus stop to go back home, but just as he got there, a bus pulled away without him.

Philip would stay in the hospital for close to two years. He began chain-smoking in the hospital, to help pass the time and because everyone else smoked too.

"Meet any nice women?" he asked Bert hopefully. He always wanted the best for Bert.

Bert's modeling work wasn't going well. Sales of crossword puzzle magazines couldn't be correlated with the economy. Not with the GNP, not with the unemployment rate, not with the nominal or real interest rates, not with the stock market, not with inflation, not with housing starts, not with the federal funds rate, not with the money supply M1, not with M2, not with anything. Not with advertising and not with promotion. Sales weren't even correlated with subscriptions, which was incomprehensible. He began searching desperately for any correlations at all, but the only ones he stumbled upon were rather baffling: the price of pork belly futures, sunspot activity, and Neil Young's quarterly ASCAP royalties — the last, Evelyn's merry suggestion.

He presented his findings to the class. Three executives from Blithedale Brothers Publishing sat stony-faced in the back, listening to his report. When he mentioned the unexpected correlation with pork bellies, the class exploded with laughter. When he plowed ahead and, with a straight face, tried to rationalize the effects of sunspot activity, the class applauded. And when he presented his coup de grâce, the amazing link with maestro Neil Young, well, the class gave him a standing ovation. Lisa beamed at him from the middle of the room, clapping wildly. The executives conferred quietly with one another in the back.

Afterward, still trying not to smile, Bert shook hands with the executives. He expected them to be polite and then to make a quick getaway. But they asked if they could take him out to lunch, and over lunch they offered him a job in the magazine division. "We like your style," the head of marketing told him. "And we need someone who knows something about crossword puzzle magazines. By now, who knows more than you?"

"The job's heavily quantitative. You'll like it," a second executive assured him.

"Heavily quantitative," Bert repeated. "Oh good."

He ended up skipping his graduation ceremony. His parents were disappointed, but Bert didn't feel like going. Instead, he spent the afternoon looking for an apartment; he wanted to find something before his job at Blithedale started and he got too busy. Back at home, Bert found a letter from Harry in the mail. He hadn't heard from Harry in months. He settled onto the couch to read the note.

Dear Bert,
I thought of you the other day, for some reason, when I was sitting in the bus on my way to work. A gang of boys — from working-class backgrounds — were making a lot of noise and annoying everybody on the bus, but they weren't really bad kids, if you know what I mean. At one point our bus passed a spot where the drain was being cleaned. (In India, or at least in Bombay, the hundred-year-old sewage system keeps getting clogged with muck. They clear the obstruction in the following way: a man — or a boy, usually — strips down to his underwear, slips down the manhole, breathing over-powering poisonous fumes, and, without the aid of a light, clears the muck ten to fifteen feet below road level with a pitchfork. His entire body is bathed in shit and filth. Frequently accidents occur and the worker dies. Almost all the workers have to prepare themselves for the job each day with a terrible alcoholic drink so that they are not overcome by the fumes. These are contract workers, and earn about half of poverty-line wages. When they die, there is no compensation.) That day, a little boy — about twelve years old — thin and dark, was emerging from the manhole, outside of which was stacked a large pile of revolting sludge which he had extracted from the drain. The boys on the bus shouted out, making fun of him, "Hey, hero! Did you find anything?" I don't think he followed what they were saying, but he just turned toward them and smiled a startlingly beautiful white-toothed smile. I suddenly felt like writing to you.

Love,
Harry

Bert heard a key turn in the lock. His mother was home. She was carrying a bag of groceries. "Hi, sweetheart." She put the bag down on the dining room table and then took off her heavy blue woolen winter coat.

"Hi, Mom. I got a letter from Harry."

"Oh, how's he doing?"

"Good, I guess."

Bert picked up the bag of groceries and brought it to the kitchen, then helped his mother put the food away. Afterward, she sat at the kitchen table, flicked off her shoes, and rubbed her swollen feet with her swollen fingers. Bert made her a cup of coffee. "Thanks, Bert. I'm so tired. If you'd gone to graduation, I could have taken the day off."

"You could have lied to your boss and taken the day off anyway."

"You're right," Evie said. "Sit down, we never get to talk anymore."

Bert poured himself some apple juice and sat down at the table with her. His mother did look tired. And she was getting older: the black hair in back was turning gray and the gray hair in front was turning white. She seemed shorter, too, as though she were starting to shrink. "What's up?"

"Your father's coming home late. He wants us to light the Chanukah candles without him. I think when he gets here, we'll splurge on a cab and all go to the hospital together."

"Great." His mother was staring at him and glowing. It made Bert uncomfortable. "What?"

"You're an M.B.A."

"Who cares."

"I care. You have no idea how much those three initials mean to people."

"I'm just glad it's over. I feel like I've lost the last year and a half of my life. It just — vanished."

"I feel that way about a lot of years of my life," Evie said.

"You do?"

"The year my brother died. The first time Philip got sick. And this year. What can you do?"

"Ma," Bert said, "every day for the past nine years, every single day, I thought I was going to go crazy."

"Oh, Bert." His mother was pained. "Why didn't you say something?"

"Most of the time I didn't even realize it myself. But I don't think that way anymore."

"That's good." She started drawing squares on a piece of scrap paper, then drew x's through the boxes. It was a nervous habit of hers. She'd doodled like this as long as Bert could remember. "That's good," she said again. "I know how you feel. When Uncle Buddy died, I thought I'd never make it to forty either. And after Philip got sick, I thought I'd get sick too."

"I just wish things had worked out differently."

"We always do." She drew some more boxes, then looked up from the paper and smiled at him. "So who's making dinner, Bert?"

She started getting dinner ready. Bert checked the answering machine in his parents' bedroom. Derek had called. Bert had apologized to Derek, but things had remained awkward between them all term. Lately, they were beginning to grow close again. Bert enjoyed the friendship, but warily.

He went back into the kitchen, lit the Chanukah candles, and said a blessing over them. His mother was making veal cutlets: dipping them into egg batter, then into bread crumbs, and then frying them in oil. As always, she worked with incredible efficiency.

"I forgot to tell you, Bert, Tom wants you to call him. He says he has an extra ticket to a Neil Young concert."

"Neil Young, huh." Bert and Tom hadn't spoken since they had met in Central Park. So he could write Harry, or call Derek, or call Tom. Harry, Derek, Tom. Tom, Derek, Harry. He watched his mother dip veal cutlet after veal cutlet. "Why are you making so much?" He put his hand over the *shammes,* the highest candle, and brought it closer and closer to the flame. He could feel the heat.

"I thought I'd bring a big batch over to the hospital tonight, for Philip and Nancy and Lawrence. I don't think they get to eat veal there very often."

"Ma," Bert decided, moving his hand away before he burned it, "could you give me Tom's number?"

"Can I get it after dinner?"

"Actually, could you get it now? Please?"

Evie rinsed her hands under the faucet, then dried them on her apron. She had always wanted Bert to be better friends with Tom, Bert knew, but now she seemed confused, even apprehensive about his sudden, urgent interest. A little trepidatious, a little triumphant, she opened her pocketbook and found Bert the phone number.

LIGHTING OUT FOR THE TERRITORY

Revolution 9

▾▾▾

I'LL MISS YOU," Ribsy said.

"We all will," Evelyn said.

"Here." Bert gave Herbert one of his ties. "Take it as a going-away present." Herbert wrapped it around his waist like a belt, then took it off and passed it to Evelyn, who wrapped it around her hair like a ribbon, then took it off and passed it to Ribsy, who knotted it around malchick's neck.

"I'll have to get a suit to go with this," Ribsy said.

"You? In a suit? I don't think so."

"Stranger things have happened," said Ribsy, peeved.

Bert's door was open and Joseph walked in. "Who are you talking to?"

"Myself."

Joseph kicked off his shoes and lay down on Philip's bed. He turned toward Bert and the aliens and smiled.

"What are you looking at?" Bert asked nervously, while the aliens, invisible, scuttled across the room and out the window.

"You, my little *sohnochikl*," Joseph replied. And then he sang a Yiddish song from the abortive Russian Revolution of 1905 which his father had taught him:

Hey, hey, arup fon tron
Men darfn nit kain Kaiser
Men darfn nit kain Hun

Schwester un Brider
Lawmer sach nit yirtzen

Funye dem Kaiser
Lawmer im die yohren kirzen

The song compared the czar to the kaiser and called openly for his assassination: "Sisters and brothers . . . let's shorten his years." Joseph's father had been arrested after the uprising and was sent to Siberia, but he had escaped from prison and fled to the United States.

"You're such a good-looking kid," Joseph told him. "How did I get to be the father of such a good-looking kid?"

"Dad," Bert said, checking his genial but plain reflection in the mirror, "you're nuts."

Evie entered the room. "So who are you boys plotting against now?"

"Czar Nicholas II," Bert told her.

Bert enjoyed the Neil Young concert, but bolted before Tom could give him more than a quick peck on the cheek. On their second date, they dressed in jackets and ties, went to the ballet, and afterward had a late supper at Sardi's, under a caricature of Jimmy Cagney. Bert walked Tom to his apartment door and kissed him on the cheek, getting a mouthful of beard.

"I think you should come in," Tom said.

"Oh you do, do you."

"I do," Tom said. "My roommates are out."

"Oh they are, are they."

Bert entered the apartment behind Tom, his heart beating just a little too fast. Bert had the strangest sense that he was playacting at dating, that he was going through the motions — that he was, in fact, an imposter. But he was sure that over time, he would come to feel more real.

As Above, So Below

▾▾▾

BERT SAID GOODBYE to the aliens in Riverside Park. A wind was up, and the day was crisp and gray, and the gray Hudson River behind them slapped angrily at the pier. Patches of snow remained on the ground from the last snowfall, but they looked small and vanquished, like the fading blemishes on a child's face on the last day of a bout of chicken pox. Blades of grass broke through the snow.

Bert helped the aliens pack the spacecraft. He carried a small valise on board, but the suitcase popped open, revealing a couple of cases of Extra-Strength Tylenol. "You just can't get Tylenol on the planet Debbie," Herbert explained.

Ribsy, wearing Bert's tie and a blue three-piece serge suit, was alternately crying and eating jumbo bars of milk chocolate. "It's to assuage my pain," malchick insisted. "It's because I hate goodbyes."

"It's because you're a pig," Evelyn said.

"You lose ten pounds, suddenly you act so high and mighty."

Evelyn laughed, threw off her heavy green wool coat, and modeled her dress girlishly. "I do look good, don't I."

"You both look good," Herbert temporized, gathering snow into a ball and throwing it at the river.

"It's just morning sickness. That's why I've lost weight." Evelyn put her coat back on.

"So, any parting words of wisdom?" Bert hurled a snowball, too, trying to throw farther than Herbert.

"Discontent is the mother of progress," Evelyn proposed.

"Bar insult, bar injury," Herbert said.

"All women become like their mothers. That is their tragedy," Ribsy advised, wiping malchick's hands clean on the snow. "No man does. That's his."

"You stole that line," Bert chastised malchick. And then, to all of them: "I want to know the big stuff. What's going to happen here? What's the future like? I know you must have some idea."

"We can't tell you that," Herbert said indignantly.

Evelyn looked over the railing at the choppy water. "Because of the Prime Directive," she explained.

"You told me you already violated it twice. What the hell, violate it a third time."

Evelyn turned around and looked at the others. "Why don't we tell him?"

"I guess it can't hurt," Herbert said. He made another snowball. Bert had thrown farther than Herbert, and a contest had begun. "I'll tell you what we're predicting. But remember, we're just dealing with probabilities." Herbert threw with all his might. "Likelihoods, not facts." The snowball passed the point Bert had reached, and Herbert grunted, satisfied. "And uncertainty increases with each successive forecast."

"Come on," Bert urged, packing another snowball. "I want to hear the good stuff."

Ribsy understood: "He wants to know about the Revolution." And then Ribsy shook malchick's head at Evelyn as Bert tried to best Herbert's record. "Men."

"The Revolution's coming, Bert," Evelyn told him.

"It's a tie," Herbert decided, watching Bert's snowball descend into the river.

But Bert didn't care. He was ebullient. "The One Big Revolution? The worldwide libertarian socialist revolution?"

"Yes."

"It's really going to happen?" Bert blew on his hands to warm them and paced excitedly up and down the walkway overlooking the river.

"Yes."

"When?" Bert demanded.

"June 2197," Herbert answered.

"Mid-June," Ribsy added.

"But that's more than two hundred years from now!"

"Of course," Evelyn said. "It's going to take generations of struggle."

"I'll be dead! I'll never get to see it!"

"Right," Evelyn agreed cheerfully. "You won't."

"Bert, take some solace from this." Herbert paused for a moment, gathering his thoughts. "Baseball's going to get amazing," he said with tremendous enthusiasm, putting an arm around Bert and walking with him on the concrete pathway. "Fielding, hitting, and pitching will all improve dramatically. Strategy will become ever more important. The Yankees will dominate the American League for two decades. Brooklyn's going to get the Dodgers back after Los Angeles falls into the Pacific. The designated hitter rule will be abolished."

"All right!"

"Gay rights will be universally recognized," Ribsy said. Malchick joined Herbert and Bert on their promenade. "There will be a queer, black, Jewish president. She'll be a former astronaut, actually. And she'll be instrumental in reducing the state's supervision of its citizens. There will only be a few more presidents after her."

"You'll finally have community-based housing for the mentally ill," Evelyn told him. She sat on a rock and huddled against the cold. "Local action committees — workers councils — with rotating directorates will take over the process of government. Workers will own the large firms that formerly employed them. Small independent businesses will flourish."

"But it's not going to happen unless you fight for it," Herbert cautioned. "Remember what Charter 77 said. 'The more citizens attempt to do, the less reason there will be for fear.' "

"And you say the Yankees are going to have some team,

huh?" asked Bert, stopping to wave at a small boat fighting the wind sweeping across the Hudson.

"Awesome," Herbert confirmed.

"On the other hand, none of this may happen," Ribsy broke in. "You could all blow yourselves up next week."

"Is that likely?"

"It's a possibility," Ribsy said, malchick's voice rising in a singsong.

"Well, assuming we don't blow ourselves up, the long-term picture looks pretty good. But what about shorter term?" Bert wondered. "What about the next fifty or a hundred years?"

"I'm afraid the news there isn't good," Evelyn said slowly, rising from the cold rock. "Not good at all."

"A plague, wars in central Europe, another depression, race riots, fascism, concentration camps, followed by four decades of crypto-fascist economic and military domination by the new superpowers —" Herbert listed.

"Oh my God," Bert said. "That's horrible."

"Well, do something about it," Ribsy prodded. "Nothing's set in stone."

"Don't mourn, Bert," Herbert said stoically. "Organize. Because you'd best believe your enemy's organizing."

Evelyn took Bert's hand and stroked it. "There's so much pain in your future. In all of your futures . . ."

"In my past, you mean," Bert said nervously.

"I'm sorry, Bert." Evelyn smiled at him. Her eyes were wet as she tapped lightly on his forehead. "Take care of yourself, okay? Look both ways when you cross the street."

"We should be going," Herbert said quietly. "Goodbye, Bert."

"Goodbye, Harold. Bye, Evelyn. Bye, Ribsy."

"Call me Rivka," Ribsy-also-known-as-Rivka said, giving him a moist kiss.

"I'll never forget you," Bert told them.

Ribsy's light green eyes darkened perceptibly. "You won't even remember us."

"Of course I will."

"No." Herbert shook Bert's hand. "We had to take certain precautions. You'll forget all about us. I'm sorry."

"I don't follow —"

"Goodbye, Bert," Evelyn said, looking away, her voice breaking a little.

Goodbye. Goodbye. Goodbye. Herbert blasted the stereo, and Bert could hear Roy Orbison singing "Dream Baby" even after the door of the spaceship closed and the engine started humming and the spaceship shook. Then, suddenly, the door burst open and Evelyn came rushing out, all four legs moving rapidly across the snow, like the tiny feet of a caterpillar. She hugged Bert tight, while Ribsy and Herbert watched from the door. Then she raced back to the spaceship. The door closed again, the ship shook again, and they were off. The ship rose into the air and Bert looked up until the spacecraft was a tiny blimp in the sky, and then a tiny point, and then nothing.

Forget them? Bert thought to himself as he walked toward Riverside Drive, humming. How could he possibly forget them? He'd never forget Herbert, the way he was always smoking that pipe. And Evelyn, working on her crossword puzzles. And Ribsy . . . something about a Norma Kamali dress. And a lecture Herbert had once given him on the Green Bank equation. And Evelyn . . . Something about Lenny Bruce. And the third one, he didn't know, exactly. And Herbert, Bert laughed, always singing those Hank Williams songs, as if they were dirges. And the other one, always drinking coffee. And Herbert — something about a haircut. And . . . and. . . . He tried to remember, he tried to think, but he couldn't quite think, the memory wouldn't quite come; and Bert gave in. He was feeling sleepy, and he had a splitting headache. He sat down on a bench on the drive. A miniature schnauzer ran up to him, slipped on some ice, started barking, and then ran away.

He couldn't remember why he'd walked to Riverside Park. But it was starting to snow again — perfect. A mother and her young son passed, both bundled up snugly against the cold. He could see they were mother and son, they had the same walk. She was carrying a large bag of groceries and the boy was carrying a small bag of groceries. Bert wondered where they'd found an open supermarket on Christmas Day. And Bert smiled, remembering. He remembered . . .

Orphans of the Storm

HE REMEMBERED a snowstorm in February 1970. He was ten years old, Philip was twelve. George Washington's birthday fell on a Sunday, and they had an extra day off from school on Monday. They had arranged to spend the long weekend at their grandparents' apartment, near Broadway and Van Cortlandt Park. Their grandparents would let them stay up late, and they'd look at old photos of their mother and Uncle Buddy, and their grandmother would smile, as always, when they looked at the photos of her son.

Bert and Philip were excited because they were going to take the bus to their grandparents' apartment all by themselves. Joseph was working an extra shift at the printer, and Evie was expecting company. Evie didn't want them to leave the apartment because the snow was starting to stick. But Philip insisted that they still go to their grandparents: a little snow wasn't going to melt them. Evie was about to relent, but then the snow started piling up in drifts along the Grand Concourse. Still Philip insisted. Then the snow fell in sheets, and cars were getting stuck, and Evie said absolutely not.

But Philip found a solution: the subway. Bert and Philip could take the D train down to 161st Street, and switch to the Number 4 train, then take the Number 4 train to 149th Street, and switch to the Number 2 train, then take the Number 2 train to 96th Street, and switch to the Number 1 train, then take the Number 1 train all the way back uptown to the last stop, 242d Street and Broadway. "That's crazy," Evie sputtered.

"That's going to take two hours!" But Philip shouted and nagged so persistently that Evie finally relented, after calling the Metropolitan Transit Authority and confirming that the subways were all running, and after making them wear boots. They promised to call her as soon as they reached their grandparents. "Be careful when you cross the street," she admonished.

Philip carried a small satchel packed with some clothes, his toothbrush, a biography of Lou Gehrig. Bert took a larger suitcase: lots of clothes, lots of books, his Slinky, his checkers set, the latest *Spiderman,* odds and ends. The suitcase was heavy, but it was so hard to know what to bring and what not to bring. Everything seemed essential.

As they set out into the snow, they realized it was going to be a true blizzard, much worse than even Evie had feared, but they decided to keep going. The snow was blanketing the city. They fought the wind to the subway station, then huddled below street level on the cold concrete platform until the train came. They had to wait a long time to make each transfer, as the trains were running slowly. When the Number 1 climbed out of the tunnel near Harlem and became an elevated, it started wheezing, like a child with asthma running, then walking, uphill. The snow was piling up on the tracks. The train moved forward sluggishly, until they approached the small bridge where the Harlem and Hudson rivers came together. The bridge was closed to subway traffic; the train whistled to a stop at 215th Street and ordered all the passengers out. Bert and Philip were still in Manhattan, and their grandparents were nearly a mile and a half away. The boys climbed down the long iron stairs from the elevated to Broadway below and then began walking. Bert was scared, but Philip said it was easy, they just had to walk in a straight line. As they trudged north, the wind rushed into their faces. Bert's eyes stung. His rubber boots were heavy and his suitcase was too bulky and the snow was too thick; Bert lagged behind his brother. Before they even reached the Broadway Bridge, they had to exchange luggage: Bert took

Philip's light satchel, and Philip took Bert's heavier valise. Bert tried to stay behind Philip, to get some shelter from the wind. They crossed the bridge on foot into the Marble Hill area and then into the Bronx. They still had almost a mile to go.

Bert started lagging behind again. "I forgot my toothbrush," he shouted through the wind to Philip ahead.

Philip turned around and grinned at him. "You goof," he whooped back, and then resumed his march.

The snow was up to Bert's knees. Philip walked slowly ahead, leaving deep depressions in the snow where he stepped. It was too hard for Bert to walk through the drifts on his own, so he stepped directly into Philip's footprints. The snow was still falling from the gray and pink skies. Bert made his way up the path Philip had cleared for him.

ACKNOWLEDGMENTS

All the poems in *Straitjacket and Tie* are written by Michael Stein, except "On Turtle Island" and "When Lee-Anne Is Eighteen," Parts One and Two, by Michael Stein and Eugene Stein.

Special thanks to Cindy Spiegel and Kelli C. Green.

Thanks also to David Alexander, Ben Baglio, Cindy Bell, Hy Bender, David Alan Black, Stu Bloomberg, Brent Coats, Dan Cohen, Janet Cohen, Geert De Turck, Matthew Eichler, Kim Fleary, Molly Friedrich, Robert Galletta, Peter Golden, Gary Green, Kent Greene, John Herman, Sheri Holman, Mizin Kawasaki, Ron Lux, F. J. Pratt, Andrew Richlin, Rod Ritchie, Carol Schlanger, Mark Schuster, Pat Sims, Girish Srinivasan, Jill Stolz, Jayne Yaffe, and all the Steins.